A
Killer
Stitch

A Killer Stitch

Maggie Sefton

BERKLEY PRIME CRIME, NEW YORK

THE BERKLEY PUBLISHING GROUP
Published by the Penguin Group
Penguin Group (USA) Inc.
375 Hudson Street, New York, New York 10014, USA
Penguin Group (Canada), 90 Eglinton Avenue East, Suite 700, Toronto, Ontario M4P 2Y3, Canada
(a division of Pearson Penguin Canada Inc.)
Penguin Books Ltd., 80 Strand, London WC2R 0RL, England
Penguin Group Ireland, 25 St. Stephen's Green, Dublin 2, Ireland (a division of Penguin Books Ltd.)
Penguin Group (Australia), 250 Camberwell Road, Camberwell, Victoria 3124, Australia
(a division of Pearson Australia Group Pty. Ltd.)
Penguin Books India Pvt. Ltd., 11 Community Centre, Panchsheel Park, New Delhi—110 017, India
Penguin Group (NZ), 67 Apollo Drive, Mairangi Bay, Auckland 1311, New Zealand
(a division of Pearson New Zealand Ltd.)
Penguin Books (South Africa) (Pty.) Ltd., 24 Sturdee Avenue, Rosebank, Johannesburg 2196, South Africa

Penguin Books Ltd., Registered Offices: 80 Strand, London WC2R 0RL, England

This book is an original publication of The Berkley Publishing Group.

This is a work of fiction. Names, characters, places, and incidents either are the product of the author's imagination or are used fictitiously, and any resemblance to actual persons, living or dead, business establishments, events, or locales is entirely coincidental. The publisher does not have any control over and does not assume any responsibility for author or third-party websites or their content.

PUBLISHER'S NOTE: The recipes contained in this book are to be followed exactly as written. The publisher is not responsible for your specific health or allergy needs that may require medical supervision. The publisher is not responsible for any adverse reactions to the recipes contained in this book.

First edition: May 2007

Library of Congress Cataloging-in-Publication Data

Sefton, Maggie.
    A killer stitch / Maggie Sefton.
        p. cm. — (Knitting mysteries)
    ISBN-13: 978-0-425-21520-3
    1. Knitters (Persons)—Fiction.   2. Knitting shops—Fiction.   3. Ranchers—Crimes
against—Fiction.   4. Triangles (Interpersonal relations)—Fiction.   5. Colorado—Fiction.
I. Title.
    PS3619.E37K55 2007
    813'.6—dc22

                                                                              2006103153

PRINTED IN THE UNITED STATES OF AMERICA

10   9   8   7   6   5   4   3   2   1

Acknowledgments

I want to thank Shirley Ellsworth, the multitalented and enthusiastic owner of Lambspun of Colorado yarn shop in Fort Collins for letting me sit in on several of her spinning classes. Watching beginning spinners try to master the wheel and listening to Shirley's patient instruction were both enjoyable and educational. And thank you, Shirley, for inviting me to accompany you to the spinners' retreat, SOAR, in Lake Tahoe, California.

Thanks also to all the spinners I encountered at Lambspun and elsewhere who willingly answered all my questions. Sitting with the spinners is always a treat for me, whether I'm chatting with them or simply knitting quietly beside them.

And thanks to Mark Sloniker, the marvelous jazz pianist at Jay's Bistro in Fort Collins, Colorado—where the martinis are icy and the jazz is hot.

A Killer Stitch

One

"That's it, Megan, keep it up. Do a little bit and send it in, a little bit and send it in," the pretty, dark-haired instructor said as she hovered over her student.

Kelly Flynn watched her friend, Megan Schmidt, frown in concentration as she fed the fluffy pink wool onto the spinning wheel's constantly turning bobbin. Slowly the pink wool slid between Megan's fingers, changing from soft and fluffy to a neatly twisted strand of pink yarn, winding around and around the maple wood bobbin.

"How am I doing, Lucy?" another spinner asked, focusing on the indigo blue wool feeding onto her wheel.

Lucy Adair moved beside the neighboring spinner who was struggling with the fleece in her lap. Instead of the smooth, slow motion Megan was managing, this spinner's fingers moved in fits and starts. Consequently, there was less blue yarn accumulating on the bobbin of her spinning wheel.

"Relax, Ellen," Lucy coached as she leaned over the wheel, her straight brown hair falling in a curtain beside her face. "Let me draft some more of the fleece for you." Reaching into Ellen's lap, Lucy gently pulled sections of the blue fleece apart, stretching the fibers into what spinners called batten or roving. "Now, loosen your fingers a little, so the twist will form smoothly. Not too much. If your fingers open too much, the twist jumps right through and winds the roving."

To her surprise, Kelly watched the yarn do exactly that. The twisted strand feeding onto the wheel seemed to bend back on itself, and then the fluffy roving in Ellen's lap started twisting. Imagine that, Kelly thought in amazement. Jumping yarn twists. Who would have thought?

"Ohhhh, noooo!" Ellen wailed, as her fluffy pile curled up like a garden snake.

Ellen loosened her fingers completely then, and the docile yarn snake suddenly writhed and twisted into a misshapen blue mass of fiber.

"Don't worry. We all do that when we start," Lucy said, her soft voice reassuring as her hand stopped the turning wheel. "It's hard to remember to keep our fingers and our feet moving at the same time."

"You're telling me," another spinner grumbled from her spot farther down the classroom. "I'm never going to finish this pile. I cannot get my hands and feet to work together. What's wrong with me?"

"Nothing at all, Anne," Lucy said as she expertly unwound the blue fibers in Ellen's lap. "It takes a while to get the rhythm of moving your feet and your hands at the same speed. If your fingers slow down and your feet speed up, then the yarn will get overtwisted and start to corkscrew."

"Like this," Ellen complained as she helped Lucy loosen the misshapen mass.

"There, now," Lucy said, handing the wool back to Ellen. "You'll want to draft some more before you try again."

Ellen gently pulled the blue fibers apart, stretching the twisted pile into roving once more. "Okay, three times is the charm, I hope."

"You'll get it, don't worry," Lucy said with a smile, giving Ellen a pat on the shoulder. "You're all doing wonderfully well for your first lesson. Just remember, keep your hands and feet moving together. If your fingers stop moving, those feet better stop right away." She gave a little laugh.

"Boy, it's a good thing I'm not one of your students, Lucy," Kelly said as she leaned back into her chair and swirled the last of the coffee in her ever-present mug. "I would never get it. I swear I wouldn't. That yarn would twist so fast, it'd wrap all of us in a knot."

"Stop that, Kelly," Megan chided. "Don't make me laugh while I'm spinning."

"I'm not trying to be funny," Kelly said after she drained her coffee. "I'd screw up the wool so badly, the spinning wheel would break. And Burt would never speak to me again."

"Why wouldn't I speak to you, Kelly? Have you been messing with my spinning wheel?" Burt spoke from the classroom doorway that led into Kelly's favorite knitting shop, House of Lambspun.

Kelly turned to see Burt Palmer, retired cop and now spinner par excellence, grinning as he carried a huge bag of multi-colored fleeces into the adjacent room.

"Your spinning wheel is safe from me, Burt," Kelly said as she crossed her heart. "Knitting provides enough challenges. Heck, I still discover new mistakes to make."

"All right, that's enough for today," Lucy announced. "You should be proud of yourselves. You've done really well. Keep practicing. I have two more classes this week, so drop in anytime."

"Hey, I can't quit now," Anne said with a good-natured laugh. "I've finally got my feet and hands together."

Kelly joined the others' laughter as she checked her watch. A quick review of her mental daytimer reminded Kelly she could visit with her friends for a little longer before racing across the driveway to her cottage and back to client accounting demands.

She'd learned that consulting had its definite benefits as well as its pitfalls. And the ticking clock inside her head that kept her on schedule all those years in the CPA firm was still ticking now that she was working on her own.

"Got time for more coffee?" Megan asked as she stuffed the pink wool and bobbin into her knitting bag.

"I've always got time for coffee."

"I haven't seen you before, Kelly. Have you been in town long?" Ellen asked as she placed the bobbin from her wheel into her knitting bag.

"Well, not exactly," Kelly replied. "I grew up in Fort Connor and came back last April for my aunt's funeral. I've been here ever since." She gave a short laugh. Had it really been only nine months since she'd returned to her childhood home? It seemed like much longer. So much had happened.

"We refused to let her leave," Megan said, shifting her bag to her shoulder. "Plus, she plays on our softball team during the season, so she's committed now. This is home, right, Kelly?"

"Absolutely."

"Well, nice to meet you, Kelly," Ellen said with a bright smile, extending her hand. "I'm Ellen Hunter, and I'm new to this shop. Lucy told me about the spinning class, and I decided to join. We met in a neighborhood coffeehouse one night when we both brought our knitting." Ellen brushed her wavy blonde hair off her face as she laughed. "I was afraid to try spinning, but Lucy is such a good teacher, I figured I'd give it a try. She's helped me a lot with my knitting."

"Lucy's a wonderful teacher," Megan said as she headed through the doorway, Kelly and Ellen following. "She's as good as Burt and almost as good as Mimi."

"Whoa, high praise," Kelly said. Mimi Shafer was the knitting shop owner and resident yarn and knitting sage. In her late fifties, Mimi also took a motherly interest in Kelly and her friends, especially in Kelly's frequent forays into investigative activities. "Sleuthing," Mimi called it.

Ellen turned in the doorway and waved at Lucy, who was still helping Anne. "See you later, Lucy. Why don't you call me tonight? Unless you've got another hot date, that is."

Lucy glanced up, and a bright pink flush colored her cheeks. She gave a quick wave and turned back to her student.

"Sounds like a boyfriend," Kelly said as they entered the knitting shop's central yarn room, noticing it was more crowded than usual for a weekday morning.

"Oh, yeah. Lucy's over the moon in love with this guy she's been seeing for the last few months," Ellen said, pausing to fondle a ball of cherry red yarn atop a pile of lollipop colors. "She goes out to his ranch all the time. She even went to Las Vegas with him."

"Wow, sounds serious," Megan observed as she stroked a tangerine fluff ball.

Kelly succumbed to the same temptation that had captured her friends. Fiber fever. She sank a free hand into the pile. Soft, soft, seductively soft.

Candy colors were everywhere. Her aunt and uncle's former farmhouse was filled to bursting with color. Yarns of every color imaginable. Tumbling from wooden crates that lined the walls, spilling out of steamer trunks tucked into corners, and scattered across antique desks. Christmas candy.

"Wow, this feels like eyelash yarn, but much thicker. Wonder what it is," Kelly said, squeezing a fluffy bundle.

"Winter eyelash," Megan joked, giving her a wink. "We'll have to ask Mimi. Mimi knows—"

"Everything," Kelly chimed in with a laugh, repeating the familiar mantra regularly heard around the knitting shop. Glancing toward the doorway, she noticed Lucy chatting with Anne. "You said Lucy's boyfriend was a rancher. He must be here in northern Colorado then."

"He has an alpaca ranch up in Bellevue Canyon. Apparently he's pretty successful. Lots of investments and stuff, too."

"Boy, I could use some investments right now," Megan said with a rueful smile. "Some of my clients are cutting back. It's going to be a lean Christmas this year."

Kelly was about to commiserate with Megan on the vagaries of consulting income, when she noticed Lucy anxiously beckoning from the classroom doorway. "Looks like Lucy wants you," she told Ellen.

"I'll see you two later," Ellen said, drawing away. "Why don't you join our spinning class, Kelly?"

"Not a chance," Kelly countered. "I'd break the wheel for sure, and I can't afford spinning wheel repairs right before the holidays."

"You, too?" Megan asked. "I thought you were doing okay with those alpaca clients Jayleen gave you."

"Well, I was until I had to pay all those professional accounting fees," Kelly admitted as they left the fluffy pile and wound through the adjoining room. "That's the thing about changing the state where you practice. New license fees, new associations, new everything." Pausing at the hallway that led to the café located at the rear of the shop, Kelly glanced around at all the shoppers. "Hey, is it my imagination, or is the shop way more crowded than usual for a Wednesday morning?"

"It's not your imagination," Megan said, smiling. "This is the holiday rush. Everyone is buying yarn and stuff to make their gifts. It gets like this every December. Right after Thanksgiving, every needleworker in the area rushes here to start their projects."

"That makes sense," Kelly said, watching the shoppers as they touched and compared yarns.

"Which reminds me. How's that scarf coming you promised to Eugene Tolliver in Denver? Is it almost finished?" Megan asked as they headed toward the café. She waved at their friend and fellow knitter, Jennifer, who was pouring coffee for a customer at a nearby table.

"No, of course not," Kelly admitted, sniffing the enticing aroma of dark, rich coffee. "You know how easily distracted I am. I keep shoving it to the bottom of the bag and go back to a froufrou yarn and knit that instead. I'm hopeless." She sighed dramatically as the caffeine lobe in her brain began to pulsate. Morning ritual. As soon as she got anywhere near the café and Eduardo's potent brew, Kelly's mug practically moved on its own.

"I've been meaning to speak to you about that," Jennifer

said as she approached, coffeepot in hand. "It's time we had a talk about dating behaviors, rituals, and all that."

"Uh-oh, sounds X-rated," Megan said, dropping her knitting bag at a corner table. "It's too early in the morning for that, Jennifer."

Jennifer stared at Megan like she'd just dropped from the sky. "Surely you're joking. It's never too early to talk about sex."

"Not without more coffee." Kelly pulled out a chair, then shoved her mug beneath the pot so Jennifer could fill it. An invisible plume of coffee aroma wound its way to her nose, tickling, inviting her to drink deep.

"Oh, brother. I've heard this before." Megan wagged her head.

"You heard the milder version, Megan. Kelly needs to hear this one," Jennifer admonished. "Now, Kelly, it has not escaped my attention that you and Steve have been dating for four months now, and you still look embarrassed when he kisses you. What's up with that?"

Kelly almost choked on her coffee. "Wh-what? When? I don't know what you're talking about," she sputtered when she could speak.

"That's true, Kelly," Megan joined in with a wicked grin. "I saw Steve steal a kiss when he was rounding your base in our final game last month, and you darn near dropped the ball."

"Hey, whose side are you on, anyway?" Kelly protested, feeling prickly. "I—I wasn't expecting that. He surprised me, that's all."

"That was over a month ago, Kelly, and you're still acting skittish. You two have been dating regularly. Twice a week or more, in fact. That's a lot of dates," Jennifer lectured, hand on her hip, looking for all the world like a slightly wayward schoolmarm.

"How do you know? Have you been checking my daytimer or something?"

"Of course. It's sticking out of your knitting bag most of the time," Jennifer readily admitted, not the slightest bit embarrassed.

Kelly scowled over her mug. "Boy, a person has no privacy around you." She pushed the incriminating daytimer farther into her bag.

"So, what's the deal?" Jennifer continued. "Why are you still acting so skittish with a great guy like Steve who really, really, *really* likes you? He's good-looking, athletic, smart, runs his own business—"

"You can stop selling, Miss Real Estate Agent," Kelly admonished, holding up her hand. "You don't have to sell me on Steve. Hey, I'm dating him. I know he's a great guy. I like him a lot."

"So why don't you kiss him more?" Jennifer pressed, brown eyes dancing. "I mean, that's what you do with a guy you like. I thought you had a boyfriend before, didn't you?"

The blush that had been creeping slowly now raced up Kelly's cheeks. "Hey, that's my business and Steve's. Not yours," she protested, hand jerking out in aggravation. "And—and how do you know we're not making out passionately already?"

"Believe me, I'd know. I have spies everywhere," Jennifer said archly, tossing her auburn hair. "Besides, lights would flash all over Fort Connor. Everyone would know."

Kelly exhaled an exasperated sigh. "Only Carl knows the truth."

"I've got Carl bribed. There's a bag of doggy bones in my trunk."

Kelly gave up and laughed, as did Megan. It was impossible to stay annoyed with Jennifer.

"Hey, Jennifer, how are you coming with that alpaca scarf you promised the Denver gallery guy?" Megan asked, clearly trying to change the subject.

"Oh, it's done and already in the mail," Jennifer replied, checking her customers. "And it's for his friend Ronnie, the psychic hairdresser. Kelly's making Eugene's scarf. Hey, gotta go, catch you later." And she was off, coffeepot in hand, heading toward another table.

Kelly took another deep drink, relaxing once more. She'd dodged the bullet. But not for long, she sensed. Jennifer was relentless.

"So, how far along are you? With the alpaca scarf, I mean." Megan asked. "Think you'll be done before Christmas?"

"I hope so. I did a little yesterday, but the soft shawl keeps tempting me, plus I've been eyeing more frothy stuff."

"You've gotta stay away from the frothy stuff until after the holidays, Kelly."

"I know, I know. No froufrou until spring. No froufrou until spring," Kelly chanted.

"Seriously, how much have you knitted?"

"About twelve inches, that's all."

Megan grinned. "Well, it's December first. You've got over three weeks until Christmas. Knit faster."

"Easy for you to say. That scarf is going slowly on those smaller needles. It'll take forever to make four feet," she grumbled.

"That's because you've gotten used to those larger needles, that's all. You've forgotten what it's like to knit with the smaller ones. Remember when you first started out?"

"Oh, yeah." Kelly nodded. "And I remember all the mistakes I made, too."

"You're doing fine, Kelly. Don't be so hard on yourself," Mimi said as she approached their table, doughnut box in hand. "What you need is one of these delectable things to restore your confidence."

"Hey, thanks, Mimi. You read my mind." Megan eagerly snatched a chocolate-coated confection.

Kelly peered into the box at the tempting pastries. She could smell the sugar. Coated, glazed, frosted, jam-filled. "Boy, I sure don't need this," she admitted as she lifted a brown sugar and cinnamon doughnut and took a bite.

"Go on. 'Tis the season of indulgence. And overindulgence," Mimi tempted.

Kelly chased the sugary bite with some coffee. What was it about coffee and doughnuts that went so well together? What fiend thought that up? A pastry chef, probably. "You're bright and cheerful," she said, observing Mimi's rosy cheeks. "All those holiday shoppers are ringing the registers, I'll bet."

"Isn't it wonderful? It seems like more and more people find us every year. More people are knitting, too," Mimi said as she continued into the café. "Jennifer, I'll bet I could interest you in one of these. Burt brought them in."

"Well, bless Burt's heart," Jennifer said, scanning the box's contents.

"Do I smell sugar?" Steve Townsend's voice sounded across the room. He appeared around the café's corner.

"Oh, please, Steve. Take two. They're small. Plus, there will be less for me to eat," Mimi said with a laugh.

Steve dutifully complied, making his selection as Jennifer refilled his coffee mug. "Oh, yeah. I definitely came in at the right time."

"What brings you here? I thought you were heading to Windsor today," Kelly asked as Steve approached, coffee in one hand, rapidly disappearing doughnuts in the other.

"I was on the way," Steve said after he swallowed. "But I thought I'd better drop by and remind you about tonight. Jazz Bistro at seven, right?"

"Got it on the daytimer," Kelly said with a nod, swirling her coffee, aware that Jennifer was grinning at her from beside the counter. Mimi had a funny grin on her face, too, as a matter of fact. "You didn't need to come out of your way for that."

"I didn't. I came for the sugar." With that, Steve leaned over and kissed her, then returned to the doughnuts and coffee.

It happened so quickly, Kelly didn't have time to react, so she sat there, looking surprised, and feeling a blush creeping up. "What was that all about?"

"I don't know. The sugar made me do it," Steve said, grinning. "See you tonight." He gave her a wink then headed for the door.

"Steve, wait," Megan called out. "I need your help."

"Sure, what's up?" he said as he paused, polishing off the last doughnut.

"You play tennis, don't you? I need some volunteers for a charity tournament at my tennis club. Can you sign up, pretty please? All proceeds go to buy toys for kids at the homeless shelter."

"Well, I haven't played for ages, but that's such a good cause I can't say no," Steve said, then drained his coffee.

"Heck, count me in, too," Kelly volunteered. "I haven't played since college, so I'll be more liability than asset, I'm sure."

"I was about to ask you next. This is great, you two. Thanks so much. You can sign up for doubles. I'll bring you the paperwork." Pushing back her chair, Megan grabbed her bag. "And speaking of work, I've gotta get back and see if I can earn enough this month to pay my yarn bill."

"Don't remind me. Client accounts are waiting for me across the driveway." Kelly pointed to her cottage.

"See you tonight," Steve said with a wave as he left. "And think of a time when we can practice."

"Practice what?" Kelly called after him but no answer floated back.

"I think he means tennis, but I could make some other suggestions," Jennifer said as she filched another doughnut from Mimi's open box.

Kelly gave Jennifer a playful frown before she headed to her cottage.

Two

Kelly slid the glass patio door open, ushering her pet Rott-weiler outside. "Here, you go, Carl. Breakfast time." She placed his nibbles-filled plastic doggie dish on the backyard patio and hastily withdrew from the icy morning chill. Carl danced about until the dish hit the concrete, hunger obviously overcoming the cold.

Brrr, she shivered. She'd need a warmer running jacket. Temperatures had dropped below freezing last night, she could tell. Frost lined her windshield. Heading for her bedroom Kelly rummaged in her closet for another jacket, then grabbed her knit hat and gloves.

She really should learn to knit one of these hats, she chided herself, admiring the neat rows of blue and green stitches. Megan was sweet to do this for her, but she couldn't keep depending on her friends' knitting "charity." She had to learn how to knit a hat. Maybe a class would help.

A loud *thump, thump* sounded at the front door. Who would be visiting this early? she wondered, yanking the door open.

"Hey, there." Steve greeted her as he leaned against the doorway, familiar grin in place. He held a cup of coffee in one hand and tennis rackets in the other. "I bet you forgot we were going to practice this morning."

She had but wasn't about to admit it, choosing distraction instead. "Not at all," she fibbed as she grabbed the coffee and took a deep drink. Ahhhh. Now she could hold up her end of the conversation. "I was coming outside to warm up now."

"Liar," Steve teased, retrieving the cup to take a drink while Kelly closed the door behind her.

"Good, you brought rackets. Mine are buried in a storage locker in Virginia," she said as she pulled the knit hat down to her ears. Feeling the cold ripple up her spine, Kelly rubbed her arms as they headed down the steps and around the cottage side yard. "Where're those courts, again?"

"On the other side of the golf course," Steve said, pointing across the frost-encrusted greens. "C'mon. We'll be warmed up by the time we get there." With that, he took off in a loping run. "Hey, Carl," he called as he passed the backyard fence. Carl immediately raced to the fence, barking at his favorite playmate.

"Another time, Carl," Kelly said to her dog as she stretched. "Steve will roll around in the grass with you next spring."

Kelly took a few more seconds to stretch then took off after Steve. She knew she could catch up with him easily. She was a sprinter. Steve was not. The golf course greens scrunched beneath her running shoes, icy coating giving way, as she lengthened her stride. A thin slice of December sunlight lightened the sky, reflecting on the greens ahead. Soon, that feeble light would be swallowed as December crept toward the winter solstice.

No golfers in sight. She wasn't surprised. Today was winter's announcement that the Indian summer temperatures and balmy weather they'd enjoyed through November were officially over. The cold had come. The ridge of mountains that rose in the distance, the foothills, were already sprinkled with snow. The Rockies that loomed behind had been glistening since September. The high country always got snow early. Yards of it, in fact.

Pulling up beside Steve, she matched her stride to his as they jogged across the empty course. "Lisa and Greg want us to go skiing with them this winter," Kelly said, watching her words form into frosty clouds on the cold air.

"Sounds good. Let's wait until after the holidays, though. My schedule is filling up. Getting crazy."

"Can you delay breaking ground on that new site in south Fort Connor? That would buy you some time."

"That's not the problem," Steve said, pointing toward the left side of the golf course then angling toward the fenced tennis courts in the distance. "Something new has come up. Something I've always wanted to do. I'll worry about finding time later."

"You're running with the Queen of Not Enough Time," Kelly joked. "I can help with that. Tell me, what's up?"

"You know that warehouse in Old Town I showed you last summer? The one close to the new lofts on the corner?"

"You mean the one you've been dreaming about? The one with all the potential? I remember what you said you could do with it."

"The same one. It's up for sale. I heard about it yesterday morning, so I went to talk to the firm handling the sale."

"Are you going to buy it?"

"I already have." Steve grinned at her as they rounded the golf clubhouse.

"Way to go, Steve!" Kelly congratulated, genuinely pleased he'd reached for his dream rather than let it pass him by. "That's fantastic. Now I know why you're feeling schedule pressure."

"Yeah, well, I'll worry about it later. Right now, I've gotta get that Wellesley site finished. Then, why don't you give me a scheduling lesson over martinis and jazz?"

"Sounds like a plan," Kelly agreed as they both slowed their pace until they reached the chain-link fence.

Steve flipped open the gate and motioned Kelly onto the courts. "We can talk while we hit. I've gotta get over to the site. We're finishing the model homes this week. People will be stampeding over the dirt by the weekend."

"Great, I'll warn Jennifer," Kelly said, unzipping the racket cover. Swinging the racket around, in front, in back, and over her head, Kelly moved her arm through long-forgotten motions. Similar to softball, but different enough to require careful attention. Tennis was a game of finesse, she remembered, not unrestrained power.

"Take it easy now," she warned Steve across the net as he bounced a ball beside him. "No points for blasting it out of the park."

"Yeah, yeah, yeah," Steve yelled as he hit the ball across the net.

As if guided by long distant memory, Kelly felt her body move toward the ball. Not smoothly, like she remembered from yesteryear, but good enough to get to the ball in time.

Her arm moved backward automatically as she ran, and she returned the ball with a solid hit. It sailed across the net.

Congratulating herself for hitting a good return, Kelly suddenly saw the ball coming back at her. That was the thing about tennis. It was so quick. No time to admire a great hit to the outfield as you rounded the bases.

Not in tennis. The ball was back in your face as soon as you returned to the center line, and you'd better be ready. Watching the ball land on her backhand side, Kelly attempted an unfamiliar shot and hit the ball weakly. It landed squarely in the middle of the net.

"Got another. Comin' atcha," Steve called out, as Kelly watched him hit another. This was going to take a lot of practice, she thought with an inward groan. And that would only get her to mediocre. Good was out of the question right now.

"I'll be over in a few minutes," Jennifer called to Kelly from the café.

Kelly lifted her newly refilled mug in reply as she headed down the hallway that led to the knitting shop. After totally reorganizing two alpaca ranchers' accounts and updating expenses, she'd earned a midday break herself. Kelly stretched her neck from side to side, loosening muscles long tensed from hours over the computer. She was going to have to invest in some new accounting software. These small accounts were taking far too much time to enter all the expenses and revenues for each client's business.

She dumped her knitting bag on the library table and indulged in a long stretch, after first waving hello to her friend Lisa, who was sitting on the other side.

"Hey, there," Lisa said, glancing up from the red and white mittens she was knitting. "I've missed you the last couple of times I came. Of course, my schedule has kind of heated up lately, so knitting time is harder to come by."

"I know how that is," Kelly replied as she settled into a chair and pulled the soft gray and white alpaca wool scarf from her bag. "But I figured I'd better get back to this if I'm going to have a prayer of finishing it in time for Christmas."

Lisa grinned, brushing her long blonde hair behind one ear. "Is that the scarf for the gallery guy?"

Kelly laughed. "The gallery guy has a name. He's Eugene Tolliver, and he was a huge help when I was poking around in Denver in the fall. You know, after Allison Dubois's death."

"You mean 'sleuthing,' don't you? I remember you and Jennifer going down there, and she came back with a whole new look."

"That was compliments of Ronnie, the psychic hairdresser," Kelly said with a sly grin. "Jennifer's knitting his scarf. Of course, she's already finished with it. I'm the slow one."

"Knit faster."

"I'm trying. Plus, I've forsworn froufrou until spring. That'll help."

Lisa chuckled. "Oh, yeah. Froufrou attacks. I know them well."

"Who are the mittens for?" Kelly asked. "They don't look big enough for Greg."

"They're for my six-year-old niece, Stephanie. After I finish these, I've got three more pairs to knit for younger cousins."

"Is this the Year of the Mitten on the Knitting Calendar?" Kelly teased.

Lisa didn't answer, because Mimi bustled into the room then, a skein of red and white yarn in one hand and an ever-present notebook in the other. She stopped abruptly when she spotted Kelly and Lisa. "Well, hello, Lisa," she sang out brightly. "I haven't seen you for a week. I've missed you."

"I've missed you guys, too. My schedule is really getting crazy," Lisa said, glancing up as her fingers worked the wool. Red and white yarn smoothly formed on the three skinny needles that created the round mitten-shape.

Kelly marveled at how Lisa could talk and barely pay attention while knitting something that complicated. Her friends scoffed at the idea of a mitten being hard to knit. But Kelly didn't buy it. Three skinny double-point needles and working in a tiny space. Just think of all the mistakes she could make. She shuddered at the thought.

"Haven't you missed *me*?" Kelly teased in a forlorn tone.

Mimi laughed her little musical laugh that trilled up the scale. "Of course I do, Kelly. I depend on seeing your smiling face every day. You're part of the shop family." She reached over and gave Kelly's shoulder a squeeze.

"Speaking of smiling faces, you certainly look all rosy-cheeked and happy," Lisa observed.

"Oh, that's because of the cash registers ringing," Kelly joked. "And Burt's also to blame."

Suddenly, Mimi's smile vanished and her eyes popped wide. "Wh-what? What do you mean?"

"The doughnuts, of course." Kelly laughed. "Burt's been bringing doughnuts to start the morning. That makes everyone happy. And fat. I have got to find some willpower somewhere." She shook her head as she went back to her scarf and found where she'd left off.

"Burt's a real sweetie," Lisa said with an enigmatic smile

as she focused on the mitten once again. "By the way, Mimi, if you need some help for the shop's Christmas party, count me in. I make a mean rum cake."

Mimi's smile returned. "Oh, thank you, Lisa. We could really use it. Every year we keep growing. Our parties are getting bigger, too."

"You have a holiday party?" Kelly fairly chirped with glee. "Fantastic! I haven't been to a happy holiday party since before my dad died four years ago. The CPA firm always had big expensive dinners for the holidays, where the senior partners drank too much and acted stupid."

Mimi giggled. "Well, we'll have a little holiday cheer, but we're all too smart to get stupid. You'll love it, Kelly. Sounds like you're due for a good time."

"You know what I've always wanted to do?" Kelly mused aloud, staring out the sock-trimmed windows to the bare branches of the cottonwood trees outside. "I want to go sleigh riding. You know, a one-horse open sleigh kind of thing."

"You can do that, Kelly. There are lots of ranches around the area that offer sleigh rides and hot chocolate beside a warm stove." Mimi closed her eyes as if remembering.

Lisa spoke up. "You know, it's too bad you couldn't get that property in the canyon you wanted so badly. It would have been perfect for sleigh rides. Greg and I cycled past the place last fall, after the woman . . . well, after she was taken away."

"You mean Geri Norbert's place?" Mimi's face paled. "That was so awful. How she could murder those women?" Mimi gave a little shiver. "I'm glad you didn't get her ranch, Kelly."

Kelly remembered anew the disappointment she'd felt when she'd learned that Geri Norbert's ranch had been bought by a real estate investor with much deeper pockets than hers. "It was a beautiful piece of property. I sure wish someone other than that developer had gotten it. Jennifer says he's going to build some mini mansion up there."

"Correction. Mini mansion plans are off the table," Jennifer declared as she pulled out the chair beside Kelly and sat down.

"What do you mean?" Kelly asked, watching Jennifer remove a blue and white wool sweater from her voluminous bag and start knitting, her needles moving at their usual lightning speed.

"Apparently, Geri Norbert's ranch is back on the market. I didn't even hear about it, and I wasn't checking the canyons this month because it's been a little slow heading into the holidays. So, imagine my surprise when another broker at my office mentioned he was taking a client up there." She shook her head. "I'm sorry, Kelly. I should have been on top of it."

"That's okay, Jen. I'm just happy to hear it's back on the market," Kelly said, the alpaca scarf dropping forgotten to her lap, excitement already racing through her veins. "Can you find out the details for me? Maybe I'll have a shot at getting it this time."

"I'll be glad to, but I heard the agent has it listed above market value. It's probably too pricey for you this time, Kelly."

"Let's wait and see," Kelly said, refusing to be deterred. "Find out how much, then I'll talk with Curt."

"Wait a minute. Curt's a rancher. You're the accountant," Lisa teased.

Kelly smiled, picturing her good friend and adviser Curt Stackhouse. Numbers she could manage. But when it came to cattle and sheep, Kelly was clueless. Without Curt's help, Kelly would have been lost when she inherited her cousin Martha's Wyoming ranch last summer. Now Curt was guiding Kelly through the wilderness of oil and gas drilling leases.

"I know, but Curt's the one who advises me on all that ranch business. Thanks to him I was able to free up enough cash to make an offer on that canyon property. He's selling off the herd."

"Okay, I'll check with the other agent then," Jennifer said. "But first, I want to find out why the developer changed his mind. I heard him talking about his plans last month, and he was all stoked about building this huge mountain home up there. True, it's got great scenery—"

"Fantastic views," Kelly corrected, feeling her excitement build.

"Take your time, Kelly," Mimi advised, a worried expression clouding her features as she headed toward the backroom. "Don't be hasty."

"Speaking of haste," Lisa chimed in, checking her watch before she rose from her chair, "I have to get back to the fitness center. Two private exercise sessions coming up."

"Wow, you'll be working late tonight," Jennifer said.

"Twice a week," Lisa said with a wave as she headed toward the main room. "See you guys later."

Kelly zeroed in on Jennifer once again. "Seriously, Jen, if that ranch is available I definitely want to make an offer. Find out the details tonight and give me a call, okay? I'll be working late."

"I thought you didn't have to work late now that you're consulting on your own. Have you gotten new clients or something?"

"Well, I've picked up a couple of small businesses here in town that Curt steered my way. Bless his heart. He—"

The rest of Kelly's sentence was blown away as Ellen suddenly raced through the classroom doorway and into the main room, hurrying over to the library table. Her face was flushed, her winter coat was hanging half off her shoulders, and a blue-green knitted scarf dangled around her neck. She leaned one hand on the table, obviously out of breath.

"Hi, Ellen," Kelly greeted, glad she'd remembered the spinner's name. "Looks like you're rushing somewhere."

"I came to see . . . if Lucy was here. Do you know . . . where she is?" she managed, catching her breath. "I called her cell, but there's no answer. She's not at home either, because I knocked on her door."

"Is she the new spinner who's helping Burt?" Jennifer asked. "Dark-haired, petite?"

"Yeah, Megan's taking her class. I sat in the other day," Kelly replied. "I'm sorry, Ellen, I haven't seen Lucy. Her class isn't until tomorrow, right?"

"It's not about class . . . ," Ellen said, collapsing into a nearby chair. "I just heard the news, and I couldn't believe it. That's why I'm trying to reach her." She stared out the window.

"Did something happen to Lucy?" Kelly let the alpaca scarf drop to her lap again. "Did she have a car accident? Is she all right?"

"It wasn't her, it was her boyfriend. Derek." Ellen leaned forward. "He's dead. I read in the paper this morning that an alpaca rancher was found dead on his ranch in Bellevue Canyon yesterday. I had a funny feeling and called Lucy. And when I didn't get an answer, I got worried. So I called this friend I have at the paper and asked if they'd released the name of the deceased. She told me she'd gotten the details today, but she couldn't reveal them yet. Then I told her Derek's name, and she went real quiet. I said I was going to assume that my guess was right. She didn't contradict me. That's when I got really worried and went looking for Lucy."

"How did he die? Was there an accident?"

Ellen shrugged. "The paper didn't say, and my friend couldn't tell me. Derek was only in his thirties."

"Did—did you say Derek?" Jennifer asked in a strangely soft voice.

"Yes. Derek Cooper. Why? Do you know him?" Ellen peered at Jennifer.

Kelly was startled to see her friend staring wide-eyed. "Did you know him, Jen?"

Jennifer nodded, staring out into the room. "Yes. I've known him for years. He used to go with one of my good friends, Diane. She was his regular girlfriend. They'd been seeing each other for ages."

Ellen sat up straight and frowned at Jennifer. "I'd heard he had a lot of old girlfriends, but he was never serious about any of them."

That comment snapped Jennifer out of her daze. *"Serious?"* she said, incredulous. "Derek Cooper would never get serious about anybody. He's the original love 'em and leave 'em guy."

"Maybe he was serious about Lucy," Ellen said in a cold voice. "But it doesn't matter now, does it?"

Jennifer stared solemnly at Ellen, but didn't say a word.

"Do you want a cup of coffee or tea, Ellen?" Kelly offered. "You look like you need to take it easy for a bit."

Ellen shook her head and rose from the chair. "I need to find Lucy. I'm still worried." With that, she flipped her scarf over her shoulder and raced from the room.

Kelly watched Jennifer pick up her needles again and begin to knit silently. Kelly followed suit. After several moments of quiet knitting, Kelly ventured, "Do you think your friend Diane knows yet? Does she live in the canyon, too?"

Jennifer shook her head and continued to knit for a minute or two before speaking. "No, Diane lives in town. But someone from the group will call her, you can be sure of that. They're the first to spread gossip and bad news."

"What group are you talking about?"

Jennifer let out a long sigh. "They're a group of people I've known for years. They meet over at a bar on the north side of town. Diane and I used to hang out with them every week. That's where she met Derek."

"Recently?"

"No, it was four years ago. He and Diane started going together as soon as they met. They were a hot couple. Couldn't keep their hands off each other. But they'd fight as much as they'd make love. Talk about a volatile relationship. She lived with him up in the canyon back then. Diane thought Derek was serious about her, too." Jennifer frowned. "Derek wasn't about to commit to anybody, despite what Ellen says. Trust me, he was a user. A real bastard. He messed up Diane, for sure. Damn him."

Kelly watched the emotions cross her friend's face. It was clear Jennifer wasn't going to mourn Derek Cooper. "How do you account for Ellen's picture of him? Sounds like two different guys."

"Oh, he was. He could be the most charming guy at the bar when he wanted you. I've watched him turn it on for some new girl who didn't know him. He was like a laser beam. He'd zero in on whomever he wanted to sleep with that night and *bam*. She'd melt like butter."

"Sounds like he melted Lucy. Did you ever see her at the bar?" Kelly pried.

"I think I remember seeing her once or twice." Jennifer shrugged. "Derek had so many girls, you lost track. I swear, he never slept alone."

"Somehow I can't picture Lucy picking up guys in a bar. She's kind of quiet and shy."

Jennifer gave a little snort. "Sometimes they're the wildest ones there. Some girls act sweet and refined during the day, then they show up at the bar ready to party."

"I still can't picture Lucy—"

"Listen, I'm going to tell Pete I have to leave early today. I need to call Diane and see how she's taking it." Jennifer shoved her knitting into its bag and pushed back her chair.

"I'm sorry about your friend, Jennifer," Kelly offered as Jennifer turned to leave.

"Diane's my friend, Kelly, not Derek," Jennifer replied tartly as she headed for the entry. "I'll call you later after I've checked on that property, okay?"

She was gone before Kelly could answer.

Three

Kelly reached across the computer keyboard and grabbed her cell phone, flipping it open. "Kelly here," she said automatically as she continued to tab through the accounting spreadsheet.

"Morning, Kelly," Curt Stackhouse's deep voice sounded. "What's got you so excited you left me a message at midnight?"

"Sorry, Curt. I couldn't help myself," Kelly said, leaning back in her desk chair. "Jennifer told me yesterday that Geri Norbert's ranch in the canyon is back on the market, and I want to make an offer."

"You do, huh?"

"Yes, Curt, I do. I lay awake half the night just thinking about it. It's a great property."

"Well, it is that. I went to take a look at it back in October when you said you wanted to buy it. It's a nice piece of land, for sure."

"I'm glad you approve, Curt, because you're going to help me find a way to pay for it all." She listened to Curt's soft laughter.

"I've already been making some plans along that line, Kelly girl, and I kept right on even when you didn't get the ranch in November. I figured it was just a matter of time until you found another place you liked. Once the mountain home bug bites you, you're a goner."

Kelly laughed. "Bless you, Curt. I couldn't do this ranch business without you. So, tell me, what ideas have you come up with?"

"The last time we talked about buying that canyon place, the plan was to sell off the rest of the herd and put the Wyoming ranch house up for sale to raise the cash you need."

"That'll be enough to buy the canyon place, right?"

"Right. But buying is just the beginning. You'll need the extra money to fix it up. Buildings are shot to hell. You need to build another ranch house, unless you plan to live in that ramshackle one. Same for the barn and stables. That'll cost."

Kelly pictured Geri Norbert, and a little shiver ran down her spine. Geri murdered two women. "No, I don't think I'd want to stay there. I'll keep living in the cottage. How long will it take to sell everything?"

"It could take longer than you think, Kelly. Holidays are coming up, then we're heading into the dead of winter."

"What about Chet? Will he want to stay on as ranch manager while we get all these sales accomplished?"

"Well, I'm hoping he will," Curt said. "I plan to recommend him to a couple of ranchers who're always looking for good men. I've been real impressed with Chet's work up there."

"Jennifer says we may want to wait for spring to sell the Wyoming house."

"She's right. You don't want to take a low offer on that place, Kelly. It's too fine a property to sell for less than it's worth."

"You know, something inside still isn't comfortable with selling Martha's ranch house," Kelly confessed. "But there's no other way to raise the cash to buy the canyon land."

"Think of it this way, Kelly. Your cousin Martha's property was left to you. You're the last of her family. It's a gift. Without it, we wouldn't be having this conversation. Your dream of a mountain home would stay just that. A dream."

Kelly found a smile. "Thanks, Curt. I needed to hear that. Now, here's the loaded question. If the Wyoming house doesn't sell until late spring or summer, how can I buy the canyon property now? I won't have enough money to bring to the closing."

"Don't be so sure."

"Will the drilling company start sending me money?"

Curt chuckled. "Not yet, Kelly. They won't start drilling until spring, and who knows when the gas will start flowing."

"Okay, I give up. You've got another plan, I can tell from the sound of your voice."

"You're right. There are private investors—"

"Whoa! Hold on, Curt. I can't take out another loan. Not with that huge mortgage Aunt Helen put on the cottage."

"These investors are different. They'll lend you the money for a short term. I figure six months should do it. The loan will be secured by the property, of course."

Kelly flinched, and the CPA lobe of her brain positively recoiled in horror.

"Yeah, but at what interest rate?"

"How badly do you want that canyon property?"

Kelly made a face into the phone. "Bad. I want it bad, Curt. It's beautiful."

"I figured. Then it'll be worth it. Don't worry. It'll probably be no more than six months."

"Okay, that sounds like a plan. But I'll depend on you to point me in the right direction, as always."

"You can depend on it."

"And you know where to find me," Kelly said with a laugh. "I'm either here with my nose to the keyboard or across the driveway in the shop knitting away. I'm trying to finish an alpaca scarf before Christmas."

"Don't worry, Kelly girl, I'll find you," Curt said with a chuckle, then hung up.

Kelly snapped her cell phone shut and wondered what she was getting into.

"**Did** you read the paper this morning?" Megan whispered as Kelly pulled up a chair beside the spinning students. "Ellen tells me that guy who was murdered in the canyon the other day was Lucy's boyfriend."

"I was here yesterday with Jennifer when Ellen came in and told us." She glanced around the classroom. "Has Lucy come in yet?"

"No, Burt's teaching her class. I overheard Ellen explaining to him that Lucy was in pretty bad shape. Apparently she's locked herself in her apartment. Ellen said she could hear her crying through the door. Won't answer the phone or anything." Megan shook her head. "Poor thing. I wish there was something we could do to help."

"It's best to leave her alone, Megan. I remember when I lost my dad, then Uncle Jim and Aunt Helen. I couldn't be around people right away. The tears kept coming. I even took a few days from the office, so I didn't have to go in and talk to people."

The sound of Burt's voice caught Kelly's attention then, as he entered the classroom with Ellen. Anne, the other student, was right behind them, looking as somber as the others. Kelly guessed that Ellen had shared the grim news.

"Anne, Ellen, why don't you two settle in and put your bobbins on the wheels," Burt instructed. "I'll be taking over for Lucy today. She's feeling a little under the weather."

Kelly's caffeine lobe chose that moment to pulsate. "I think I'll go for coffee," she excused herself as she rose. "See you guys after class."

Retrieving her mug, Kelly was headed toward the café when a familiar voice called out from an adjoining yarn room. "Hey, Kelly, how've you been?"

She turned to see Jayleen Swinson saunter past the yarn bins piled high with holiday fibers. "Hi, Jayleen. Join me for coffee?"

Jayleen shoved her hands in the back pockets of her jeans in her usual fashion. "I reckon I could use a little sit-down. I've been runnin' nonstop most of the day." She tossed her still-blonde curls over her shoulder.

Kelly headed down the hallway toward the café, Jayleen following. "What's up? I thought you were settling into your new place pretty well. Are you rattling around now with all the extra space?"

"Oh, that part is fine. Great, actually. The animals sure like the bigger barn and pastures, too," Jayleen said as she pulled up a chair at the table Kelly had chosen. "Something else is on my mind. I volunteered to run my charity's holiday party for kids this month. Someone backed out at the last minute, and I stepped in. Now I'm scrambling to get it all together, and I've only got a week and a half. It's set for Sunday after next."

"Sounds like you need help. What can I do?"

Jayleen's sun-lined face broke into a big grin. "Thanks, Kelly. I was about to ask you. In fact, that's why I'm here. I plan to corral as many folks into helping that I can find. Are any of the other gals here?" She craned her neck, peering around the café. "I don't see Jennifer."

"Afternoons Jen works real estate, remember? And she's actually in her office writing a purchase offer for me." Kelly held up her mug so the waitress could fill it. "Thanks, Julie."

"Whoa, girl," Jayleen exclaimed. "Don't tell me you found another mountain place. Where is it?"

"Right up the road from you," Kelly said. "Geri Norbert's place went back on the market. It seems the real estate developer changed his mind about building his mini mansion. So we're making another offer. Keep your fingers crossed, Jayleen. Maybe I'll snag it this time." She leaned out of the way so the waitress could pour coffee for them both.

Jayleen's surprise was evident. "When did this happen? I hadn't heard a thing."

"It only came on the market this week, according to Jen. Of course, it's listed a lot higher this time, but I've checked with Curt, and he says I'll have enough to make an offer."

"Kelly, that's great. I know how much you wanted that

place. Hell, it'll be much better having you build a home up there rather than Mr. Big Shot. I asked Bobby what the guy was like, and he said a typical CEO type. Barking orders and a short temper."

"Who's Bobby?" Kelly asked.

"Oh, he's the part-time guy the bank hired to take care of Geri's livestock. He comes out twice a day. Apparently the big shot hadn't decided if he was going to keep the animals or not, so he kept Bobby on. Now that he's selling the ranch, you may be able to expand your herd. Providing you get it this time."

"That's an idea," Kelly mused out loud.

"Geri had some good females, too."

"Wow, I wonder if I could afford them."

Jayleen's smile turned sly. "Well, they'll be more expensive now that the real estate guy is selling."

Kelly took a long drink of coffee. Her pulse had speeded up so much she couldn't tell if it was excitement or the caffeine. She was getting way ahead of herself. She didn't know if she'd even get the property. There would be plenty of time to check out Geri's alpacas. Then she'd talk to Curt. Again.

"I was visiting with Mimi when I first came in, and I spotted Burt walking by. Is he all right? He was frowning about something. Didn't even hear me say hello."

"He's fine, Jayleen. Burt had just heard the same bad news we all did. One of our spinning teachers was dating that guy who was killed in the canyon the other day. Apparently she was really serious about him, too. He was an alpaca rancher, so you probably knew him. Derek Cooper."

This time, Jayleen's eyes popped wide. "Lord a'mighty! I read about it this morning. It made my blood run cold, thinking there was a killer running around the canyon." She shivered. "Who would have done such a thing? And which one of Mimi's gals was going with him?"

"Lucy. The dark-haired, quiet one who helps Burt. She's taking it pretty hard."

"I know Lucy. She's helped me out with the spinning since fall. Lucy's a real sweetheart."

"Did you know Derek Cooper at all?"

"Didn't know him real well. Saw him at several breeders' association dinners, talked to him at a few meetings, that's all. He seemed like a nice enough young man. In fact, that's where Lucy met him. I had an extra ticket for a banquet one time and invited her to come along. Next thing I know, Derek had her sitting next to him." She shook her head, still only a trace of gray running through her blonde curls. "That's a damn shame. I didn't even know she was seeing him."

"She's kind of shy. I think she only told Ellen she was dating him." Glancing at the doorway, Kelly spotted Ellen walking by. "Hey, Ellen," she called, "skipping class? Come over here and meet someone."

"I'm looking for a yarn I saw yesterday," Ellen said as she approached.

"I want you to meet another Lambspun regular—Jayleen Swinson. She has a ranch up in Bellevue Canyon, too. Jayleen, Ellen Hunter. She's another spinner in Lucy's class."

"Nice to meet you, Ellen," Jayleen said. "I sure was sorry to hear about Derek Cooper getting killed up in the canyon. That's awful. And I'm sorry poor Lucy was involved with him."

Ellen nodded solemnly. "So am I. It's been awful."

Jayleen peered at Ellen for a minute, then smiled. "You know, you look real familiar to me. Have we met before? Are you a rancher, too?"

Ellen smiled as she shook her head. "Not me. I'm not much for taking care of livestock. You probably have me mixed up with someone else."

"I don't know, I've got a pretty good memory for faces." Jayleen checked her watch, then fairly leaped from the chair. "Whoa, I've gotta get going. I'm still trying to figure out where I'll put all those kids. Hell, I'm barely settled in myself, and the ranch house is still filled with unpacked boxes. I don't know when I'll have time to get ready. Catch you later, Kelly. Tell the others about the charity event for me, okay?" She gave a quick wave as she hurried off.

"Gotta get back to class," Ellen said, drawing away.

Dropping some bills on the table, Kelly checked her own mental daytimer as she walked toward the knitting shop again. If she returned to her cottage-office now, she could start another client account before meeting Steve for quick tennis practice and a quicker dinner.

Edging close to the classroom, Kelly spotted Burt quietly monitoring the spinners. She leaned around the corner and motioned Burt closer.

"Hi, Kelly. Want to learn to spin?" Burt asked, a twinkle in his eyes.

"I wouldn't do that to Mimi's spinning wheels. No, I was wondering if you could do something for me, Burt. You read about that rancher in the canyon, right?"

Burt nodded. "Did you know him, Kelly? I figure you're about to ask me to look into it for you, am I right?"

"Burt, you are reading my mind far too easily nowadays. You're right. I was curious as to how Derek Cooper was killed. The paper said it was a homicide."

"Why are you interested, Kelly? For Lucy's sake?"

She shrugged. "Yes, and Jennifer knew him, too. So, I'm curious."

Burt observed her with a wry smile. "That curiosity of yours never sleeps, does it?"

"Nope, I guess I can't help myself," Kelly said, wondering herself.

Four

"**Did** he say anything when you gave him the offer last night?" Kelly asked, extending her mug so Jennifer could fill it.

Midmorning coffee break. Only Eduardo's black gold could enable her to face the shoebox full of receipts her new client had brought yesterday. Talk about disorganized. She was going to have to have a long talk with this rancher.

"No. He'd already left, so I gave it to his assistant, Rodney. Rod's a good guy. He indicated that we were 'in the ballpark.'"

"Good. Maybe we have a chance this time."

"Let's hope." Jennifer replaced the pot and called over her shoulder to the café owner. "Pete, I'm going to take a break now, okay? Be back in a few minutes."

"Take your time, Jen. It's quiet," Pete said as he arranged salads in a glass case.

Jennifer snatched her knitting bag from behind the counter and followed Kelly into the shop. "Listen, I've been asking around to find out why that guy changed his plans for the property. And, you know, all I'm getting is vague answers. I asked the diva in our office what she knew. She's been around since forever—"

"Diva?" Kelly laughed as she settled at the empty library table.

Jennifer sat beside her. "Oh, yeah, every office has an old-timer who's been selling real estate since dirt. They know everything and everybody. Who's doing what to whom, you know." She pulled out the blue and white patterned sweater and began to knit.

Kelly noticed that one sweater sleeve was completely finished. A long sleeve, too. Sleeves. She needed to learn to knit long sleeves. It was winter, for Pete's sake. She could use a pretty sweater like that one, she thought, returning to Eugene Tolliver's alpaca scarf. Unfortunately she couldn't stop looking at the intricate pattern Jennifer was deftly knitting, blue yarn working a design with the white. Kelly wondered if she could manage both challenges: long sleeves and a design. After a minute of self-reflection, she sighed. *Nah.* She'd wind up botching both the design and the sleeves. Better try one at a time. First, sleeves. Definitely sleeves. If she started after Christmas, maybe she could finish a simple one-color sweater before spring. Maybe.

"Anyway, all Maya said was she'd heard he lost interest in the mountain place after one of his commercial properties was vandalized."

"Really? What happened?"

"I remember hearing something about a fire," Jennifer said. "Maya confirmed that his new apartment complex out near the interstate was torched. Luckily, some drivers on the interstate noticed and called 911. Firemen were able to get there before it was completely destroyed. That's good, but it'll still be costly to rebuild."

Kelly reflected on that scary scenario, wondering if Steve had ever experienced any vandalism at his building sites. "Maybe that's why he changed his plans. He can't afford to build the mountain home now."

Jennifer sent her a wry smile. "Mr. Deep Pockets? No, Kelly. Something else changed his mind; I can tell. I asked Rod why the change of plans, and Rod turned away and started shuffling papers on his desk. My instinct says there's more here than meets the eye."

"You're starting to sound like me when I'm searching for clues," Kelly joked.

Jennifer stared across the table, her smile disappearing. "You know, I spoke with my friend Diane yesterday. She's a wreck. Crying and almost hysterical when I finally reached her. She kept saying, 'I can't believe he's dead,' over and over, and 'I should have stayed, I should have stayed.' That worried me, so I asked what she meant, and she couldn't even answer at first. Then she blurted out she had gone over to Derek's place that night."

Kelly's needles stopped their rhythmic movements. "You mean the night Derek was killed?"

Jennifer nodded, staring at the blue and white yarn in her lap, needles moving slower now. "Yeah. I asked her why, and she told me Derek had called and begged her to come out. Said he wanted to make up after their last fight. So she drove up to his ranch. But when she got there, they started fighting again so she left."

"I thought he was going with Lucy. What's he doing, keeping two girls at the same time?"

"I told you. That's Derek's style. I'm sorry Lucy got involved with him, but I'm sorrier for Diane. Derek was up to his old tricks with her. Fighting with her, then begging Diane to come back to him, then he walks all over her again." Jennifer's tone had grown increasingly bitter.

"Derek sounds like a real bastard."

"Ohhhh, he was a piece of work, for sure."

Kelly chose her next words carefully. "Sounds like he and Diane had a love-hate relationship."

"That's pretty accurate. And I can tell what you're thinking, Kelly, and there's no way Diane could have killed Derek. She's hotheaded, sure, but she's not violent. Not really."

"Do the police know Diane went up there that night?"

Jennifer's shoulders drooped. "No, but they will. I'm sure they're interviewing everybody at the bar. They'll be eager to tell the cops about Diane and Derek."

"Where did Diane go after she left Derek? Did she tell you?"

Jennifer shook her head. "I didn't ask her, but I should have." Jennifer stared across the table once more, then stuffed her knitting into the bag. "I should call her. In fact, I'd better go over there right now before she goes into a dive."

"A dive?"

Jennifer rose from her chair. "Yeah, whenever she and Derek would have a blowout, Diane would go out on a binge, drinking. Then she'd sink even lower when she sobered up. Maybe I can reach her beforehand. The last thing she needs is for the police to knock on her door with questions, and she's passed out, drunk. I'll talk to you later, Kelly." With that, she hurried from the room.

Kelly let Jennifer's words filter through her mind. They certainly didn't paint a very flattering picture of Diane. Binge-drinking, passing out drunk. Jennifer made it sound like this had been happening for quite a while. Not good. Particularly if the police come calling. Diane would definitely need a clear head for *their* questions.

She took a long sip of her coffee and wondered if Lucy knew anything about Derek's other lovers. Some women were drawn to the "bad boys," and would forgive them anything. Kelly remembered some of the various and sundry bad boys who had flitted through her life. Most had never stayed around long, no doubt sensing that she would be less than tolerant of their transgressions.

All except one. Jeff the Slime. Smooth, and very, very clever at concealing his sneaky side. Old memories darted from the bushes, aiming their barbs at her like before. But their sting was weaker now, Kelly noticed. Barely skin-deep.

"Kelly, have you seen my knitting bag? I misplaced it," Megan's voice interrupted as she raced into the room.

Kelly glanced about the familiar clutter in the middle of the knitting table. "Nope. Afraid not."

Megan scurried around the table, sapphire blue knit scarf wrapped tightly around her neck as if she'd rushed in from the winter cold that very minute. She anxiously checked under chairs and behind yarn bins. "Darn, I'm running late already. Now, where is it?" she fussed, dropping to the floor to peer under the table. "Ah-ha! There it is," she crowed triumphantly as she reached beneath a chair and retrieved the missing bag.

"What's the big hurry?" Kelly asked, observing that

Megan looked uncharacteristically scattered. "Have you got an important appointment or something?"

Megan rounded the table quickly, clearly ready to race from the shop. Pausing beside Kelly's chair, she hesitated before answering. "I'm trying to get all my work done by the afternoon, so I can go with Lisa and Greg to the movies tonight."

"That sounds like fun," Kelly said, noticing that Megan hadn't made eye contact with her yet. Something was up. Megan was unusually flustered. Going to the movies with Lisa and Greg wouldn't elicit this reaction. Unless . . .

Instantly, Kelly knew what was bothering Megan. Lisa and Greg were fixing her up with a guy. It had to be.

"Yeah, we're going for pizza in Old Town first." Megan stared at her car keys as she turned them over in her hand. "And . . . and they're bringing some guy they want me to meet. He's a colleague of Greg's at the university. I think he cycles with him, too."

Kelly shined her most encouraging smile, hoping to penetrate the barrier that Megan was hiding behind. "That's great, Megan! I'm sure you'll have a lot of fun. Sounds like the guy is athletic, like you. I bet you two will hit it off. I'm sure that's why Steve and I get along so well. We're both jocks."

Megan exhaled a big sigh and finally met Kelly's gaze, her fair skin making her blue eyes look huge. "I don't 'hit it off' with guys, Kelly. You know that. That's why I hate blind dates. Whenever I meet a guy on a date, I freeze up. I stammer like I can't talk, and I turn red as a beet." She shrugged. "I'm only going tonight because Lisa begged me."

Kelly searched for something encouraging to say, something that would help Megan conquer her shyness. She could see Megan retreating into her shell already. "Megan, you only freeze up when you know it's a date or the guy is coming on to you; I've watched it. But you have no problem at all talking with guys who are friends. Steve, Greg, all the guys on the team. Your tennis buddies. Why don't you tell yourself this guy is not a date. He's only a friend, only a friend. See if that helps."

Finally a smile peeked out as Megan repeated the mantra. "He's only a friend. He's only a friend. He's not a date. Not a date." Her smile spread, much to Kelly's relief. Smiles were a start. "Self-hypnosis, huh? Okay, I'll give it a try. Wish me luck," she said as she walked away. "Oh, and tell Steve that Sam and I will practice doubles with you two tomorrow night. You've got your first match the following night."

"Don't remind me. We're still barely competent," Kelly called over her shoulder.

"Kelly, you mustn't be so hard on yourself. You're doing very well indeed," a deep, throaty woman's voice sounded behind her.

"Yes, dear. Your sweater-in-the-round turned out quite nicely," a birdlike chirp floated past.

Kelly recognized the voices before the two elderly women approached the table. Hilda and Lizzie von Steuben. Spinster sisters, retired schoolteachers, and knitters of the highest level. Others knitted yarns. Hilda and Lizzie could knit cobwebs.

"Hello, ladies, how're you doing?" Kelly greeted as the two women pulled out nearby chairs. Hilda, tall and raw-boned, and rosy-cheeked, plump-as-a-dumpling Lizzie. They barely resembled each other except in talent and kindness as well as genuine concern for the knitting shop family.

Almost as if she read Kelly's mind, Lizzie spoke up while she lifted a white, gauzy creation from her bag. "We're doing well, dear. But I'm concerned about that dear child, Lucy. Mimi told us what happened, and we were both shocked. Simply shocked."

"Murder most foul," Hilda intoned from her end of the table, fingers nimbly turning green and white yarns into a sweater. "Who could do such a thing, especially in a tranquil setting like Bellevue Canyon?"

"Well, Hilda, I don't think setting is too important to a killer when they decide to murder someone. If you recall, Vickie Claymore was killed in her canyon home last summer. And her daughter, Debbie."

Lizzie shivered, causing the bits of red and white lace that adorned her upswept silvery hair to bounce. "Ooooh, that was simply dreadful. That awful woman, Geri Norbert. Killing both those lovely women. Horrible."

"How was the young man killed, Kelly? I assumed you'd be checking into the details for us," Hilda commented in a matter-of-fact voice.

"You know me too well, Hilda," Kelly confessed with a grin. "I asked Burt to find out. After all, Lucy is one of our own."

"You're right, dear. We need to make sure she's not alone in this crisis." Lizzie's tiny needles deftly worked the white yarn. "Where is she, anyway? Has she been to the shop?"

"Apparently she's still grieving at home. Ellen, one of the other spinning students, is a good friend of Lucy's, and she says Lucy doesn't want to talk to anyone right now."

"Poor dear." Lizzie tsked. "We should do something, don't you think? We shouldn't leave her alone like that."

"Sometimes that's exactly what should be done. Each person needs to grieve in peace. Lucy will rejoin her friends when she's ready," Hilda decreed.

Kelly nodded her agreement, letting the rhythm of the stitches work their relaxing magic. She needed some relaxation after trying to make sense of her newest client's messy accounts. She might have to recommend a bookkeeper for this one.

The reminder of client accounts caused the ticking clock inside her head to buzz. Time to get back to work. Nose to the keyboard. She stuffed the alpaca scarf back into its bag and rose to leave. "Ladies, I'm afraid I have to return to work. See you later."

The sound of goodbyes floated after her as Kelly wandered through the main yarn room, fondling and stroking the brightly colored wools, mohairs, alpaca, and silks that were scattered on tables, stacked in piles on cupboards, and spilling from shelves. Holiday sweaters adorned the walls, festive socks dangled like ornaments, and matching hats and mittens bloomed in the corners like Christmas poinsettias.

Slowly she made her way to the foyer, reveling in the sensuous softness surrounding her. A multihued skein of recycled sari silk begged to be stroked. Luscious shamrock green mohair called next. Champagne-colored cashmere glistened in billowy bunches, almost as if the bubbly wine were captured in the fibers. Kelly indulged herself, sinking her hands into the seductive yarns.

Lingering over a particularly tempting pile of froth, Kelly detected the low murmur of voices, a man's and a woman's, coming from the adjoining room. She glanced about the shop, which was uncharacteristically empty at the moment. A girlish giggle floated from the room, and Kelly peered around the corner, curious for some unknown reason.

Mimi and Burt stood across the room, talking softly to each other. Mimi's face was flushed, as was Burt's, Kelly noticed. And they were looking at each other in the way people do when there's more going on in a conversation than talking.

Kelly observed them for a second more, then withdrew and tiptoed to the door, not wanting to disturb their absorption with one another. *Well, well, well,* she thought with a smile as she hurried across the driveway.

Five

"**I'm** so sorry it didn't work out, Kelly," Mimi said, patting Kelly's hand. "I know how much you wanted that place. But maybe . . . maybe it wasn't meant to be."

Kelly smiled across the café table at Mimi, who was obviously trying to make her feel better. Mother Mimi. Not having had a mother when she was growing up, Kelly had learned how to soothe her own hurts over the years. She'd actually believed she didn't need motherly attention. Now Kelly knew better. Simply sitting with Mimi, who listened attentively while she shared her disappointment about losing Geri Norbert's canyon property again, made Kelly feel better. Comforted.

"Maybe so, Mimi," she said as she lifted another bite of the western omelet. "But it's still hard to watch it slip away again."

Mimi patted, but said nothing this time. Jennifer

approached their table, coffeepot in hand, and gave Kelly a big smile. "I knew Eduardo's omelet would make you feel better. More coffee?"

"Always." Kelly shoved her mug forward.

"I'd better get back to the shop," Mimi said, rising from the chair. "It's nice to share breakfast with you, Kelly. Let's do this another time, okay?"

"You bet. I didn't know what I was missing," she said, before she finished off the homemade sausage.

"See you later, Mimi," Jennifer said as Mimi walked away. "Don't worry, Kelly, I promise to keep a wary eye on the mountain property listings from now on."

Kelly glanced out the window at the barren and empty café patio. A light covering of snow on the concrete hinted at more to come. Tables and chairs were stored behind the garage and covered with a tarp—waiting for spring. Just like Pete's plans for expanding the café. Waiting for warm weather to return.

"I know you will, Jen. It's not your fault. My offer was lower, that's all. I can't fault the seller for taking a much higher offer." She took a long sip of coffee, then deliberately shifted her attention back to the café, changing the subject. "You know, I spotted Mimi and Burt talking with each other yesterday afternoon. Except they weren't simply talking, if you know what I mean." She grinned up at Jennifer.

Jennifer grinned back. "Oh, yeah. I've seen them having lunch here at that corner table in the back." She gestured over her shoulder. "They're definitely looking like lovers to me."

"Whoa! You think?" Kelly sat up straight.

"If not, they're headed that way fast. They've got 'the look.' " Jennifer gave her a sly smile. "It's a dead giveaway."

Kelly sensed she'd better change the subject again before

Jennifer started teasing her about Steve. She never got the chance. Jennifer set the pot on the table and sat down, a concerned look on her face.

"Kelly, I'm worried about Diane," she said as she leaned forward. "The police questioned her yesterday afternoon. She called me right afterward, scared to death. They'd asked her where she was the night of Derek's death, and she told them she was at home, asleep."

"You mean she didn't tell them about going over to his place?" Kelly asked in a low voice.

"No, and what's worse is they probably already know she's not telling the truth. I had a call from one of the girls at the bar, and she said Diane was there when she got Derek's call. Furthermore, she told several people she was going up to his place."

"Oh, no," Kelly breathed. "That will make her look even worse to the police. They've caught her in a lie."

Jennifer nodded. "It gets even worse. My friend also told me Diane and Derek 'had it out' in the bar last week. Same old thing, but this time Diane threatened Derek and came at him with a broken glass, screaming 'I oughta bash that pretty face in.' The others had to hold her back."

"Whoa . . . that's bad, Jen. Really bad. I hate to say it but Diane is going to wind up Lieutenant Peterson's chief suspect."

"Peterson? The same detective who interviewed us at Vickie Claymore's ranch last July?"

"Yep. This crime happened in the county, so it's on Peterson's desk. And he doesn't miss a trick as I recall. He'll interview everyone at that bar and learn all about Diane and Derek's volatile history and Diane's drunken binges."

Jennifer's mouth tightened. "Damn it. I know she didn't

kill Derek. She couldn't. She was probably passed out drunk on her sofa."

Kelly took a deep breath and spoke the thoughts she knew Jennifer didn't want to acknowledge. "Jen, have you considered that maybe the reason Diane came back to her place and drank herself into a stupor was because she'd just killed Derek?"

Jennifer stared into Kelly's eyes. Kelly watched doubt flit through her troubled gaze. "Of course I've thought of that, but . . . but I couldn't believe it. Diane couldn't kill Derek. I know she couldn't."

"You don't know that, Jen," Kelly countered, hoping to penetrate her friend's denial. "Anyone is capable of murder. Sounds like Diane was already drinking at the bar, then she goes up to the canyon where she and Derek have another blowout. Maybe she doesn't remember killing him; I don't know. I've never been that drunk."

"I have," Jennifer admitted softly, staring out into the cold December sunlight. "And I'd remember. I know I would."

Kelly reached over and patted her friend's arm, much as Mimi had patted hers earlier. "I don't think you're as bad off as your friend Diane, judging from what you've told me. I mean, you don't go on drunken binges. We'd all know if you did. You know the Lambspun network. No one can keep a secret here."

Jennifer gave Kelly a wry smile. "You've got that right." She glanced over her shoulder and pushed away from the cozy corner table. "I'd better get back to my customers."

"Me, too. But first, I need a few minutes of quiet before I return to this messy client's file. I stopped working last night after your phone call."

Jennifer retrieved the coffeepot then walked beside Kelly

toward the hallway. "By the way, did you find out how Derek was killed? I mean, was he shot, stabbed, what?"

"I'm waiting to hear from Burt on that. Did Diane have a gun? Did Derek?"

Jennifer shrugged. "I can't imagine Diane with a gun. But I know Derek had a shotgun and a rifle, because he talked about shooting scavengers. Listen, I'll see you later," she said as she headed toward another table.

Rounding the corner into the main room, Kelly settled at the empty library table, anticipating the meditative relaxation that knitting quietly could bring. But this time it didn't come. Her mind would not slow down. Bits and pieces of the conversation with Jennifer kept flitting through her brain.

Diane threatening Derek at the bar. Diane returning home and passing out drunk. Diane having it out with Derek at his ranch. Diane lying to the police. Jennifer's worried expression and defense of her troubled friend. Had Diane killed Derek? How? Did she shoot him? Where did she get the gun? Kelly knitted another row of stitches, but her thoughts didn't slow down. Where was Burt anyway? The last she saw him, he was flirting with Mimi over the yarn bins. Where was he when she needed him?

"Good, I was hoping I'd find you here alone." Burt's voice startled her as he walked up from behind. Pulling up a chair beside her, he sat down, hands clasped between his knees in what Kelly recognized as his "talking pose."

She released an audible sigh. "Burt, I must have summoned you telepathically. I swear my curiosity won't let me alone about this Derek Cooper murder."

"I figured," Burt said with a grin.

"So, tell me. How was Derek Cooper killed? The newspapers aren't giving any details except that it was a homicide."

"Well, they were told to wait until the next of kin is notified. It seems Derek's mother and father were on a cruise in the Caribbean, so it took a while to reach them. They'll be coming later this week to take his body back to California for burial."

"Was he shot?"

"Nope. He died from a severe blow to the head, which led to fatal bleeding inside the brain. The weapon was an old shovel found on the barn floor, still bloody. No good fingerprints, unfortunately."

"A shovel?"

Burt nodded. "He died within minutes, apparently. Too bad there was no snow on the ground. They could have gotten some footprints. As it was, there was nothing found near his body except the shovel and a lot of cash lying around."

"They found money?"

"Yep. Lots of dollar bills scattered around. Derek's wallet was empty, too, so they figured it was his money."

Kelly tried to picture womanizing Derek Cooper, lying dead in a pile of his own cash. "That's strange, don't you think?"

"Well, it's different, I'll say that," Burt admitted with a smile.

"It couldn't be a robbery gone bad," Kelly mused out loud. "Otherwise, the killer would have taken the cash. And I can't imagine a killer carrying around a shovel as a weapon, can you?"

"It would be a little awkward."

Kelly pondered another minute. "Sounds to me like a

crime of passion, Burt. I mean, shovels are naturally found in barns. Derek and the killer are having an argument or a fight, and the killer reaches out for whatever is handy. Wham! Derek's dead."

Burt's careworn face crinkled into a grin. "Right as usual, Kelly. That's exactly what the investigators are thinking. There's certainly no way this was accidental. You have to hit someone really hard to kill them. Exam showed that Derek was hit on the right side of the head. Death was quick."

"If Derek was hit on the side of his head, he was probably turning away or walking away from the killer."

"Most likely."

Kelly pondered for another minute. "There's no way Derek Cooper would turn his back on a menacing stranger, certainly not if they were having a heated argument. That means the killer was not a stranger. It was someone Derek knew. Someone he felt safe walking away from."

Burt chuckled. "Sharp eye, Kelly. The investigators are looking at everyone, though. They can't afford to rule out any possibility, even the intruder theory. They're interviewing Derek's friends and business acquaintances right now."

Remembering that Jennifer's friend Diane had lied to the police, Kelly deliberately kept quiet. The detectives would find out soon enough about Diane. She didn't need to point them in that direction. "Keep me posted, will you?"

"You bet," he said as he stood up. "Right now, I'm going to spin some of those fleeces that have piled up in the storage room. See you later, Kelly."

"Thanks, Burt," Kelly said as he left.

Picking up the gray and white alpaca scarf in her lap, Kelly began to knit while her mind sifted through everything Burt had said about Derek Cooper's death. A crime of passion. It had to be. A violent argument taking a nasty turn into murder. A little shiver ran through her, recalling what Jennifer had said about Diane and Derek's many fights. The last argument sounded pretty violent. Diane tried to attack Derek, threatening him. That on its own looked bad. Then Diane lied to the police about her whereabouts that night, when there were plenty of witnesses ready to contradict her story. Not good, not good at all.

Not knowing Diane personally, Kelly didn't know how to feel about Diane. But she did know Jennifer, and Kelly trusted Jennifer's judgment. Jennifer might be a free-spirited party girl, but she was also smart and an extremely shrewd observer of people. Had Jennifer's friendship with Diane blinded her keen vision in this situation?

Too many questions buzzed inside Kelly's head now, darting around like summer mosquitoes. So much so, she decided the only way to clear her head would be to return to her client account files. Nothing like numbers to restore order.

She shoved the woolen scarf into her bag and rose to leave, when Curt Stackhouse strode into the room. Tall, burly, and silver-haired, Curt was the image of a Colorado rancher, his face weathered from years outside with herds of cattle, flocks of sheep, and riding the range.

"Not so fast, Kelly. That computer work can wait," Curt announced as he pulled up the chair beside her, setting his Stetson on the table.

"Hey, Curt. You're reading my mind again," Kelly said as she plopped her bag back on the floor. Curt was here to talk, she could tell. Next to client account files, she couldn't think of anything that cleared her head faster than hearing details of the Wyoming ranch she inherited when her cousin Martha died.

"First, let me tell you how sorry I am you didn't get that canyon property, Kelly. I could tell you had your heart set on it."

"Thanks, Curt. I guess this kind of changes our plans, right?"

Curt rested one leg on his knee. "Kelly, I've decided to proceed with the same plans, only go a little slower. There's no need for us to sell what's left of the herd right away. We've already reduced it to a manageable size. And we can take our time selling that fine ranch house. Now we can wait for the right buyers and the right prices for both. I'm sure you'll agree that's a wiser decision."

"I trust your judgment implicitly, Curt. Whatever you think best. I certainly won't be needing a lot of cash right away like before."

"Well, I figure it's only a matter of time before you find another canyon place that tickles your fancy. Who knows? You may find someplace this spring. And in case you find a place sooner, we'll proceed with our original plan."

"With the private investors, right?"

Curt nodded. "That way, you'll have time to sell the ranch and herd for a good price."

"Well, it's certainly an option, but I don't think I'll even be looking until the springtime, Curt. Meanwhile, Jennifer plans to keep an eagle eye on the mountain listings, just in case."

"Hey, looky here," Jayleen's voice called out from the adjoining room. She strode toward them, boots tapping a quick staccato. "I was hoping to see you folks."

"How're the plans for the children's party going?" Kelly greeted her, noticing snowflakes on Jayleen's denim jacket. She glanced outside. Tiny flakes drifted down. Tennis would be chilly tonight. Hopefully she and Steve would lose quickly to Megan and her partner, so they could head to dinner to warm up.

Jayleen tossed her cowboy hat to the table, grabbed a chair, and straddled it backward all in one smooth movement. "Well, if I can get a few more volunteers, I'll feel much better. That's why I came here. I figured I could snag some folks who'd like to help out with the kids."

"What are you up to, Jayleen?" Curt asked.

"Oh, I stepped in at the last minute to help run a Christmas party for kids run by a local charity. And now I'm running around like a chicken with its head cut off. I barely have time to get my work done at the ranch. God knows when I'll ever be able to clear out all those packing boxes from my house. I may have to carry them to the barn, so we'll have room for the party."

"We can help with that, Jayleen," Kelly offered. "I'll get Megan and Lisa and Jennifer to come along early. We can help you clean up beforehand."

"I've got a better idea. Why don't you leave those boxes be and bring those kids and everyone else out to my ranch?" Curt suggested. "I've got more space than I know what to do with."

"Lord, Curt, we couldn't impose like that," Jayleen objected. "I was hoping you'd help with the kids. No need to go to all that trouble."

"No trouble at all, Jayleen," Curt said with a lazy grin. "I miss having folks over. Only one thing—my grandkids have to come along, too."

"Hell, yes," Jayleen exclaimed. "Bring 'em along. But are you sure you want a whole passel of kids runnin' around your place? Now, me, I don't have much they can mess up, but your house is all neat and tidy."

"And too damn quiet," Curt said. "I'm rattling around there like a bean in a can. I'd welcome the commotion. Truth be told, the place is feeling pretty empty, especially with the holiday coming and all. By now, Ruthie would have the house all decorated. Hell, I may not even put up a tree this year."

"Now hold on, we can't have that kinda talk," Jayleen scolded. "Tell you what we'll do. You buy the tree, and we'll all come out early to decorate. The kids won't be coming until two o'clock."

"Hey, that's a great idea," Kelly joined in. "We can take over Curt's kitchen and make brunch. If we have food, we'll get more helpers. Then we'll decorate Curt's entire house before the kids show up."

"You don't have to do that, Kelly," Curt protested.

Kelly gave him a big grin. "Are you kidding? It'll be a lot of fun, and, to quote your words, 'it'll be no trouble at all.'"

"It's really coming down now," Steve said, pointing through the windows at the falling snow.

Kelly sipped her vodka martini and watched the snowstorm from their cozy corner booth in the Jazz Bistro's lounge. Enticing rhythms pulsed through the air from the trio across the room. "I'm glad we've got that big, badass truck of yours to drive home tonight," she said. "I'm also glad Megan and Sam worked us over quickly so we could have dinner."

Steve chuckled and settled back into the curved cushioned leather, resting his arm above Kelly's shoulders. "They were merciful, that's for sure. But we're getting better, too, don't you think?" He took a sip of his drink.

"There was only one way for us to go, and that's up." She

nibbled a slice of baked Brie with raspberry sauce drizzled over it.

"You sound like you're feeling better. Yesterday when you called me, you were pretty low."

Kelly gave a little shrug, then sipped her martini. "I'm all right now. It was just so frustrating to lose that great property a second time. But I was outbid, simple as that."

"Any idea who got the place?"

"Jennifer said some woman from the Midwest bought it for her retirement dream home. Apparently she's coming out this week to talk with builders and stuff." She eyed him over the top of her glass. "You want to audition for the job? Jennifer heard she's got money to burn."

"Naw, not interested," Steve said, leaning closer. "The only canyon house I'd be willing to build would be yours."

Kelly looked into Steve's warm gaze. "Really? You'd build a mountain house for me?"

"Sure I would. In fact, I wouldn't want anyone else building it," he said, laughing softly.

"Steve, you can't take time from all your building sites to drive up into the canyon every day. You're about to begin a new project in Old Town, for heaven's sake," Kelly reminded him.

"Let me worry about that. Besides, I may be getting some help. I'm seriously thinking about hiring a supervisor for the housing sites, someone with experience I could trust, so I could free up the time to get this loft project developed."

Kelly gave him a sly smile. "You? Are you sure you could hand over control to someone else? I'll believe that when I see it."

"Spoken by the Queen of Control Freaks, right?"

"It takes one to know one." She laughed softly, relaxing into the moment.

"I'll make you a promise, Kelly," he said, so close to her face she could feel his warm breath. "You find the land, and I'll build your dream house."

Jazz rhythms swirled in the air around them, like the snowflakes flurrying outside. She smiled into Steve's eyes. "Promise?"

"Promise," he whispered, then leaned forward and kissed her, lingering just long enough before he drew back.

Nice. Very, very nice. And warm. Kelly wondered if Jennifer had any spies in the lounge tonight. Lifting her martini glass, she glanced around the crowded room and noticed the jazz pianist, Mark, grinning at her. She could swear he gave her a wink.

"I saw Mark grinning at us. Maybe he's one of Jennifer's spies," she teased.

"Not a chance. Mark's a jazzman. He simply appreciates good timing," Steve said, giving her a wink of his own.

Together they lifted their glasses toward the piano as very, very good jazz wrapped around them.

Six

"They've got a head start, Carl. You'll never catch them," Kelly said as she slid the patio door open.

Carl bounded outside into the snow, barking furiously as he raced toward the parade of squirrels trooping along the fence. The squirrels, of course, were as fleet-footed as usual, so even Carl's enthusiastic shaking of the chain-link as he jumped against it couldn't thwart their escape. One by one, they reached the corner post, where they skittered and hopped through the snow and up the adjacent cottonwood tree. Kelly could have sworn the last squirrel deliberately shook his rear end at Carl, tail up, taunting.

"I think that last squirrel mooned you, Carl," Kelly called to her barking dog. Undaunted and oblivious to insult, Carl stood, paws up on the fence, barking doggie threats into the snow-laden branches above. Each bark created little clouds of frozen dog breath in the icy air.

Leaving Carl to his wintry patrol of the backyard, Kelly escaped the cold and refilled her coffee mug before she returned to her desk and accounts. She clicked on the computer screen and entered additional figures, moving quickly through the spreadsheet. A snowy, cold day was perfect for holing up and digging into her accounts. If she kept at it, she'd have these clients finished by midafternoon.

The sound of her cell phone interrupted. "Kelly here," she answered automatically, continuing to cruise the spreadsheet.

"Hey, Kelly, have you got a minute?" Jennifer's voice came through.

Kelly stopped her calculations and focused her attention. "What's up, Jen? You sound upset."

"Well, you would be, too, if you'd just been interviewed by the police."

"What? Just now?" Kelly quickly set her mug on the desk.

"Yes, Lieutenant Peterson came to the café this morning and asked to speak with me. I've gotta admit, that spooked the living hell out of me, Kelly."

Concerned, Kelly hunched over the little phone. "I can imagine. It would scare me, too. What did Peterson ask about? Derek and Diane and . . . and all that?"

"Ohhhh, yeah." Jennifer exhaled a long, audible sigh. "Believe me, Kelly, Peterson knows all about Diane and Derek and her going up to Derek's place that night. He said he'd talked to all the regulars at the bar, and they gave him an earful." She snorted. "Of course they told him all about Diane and Derek's 'tempestuous relationship,' as he called it. Their fights, their breakups, their reconciliations. And he heard lots about Diane's partying and drinking habits."

"So he wanted to hear your version, is that it?" Kelly probed.

"Yes, and he wanted to know more about Diane herself, since everyone had told him I was her closest friend." Jennifer paused for a second. "So I told Peterson about the two of them. Why they fought so much, the crappy way Derek treated Diane, swearing he loved her, then dumping her whenever a new girl came along, then jerking her back, over and over, and Diane sinking lower and lower each time." She exhaled a long sigh.

Kelly waited for her to continue, and when she didn't, Kelly interjected quietly, "You had to tell the truth, Jen. Peterson already knew it. He was simply looking for confirmation from someone he knew to be trustworthy. You."

"Me?" Jennnifer sounded startled.

"Yes, you," Kelly repeated. "Peterson met you last summer, Jennifer, and he knew you to be a credible, reliable witness and observer. That's worth more to a detective than the gossip of barflies."

Jennifer's chuckle sounded over the line. "Did you learn that from Burt?"

"Yeah, it's part of my junior detective training."

Jennifer sighed. "You know, Peterson said something to me after the interview that was kind of funny. He smiled and asked if he could give me some 'fatherly advice.' "

"You're kidding."

"Nope, honest. So I said, sure. I mean, what else would you say to a cop, right? Then he looks me right in the eye and tells me he thinks I'm much too smart a girl to be hanging out with that bar crowd. His advice was to 'cut them loose before they drag you down.' "

Kelly caught her breath. *Way to go, Lieutenant Peterson!* She'd been wanting to say that to Jennifer for months. "Sounds like good advice to me, Jen. Peterson's got a good eye. Besides, everyone can use fatherly advice."

Jennifer laughed softly. "Are you kidding? What with Burt in the shop and Curt Stackhouse watching over us, we've got fatherly advice coming out the ying-yang."

"So, you knew about Mimi and Burt?" Kelly asked, leaning closer to Lisa as they sat knitting beside the library table.

Lisa glanced at the various knitters who flanked them, chattering away as they knitted, then spoke in a low voice. "Yeah, Greg and I spotted them at a restaurant one night. They were sitting in a corner booth in the back, gazing at each other in the candlelight." She grinned as her fingers worked their magic in the red and green wool. "It was so romantic. And cute."

Kelly noticed another pair of mittens were nearing completion. Ahhhh, to be able to knit that fast and still be good, she thought enviously. "Wow, I hadn't noticed a thing. I wonder how long they've been dating," she said, working another row of gray and white stitches in the alpaca wool scarf. She was making progress. Two and a half feet done. Only eighteen inches to go.

"From the way they were looking at each other, I figure they've been sneaking out behind our backs for a while now. And you didn't notice because you're oblivious to that sort of thing."

"I am not," Kelly protested. "I'm just as observant as you and Jennifer."

"When you're off detecting clues and sleuthing, yeah," Lisa teased. "But you're absolutely clueless when it comes to something romantic. You never see those looks Steve throws your way."

Some of the knitters seated across the table turned their heads. One of them giggled, then quickly looked away. Kelly felt a slight flush creep up her cheeks. "Your imagination is on overload. You've been working too much, Lisa."

"Everyone notices except you, Miss Workaholic," Lisa zeroed in, with a wicked smile. "You've got to get your nose off that computer screen."

Deciding diversion would be the best strategy in this instance, Kelly asked, "Tell me, how did Megan like the guy you and Greg fixed her up with? Was he nice? Did she retreat into her shell?"

Lisa's grin disappeared. "She liked him okay, I guess. He was nice and friendly and nonthreatening and acted really interested in her, but Megan shrank right into her shell like she always does. Blushing and responding in monosyllables." She shook her head. "I don't know what we can do to help her, Kelly."

"I don't think *we* can do anything, Lisa," Kelly admitted with a sigh. "This is something Megan is going to have to conquer herself."

"It's so painful to watch, though," Lisa said. "She's such a great girl and she deserves someone in her life who appreciates how special she is."

"I agree, and—"

Kelly broke off when she spotted Lucy come through the classroom doorway, Ellen close behind. They both found chairs at the end of the long table.

Lucy's dark hair was pulled into a long braid down her back, and Kelly noticed she looked wan and pale. Waiflike. Lucy kept her eyes downcast and didn't glance toward the others until she removed a butterscotch cream wool from her bag and began to knit. Only then did she lift her gaze.

Kelly gave Lucy an encouraging smile. "Welcome back, Lucy. It's good to see you again," she said in a gentle voice.

The sound of soft greetings and condolences echoed around the table. For a moment, Lucy looked like she would bolt. Kelly detected a quiver of her lower lip. Once or twice, Ellen placed her hand on her friend's arm, clearly reassuring.

"Would you like some tea?" Kelly gestured to the pot in the middle of the table, surrounded by cookies and assorted edibles.

"No, thanks," Lucy murmured, giving Kelly a small smile.

Lisa leaned forward. "Hi, Lucy, remember me, Lisa Gerrard? We were in the same group at the fitness center a couple of years ago."

A spark of recognition flitted across Lucy's face. "Yes, yes, I do." Again, her gaze dropped.

"I'm so glad you've started teaching classes here now," Lisa continued. "I've heard wonderful things—"

The rest of Lisa's sentence was drowned out by the booming voice of Hilda von Steuben as she steamed into the knitting shop harbor. "Good morning, ladies," Hilda said. "I see you're all busy at work on your holiday projects. I trust they are proceeding apace." She unceremoniously plopped her knitting bag at the other end of the library table across from Ellen and Lucy.

Kelly couldn't resist. "If 'apace' means struggling along as usual, then I am apacing."

Lizzie drifted into the room next, darting into corners to

check yarns and fibers like a sailboat skimming around a lake, checking the coves. Kelly waved her over and gestured for Lizzie to lean closer.

"What is it, dear?" Lizzie asked in a dramatic whisper as she bent beside Kelly's shoulder.

"This must be Lucy's first day back." Kelly indicated the end of the table where Ellen was clearly trying to involve Lucy in a conversation. Lucy nodded instead of talking, Kelly noticed. "We've all welcomed her, but she still looks an inch away from crying. I was hoping you might take a few moments and send some of your motherly warmth Lucy's way. It looks like she needs it."

Lizzie's bright blue eyes lit up as she smiled. "That's sweet of you to say, Kelly, but you know I've never been a mother. So I doubt I'd be much help."

"I've seen you in action, Lizzie. You're a natural mom." Kelly winked.

Clearly flattered by Kelly's words, Lizzie patted her on the shoulder. "I'll do my best, dear." She moved a chair beside Lucy and settled, withdrawing the frothy white baby blanket she was working on, all the while smiling and chatting gaily beside Ellen and Lucy.

Lisa glanced at her watch, then shoved the mittens into her bag. "I've got a client in half an hour, so I'd better leave."

She pushed back her chair and was clearly about to leave when Kelly leaned toward her. "Before you go, tell me how you know Lucy. You mentioned that the two of you were in a class together at the fitness center. Were you teaching an exercise class or something?"

Lisa set her bag in the middle of her lap and leaned on it, glancing across the table at Lucy. "Or something. It was a little more complicated than that. Two years ago I was assisting a counselor with group therapy sessions. I'd come in and lead the group through some relaxation techniques. Some of the women needed a lot of help 'letting go' and sharing in the group."

"Was Lucy one of them?"

"Oh, yeah," Lisa said with a sigh. "She had lots and lots of personal issues she was wrestling with. I stayed with the group for nearly a year, then my schedule shifted and someone else took my spot. I haven't seen Lucy since then. In fact, I've never been here when she's taught a class, so I didn't even know she was part of the 'shop family' until Megan told me."

Kelly glanced to the end of the table, watching Lizzie try to draw Lucy into conversation. "Maybe she could use some counseling now, Lisa. You know, like grief counseling. She looks like a beaten puppy. So sad, she almost makes me want to cry."

Lisa looked over and nodded. "That's a good suggestion, Kelly. Maybe I can mention it to her on the way out. Tell her if she wants to talk with anyone to give me a call, and I'll arrange it." With that, Lisa rose and walked slowly to the end of the table.

Kelly watched as Lisa greeted Lucy and the others, engaged them in conversation for a couple of moments, then leaned down beside Lucy's chair. After a moment, Lucy's blue eyes widened in her pale face before she dropped her head and stared at her knitting once again. Lisa patted Lucy on the shoulder before she left the room.

Good job, Lisa, Kelly mentally congratulated her friend. Maybe Lucy will take Lisa up on the offer, grab at the helping hands that are offered, maybe . . .

The rest of Kelly's encouraging ideas evaporated when she saw Lucy abruptly push back her chair, shove her knitting haphazardly into her bag, and race from the knitting table. Her face was red and wet with tears.

So much for good intentions, Kelly thought sadly.

Seven

"Tell Jennifer I'll see her on break, Pete. I want to catch the spinning class before it's over," Kelly said as she sped down the hallway to the shop. Rounding a corner near the bathroom, Kelly nearly bumped into Megan.

"Whoa, sorry, my fault. I've gotta watch the curves," Kelly said as Megan backed up.

"No problem. You coming to see the class? Lucy's back."

"How's she doing?"

"She's really wound tight," Megan whispered as she headed through the doorway. Kelly could hear the spinning class in session.

Kelly followed Megan into the classroom where four other spinners sat beside their wheels. Each one of them was immersed in various stages of drafting fleece into roving or attempting to feed the roving through their fingers onto the wheel. Both Anne and Ellen seemed to be succeeding, for Kelly noticed much more yarn wound around their bobbins.

Megan returned to her spinning wheel, and Kelly observed that her friend had exceeded all others in spinning. Her bobbin was fat with pink yarn—bubble gum, cotton candy pink. Kelly wasn't surprised. Megan was a classic overachiever.

Megan might be shy and awkward in certain social situations, but put her in a competitive environment like sports and watch out. Megan could outplay anyone. Kelly already knew how good Megan was at softball, having played all summer and fall on the same team. Now, however, Kelly got to witness Megan in action on the tennis court and was extremely grateful she wouldn't have to face her friend across the net in a real game. Megan would wipe up the court with her.

"All right, everyone, keep your hands and feet together," Lucy instructed as she hovered over each spinner in turn. "That's right, Ellen, fingers open a little, just a little. That's good."

Kelly leaned against the doorway watching the blue wool gathering slowly on Ellen's bobbin. Catching Lucy's gaze when she glanced her way, Kelly gave her a smile. "Wow, everyone's doing so much better than when I last visited."

The words had barely left Kelly's mouth when one of the newer spinners cried out, "Oh, no! It's twisting. Make it stop, Lucy!"

Kelly watched the spinner release her fingers' grip while her feet kept working the wheel's treadle, and sure enough, the fluffy gray roving in her lap coiled up like an angry snake.

Lucy rushed beside her to stop the wheel, but nothing could stop the spinner's wailing. "Ohhhh, noooo!"

The other new spinner glanced to her fellow student, gave a start, then let the wool drop from her hands while the treadle kept moving. In the blink of an eye, the roving in her lap began to corkscrew, too. This spinner emitted a high-pitched shriek. "Make it stop, make it *stop!*"

Lucy tried to reach out and stop that wheel, but it was too late. The white roving was already twisted in the spinner's lap, sending her into even louder squeals. Lucy stared at the chaos, a panicked expression claiming her face. She backed away from the others, her hands at her throat, then fled from the room, nearly knocking over Megan's spinning wheel as she ran.

"Oh, my God! What happened?" cried the first casualty. "I thought she was feeling better."

"Well, you thought wrong," Ellen retorted. "Lucy's still not herself. And all this screaming doesn't help."

"I'm sorry," the second casualty apologized meekly. "I didn't mean to shriek. I—I—I never saw anything like that before. It was like the yarn was alive in my lap!" She gave an exaggerated shiver.

Megan rose from her wheel. "Okay, okay, settle down, everybody. Let's get started again. Lucy needs more time to calm down. Meanwhile, we can do our part by practicing, so we won't freak out, okay?"

The others murmured agreement as Megan stood between the two new spinners, guiding each one through the basic movements. Kelly watched her friend coaching and encouraging, exactly like she would a new player on the field.

"Good luck," Kelly said as she headed toward the knitting table. She needed some peace and quiet after all that shrieking. Who would have thought spinning could make someone scream?

Finding the table empty, Kelly settled and resumed her scarf. Only twelve inches to go. She'd definitely finish Eugene's present in time for the holidays. Several peaceful, relaxed minutes passed before she heard Jennifer's voice sound behind her.

"What was all that noise in class? Pete was about to call the cops." Jennifer settled into a chair beside Kelly and resumed knitting the blue and white patterned sweater. It looked almost finished to Kelly.

"Oh, a couple of novice spinners got their yarn all in a twist. It would have been funny, except their shrieking sent poor Lucy over the edge and she went racing from the room. Poor thing. She's hanging on by her fingernails, it seems."

"You know, I'm sick and tired of hearing everybody talk about 'poor little Lucy,' who's crying all the time. She's not the only one who was hurt by Derek's death. I'm a lot more concerned about Diane. She's sinking lower and lower."

"Is she drinking?"

"Oh, yeah. That's all Diane knows to do when she's depressed, and of course that only makes her more depressed." Jennifer shook her head sadly. "I took her out for dinner last night and told her she's got to try and stay sober so she can think clearly. The police will probably want to question her again. I mean, they already caught her in a lie, so you know Peterson will follow up on that."

"Definitely."

Jennifer's needles slowed. "Kelly, can I ask you a favor?"

"Sure," Kelly responded automatically as she examined the neat rows of gray and white stitches she'd created. The scarf was turning out better than she imagined. Eugene Tolliver would love it.

"Would you poke around and see what you find? You're so good at seeing things that others don't pick up on, including the police."

Kelly looked up, startled. "You mean look into Derek's death? I wouldn't know where to begin."

"I didn't mean you'd be doing it alone," Jennifer said. "I've already started poking around myself. Asking questions and all that. I simply wanted your help in case I turn up something."

Feeling more comfortable with that suggestion, Kelly nodded. "Sure. I'll be glad to help you any way I can, Jennifer. Have you turned up anything yet?"

"Actually, I have." Jennifer gave her a sly smile. "I learned from the bartender that one of the guys who hangs out pretty regularly had tried to do a deal with Derek earlier this year. Some guy named Gary. He wanted Derek to buy into this franchise he was selling. Apparently, Derek strung this Gary along for months, telling him he would definitely be joining him as a partner or something, then wham! Derek pulls out. Tells the guy about it at the bar. And get this, he laughs as the guy is sputtering, getting madder and madder. But that was Derek's style. I think he really enjoyed being cruel to people."

Intrigued, Kelly probed, "Did this Gary guy threaten Derek in front of others?"

Jennifer looked her in the eye. "Oh, yeah. Seems he'd made some big financial commitments based on Derek's promises. The bartender said Gary lunged for Derek, but another guy held him back. While Derek laughed, of course. He was such a bastard."

"But did Gary actually threaten him, Jen?"

"Not then, no," Jennifer admitted with a sigh. "A couple of guys took him outside to cool down. But the next time this Gary came in, he was bad-mouthing Derek a lot, saying 'one of these days Derek Cooper will get payback.'"

"Hmmmm."

"That's what I thought," Jennifer said, fingers moving faster. "It sounds suspicious to me. So I'm poking around and asking questions. Trying to find out more about this Gary. What kind of business he does, see what I can find."

"Let me know what you turn up, okay?" Kelly said.

"That's what I was hoping you'd say. Oh, and you'll keep asking Burt about the murder, right?"

"Absolutely. He already knows I'm curious and want to find out for Lucy's sake. So he'll keep me in the loop."

Jennifer sighed. "I know I'm reaching for straws, Kelly, but Diane is deep in depression, and she's not able to look out for herself. I have to do something to help her. I know she didn't do it."

The impassioned tone of Jennifer's voice touched something within Kelly. Jennifer thought Diane was innocent and needed help. Perhaps Kelly was being too hasty. She decided to shed all former opinions of Jennifer's friend and take a look herself.

"Listen, Jen, I want you to do something for me."

"Anything."

"I want you to bring Diane here tomorrow for lunch, so I can meet her face-to-face. If I'm going to try and help this woman, then I need to know who she is. I need to talk with her. Listen to her side of the story."

Jennifer smiled warmly at Kelly. "You've got it. I'll bring her for lunch tomorrow if I have to go drive her here myself."

Voices spilled through the doorway then as the spinners spilled into the room, converging on the yarn bins and bookshelves, sharing their obvious excitement and newly discovered appetites for fibers and textures.

"Break's over," Jennifer said, rising from her chair as she slung her knitting bag over her shoulder. "See you tomorrow for lunch."

Kelly waved goodbye to Jennifer then gestured to Megan across the room. "Thank goodness you were able to take over for Lucy," she said as Megan appropriated Jennifer's chair. Chairs around the Lambspun knitting table didn't stay empty for long. Two of the spinners had already spread out magazines, enthusiastically sharing project ideas with one another, pointing at colorful yarns.

"Yeah, I got them all back on track. Hopefully, they'll be calmer for the next class." She looked at Kelly with concern. "You know, I'm beginning to worry about Lucy. She's wound so tight I'm afraid she'll snap."

"Maybe that's what we saw today," Kelly suggested, continuing to work the stitches. Noticing Ellen nearby, Kelly gestured her over. "Ellen, you're Lucy's best friend. How do you think she's doing? I mean, it looks to Megan and me like she's losing it."

Ellen stared across the room at the bookshelves before she spoke. "I know; I'm worried about Lucy, too. I've tried talking with her about Derek's death, but she usually bursts into tears."

"She needs to see someone. A counseler, someone she can talk to, to lift this cloud of grief she's living under," Megan suggested.

Ellen closed her eyes and released a huge sigh. "Believe

me, I've suggested it, but Lucy gets this terrified look and closes off. She refuses to consider it."

"Does she have any family you can contact?" Megan suggested. "Maybe they can get through to her."

"Unfortunately, no," Ellen said as she pulled a chair closer. "Her mom died years ago and her dad remarried and started a whole new family. Lucy's been totally shut out ever since. They don't even stay in touch anymore."

Kelly felt a little tug inside. She knew what it felt like to have no family left. How alone she felt. Until she returned to Colorado after her aunt's death and walked into the Lambspun shop. Kelly hadn't felt alone since. She had friends now. People who cared about her. And she'd never been happier.

"You know, Lisa shared a workshop or therapy session with Lucy two years ago. Maybe she can reach her," Kelly offered.

"I hope so. She's going to need someone to help her, especially . . . especially now."

Curious, Kelly probed, "What do you mean, 'especially now'?"

Ellen stared silently at the bookshelves for a full minute, then turned to Kelly and Megan. Brushing her hair away from her face, she leaned forward and whispered, "Lucy's pregnant. She found out right before Derek died. That's what she was telling me after class the other day. And that's the real reason she's so upset."

"Poor thing," Megan whispered, her face revealing her concern. "No wonder she's wound so tight."

Kelly stared at Ellen. "Did she tell Derek?"

"She tried to call him but couldn't get through," Ellen said. "Don't let it out to everyone, okay? She told me in strictest confidence. Lucy doesn't need people gossiping about her."

"I understand, but we should tell Lisa. She's a professional who could get Lucy the help she needs," Kelly said.

Ellen nodded. "That's a good idea. Lucy doesn't listen to me anymore, but she might listen to Lisa. Maybe she can convince Lucy to see a counselor, for her baby's sake if nothing else."

Kelly sat silently knitting for several moments more, letting Ellen's news filter through. Lucy definitely needed help. With no family or support system in place, it was no wonder she felt adrift and alone. She needed to know there was help available, people who cared about her. People she could turn to in what must surely be the scariest time in Lucy's life. Alone and bearing her lover's child.

Mimi bustled into the room then, arms filled with red and white striped yarn. Peppermint candy yarn. "Are you planning to knit some candy canes, Mimi?" Kelly joked. She really wished she could confide in Mimi about Lucy's plight. If anyone needed some motherly attention right now, it was Lucy.

Mimi gave her familiar bright smile. "Oh, no, we'll have the real kind for our party. But I'd be glad to knit some for decorations, if you'd like."

"You can actually do that?" Kelly said, as she shoved her nearly finished alpaca scarf into her bag and prepared to leave. Client accounts were calling, and she needed time to speak with Lisa.

"Sure, I'll make some for fun. By the way, Burt and I will bring two breakfast hot dishes, which should serve all of us for that brunch at Curt's on Sunday. You girls can bring the rest," Mimi suggested as she headed toward the adjoining classroom.

"Thanks, Mimi, I'll let everyone know," Kelly said as she rose to leave. "Ellen, thank you for sharing with us. I'll let Lisa know right away. Megan, see you tomorrow, probably. If not in the shop, then on the court. Steve and I have another doubles match tomorrow night. Wish us luck."

The moment Kelly stepped outside, however, she wished she'd brought a coat. Regularly eschewing a coat for such a short walk, Kelly had been racing through the frigid winter air between the shop and her cottage every day. Reminding herself for the umpteenth time that she needed to wear a jacket, Kelly was halfway across the driveway when she spotted Burt walking from the shop storage building.

Kelly debated for a second whether she should talk to Burt now and freeze or call him later when she was warm and cozy inside. As always, the pressure to act immediately won out. She backtracked to intercept his path. "Hey, Burt, got a minute?"

Burt appeared lost in thought and didn't respond at first, until Kelly got closer and called him again.

This time Burt wheeled around, and his face broke into a smile. "Hey, Kelly, how're you doing?"

"Doing great," she said, rubbing her arms. Her long-sleeved sweater was no match for Colorado's December.

"C'mon inside, Kelly; you're shivering," Burt suggested, gesturing to the shop.

"C-can't. G-gotta get back to my accounts," she said through chattering teeth. "I just wanted to ask you a f-f-favor."

"Shoot."

"C-c-could you check with your f-friend and see how Derek C-Cooper's investigation is c-coming? Do they have any suspects?"

"Ok-k-kay, K-Kelly," Burt imitated with a big grin as he continued toward the entrance, looking comfortably warm in his sensible Colorado ski jacket. "Now go inside."

Kelly did what she was told, without another word.

Eight

"**Pete,** we're taking the table in the alcove, okay? We need a quiet place to talk," Jennifer said as she wound her way through the café, Kelly and Diane Perkins following close behind.

Jennifer had chosen well, Kelly decided, as the three of them settled into a cozy corner. The café was buzzing with lunchtime noise, but this corner had a little buffer of space around it. Perfect if you wanted a quiet conversation.

Diane Perkins was tall, almost rangy, with blonde shoulder-length hair, Kelly observed. She was probably very pretty under normal circumstances, but now there were dark blue shadows beneath her eyes and her skin was pale and drawn. She also didn't hold Kelly's gaze when they first met and shook hands. Diane's eyes darted away quickly. Kelly did feel Diane watching her while she and Jennifer spoke.

Kelly gave her order to the waitress and surreptitiously observed Diane while she and Jennifer placed their orders. She toyed with the nice-and-easy approach to getting to know Diane, then decided against it. She needed to get a feel for this woman, and the best way would be to see how she responded to questions—uncomfortable questions.

"I'm glad you could come, Diane," Kelly began, leaning back into her chair, trying to appear relaxed. "Jennifer's told me a lot about you, so I wanted to meet you in person, get to know you a little."

Diane glanced to Kelly, and she caught a flash of fear in Diane's sea green eyes. "See if I look like a murderer, right?"

"C'mon, Diane, be nice," Jennifer chided.

Kelly gave Diane a warm smile. "I'm here because Jennifer believes in you, and I believe in Jennifer. I trust her judgment, and she says you didn't murder Derek Cooper."

Diane stared deeply into Kelly's eyes, her gaze never wavering. "Thank you, Kelly," she said softly. "You don't know how much it means to hear someone say they believe me when I tell them I didn't kill Derek." Her mouth tightened. "The other night at the bar, no one wanted to stand near me, let alone talk to me. Oh, they'd say 'hi' and a few words, then they'd inch away and stare at me from across the bar . . . and whisper. So, I left."

"Blow 'em off, Diane," Jennifer said, repeating Peterson's advice. "They were never your friends, anyway."

"Yeah, I know that now. Apparently they've really enjoyed telling the police about . . . you know, Derek and me fighting and all." She gave a disgusted snort. "I can hear them now, blowing everything out of proportion, and making it . . . making it sound even worse."

"Jennifer told me you and Derek had a rather, uh, stormy relationship," Kelly ventured. "Apparently he was quite a womanizer."

Diane looked up at Kelly, and something resembling a smile tweaked her lips. For the first time since they met, Kelly could see that Diane was a very pretty woman. "Stormy, yeah, you might say that. In the good times, when we were together, it was fantastic. But those never lasted too long." She stared out into the café. "He'd start sneaking off with other girls, and I'd rag him about it, even though I knew that wouldn't help."

"Derek couldn't keep his pants on," Jennifer interjected.

Diane shook her head, as if all those bad times and good times were jumbled together in her mind. "And then, he'd start going after other girls right in front of me, at the bar, for instance. Or anywhere we'd go. I remember when we stopped for dinner on the way back from a concert in Denver, and he put the moves on a waitress right in front of me." Her tone turned bitter.

Jennifer caught Kelly's eye. "I told you he was a bastard."

"He sure sounds like it," Kelly agreed with a wry smile. "But, you know, that doesn't mean a damn."

Both Jennifer and Diane stared back.

Now that she had Diane's attention, Kelly zeroed in. "It doesn't mean a damn, because Derek's dead now, and the police are looking for the killer. And because of that stormy past you two shared, you can understand why the police have questioned you, can't you, Diane?"

Diane's mouth tightened. "Yes."

Kelly leaned forward, crossing her arms on the table. "Why don't you tell me about your fight with Derek at the bar? What happened that night?" she asked in a gentle tone.

Diane took a breath. "Derek and I had broken up again and hadn't dated for a couple of months. Whenever he showed up at the bar, he always had a new girl with him so I stayed out of his way. Then that night, he shows up alone." She began tracing invisible patterns on the tablecloth. "I'd already had too much to drink by the time he showed up, so I must have smarted off to him or something, because he starts in on me. Taunting me, telling me how glad he was to be rid of me, how bad I was in bed, and how I'd be passed out drunk half the time he was with me."

Diane's voice had dropped so low that Kelly had to strain to hear her over the lunchtime noise.

"Anyway, I just snapped. I don't know. I was sick and tired of his bad-mouthing me to my face, and now, now he was doing it in front of others." She closed her eyes. "I don't remember exactly what happened next, but I must have gone for him, I guess. That's what Ted, the bartender, told me later. He said I smashed the glass I had in my hand and lunged for Derek. Ted said one of the guys held me back, but I guess I shouted something. Something like, 'I oughta bash that pretty face in.' I don't know. . . ." Her voice drifted off, eyes still closed, as if afraid the vivid memories would reappear.

Kelly, however, saw the violent images forming in her own mind. An ugly, drunken bar scene. "Do you remember anything else?"

Diane's mouth twisted. "Yeah, I remember Derek laughing. Laughing his head off as I left the bar."

"Bastard," Jennifer hissed.

"How'd you get home? Please tell me you didn't drive," Kelly asked.

The lighter tone seemed to penetrate Diane's ugly memories, and she opened her eyes. Kelly glimpsed some of the pain of that experience before Diane stared at her hands, which were clasped tightly on the tabletop.

"One of the girls—Cindy, I think—drove me home."

Kelly leaned back in her chair, letting Diane's story filter through her mind, while the waitress served their salads and soups. She deliberately turned her attention to Eduardo's good cooking and away from painful memories while they enjoyed their meal.

From what she'd heard so far, Kelly was surprised Lieutenant Peterson hadn't already questioned Diane a second time, especially since she'd lied in the first interview. Kelly poked through the romaine lettuce, searching for a juicy morsel of mozzarella, picturing Peterson's quiet, burrowing interview style. Judging from how anxious Diane was now, Kelly figured she would crumple like a dry leaf if Peterson went after her.

Waiting until they'd finished eating before she resumed her questions, Kelly sipped her coffee and ventured into neutral territory. "What kind of work do you do, Diane?"

Diane hesitated before she answered. "I'm a landscaper. Got my degree from the university years ago. That's where Jennifer and I met." She gave her friend a quick smile. "I've been working with a local landscaping company for several years, but . . . but I've missed work recently and been late a lot, and my boss kind of gave me a warning the other day. So I'm getting kind of nervous now. I mean, I can't afford to lose my job."

"Why'd you miss work? Were you sick?" Kelly probed, even though she sensed she knew the answer. She wanted to hear Diane say it out loud.

"I'd . . . I'd had too much to drink the night before and slept right through the next morning," she admitted in a soft voice as she stared at her clasped hands.

"Not good, Diane," Jennifer said. "You know that."

Diane's head dropped lower. "Yeah, I know."

Kelly could feel Diane's despair coming at her in a wave. Jennifer was right. Diane was deep into depression and despair. And if she had been drinking so much she would sleep the next day away, that only made it worse.

Even though she knew her questions were forcing Diane to confront the very things that had sent her into a tailspin, Kelly knew she had to continue. How else could she help her? And maybe, this sober questioning in the harsh light of day would cause Diane to rethink her self-destructive behavior. Maybe.

"Why don't you tell me about the night of Derek's death," she ventured in a gentle voice. "Jennifer said he called you while you were at the bar, right?"

Diane looked out into the café. "Yes, he called while I was there. I couldn't believe it. I mean, we'd had that awful fight the week before, and there he was on the phone, sweet-talking me like always. Like nothing happened." Her bitter tone returned.

"What'd he want?"

"He wanted to get laid, that's all," she said with a disgusted snort. "Begged me to come on out to his place. He wanted to make up. Promised we'd have a new start. He said he was only joking that night at the bar. He knew that I'm the only one who really loved him."

"What'd you say?"

"I told him he was a lying bastard, and I wasn't going up there. I told him he could screw himself."

Kelly glimpsed a spark within Diane that she hadn't seen as yet. Anger. Normally, that could be a good sign for someone who was putting an end to a bad relationship. But in this case . . .

"Good for you," she told Diane. "Sounds like you'd had it."

"Damn right. He'd been using me for three years, and I was sick of it."

Kelly paused. "Then why did you go up there that night? What happened to change your mind?"

Diane shook her head, as if she couldn't believe what she was about to say. "Everyone at the bar had heard my conversation with Derek, and they were laughing and all. But a couple of guys told me I should give him another chance. One guy said I should at least hear what Derek had to say." She closed her eyes, clearly not wanting to see what was in her head. "I can't believe I let them change my mind."

"Had you been drinking?" Kelly probed.

"Ohhhh, yeah," she admitted. "I had a couple more after the phone call. The guy kept on trying to persuade me. Jeeeez. He was like a salesman, almost."

Jennifer leaned closer. "Do you remember the guy's name? Was he a regular?"

Diane nodded. "Yeah, he was. Gary something or other. I don't know."

Jennifer sent Kelly a sharp look. Gary, Gary . . . Kelly mulled the name. Gary was the guy that Derek burned in a business deal. The guy who threatened that "one of these days Derek Cooper will get payback."

"Did you go up to Derek's place alone?" Kelly continued.

"Yeah, I was still okay to drive," Diane said with a nonchalant nod. "But as I drove up the canyon, I got angrier and angrier every mile. I was finished with that bastard for good. He'd used me for the last time, and I was going to let him know." She glanced to Kelly with an apologetic smile. "Don't worry, I didn't run anyone off the road. Believe me, every drop of alcohol was burned out of my system by the time I reached his ranch."

Not sure whether she should believe that description or not, Kelly continued. "Was he alone?"

"Oh, yeah. He was in the barn, and I let him have it." Diane's eyes sparked with fire this time.

"Uhhh, you mean you told him off, right?" Jennifer prodded.

"You bet!" Diane's eyes narrowed. "I told him exactly what I thought of him *and* how he'd treated me. I told him he could find some other girl to jerk around, because I was through with him."

"I bet that felt good, didn't it? To finally tell Derek off, I mean," Kelly said.

"Boy, did it ever." Diane's face was flushed with color, revealing the good looks that depression had cloaked until now.

"What did he say?" Jennifer probed. "I would have given anything to see you tell off that bastard at last."

"You know, I didn't wait to hear. I cussed him out, then turned my back and left." Diane closed her eyes, as if savoring that moment. "God, that felt good."

"Did you leave then?" Kelly asked, watching Diane's expression carefully for any sign of deliberate evasion, anything that might hint Diane was lying to them. After all, she'd lied to Lieutenant Peterson. Maybe Diane was lying now. But Kelly saw nothing, no shifting glance, no nervous mannerisms, nothing that aroused Kelly's naturally suspicious nature.

Diane looked Kelly straight in the eye. "Yes. I drove down that canyon as fast as I drove up, but I felt a helluva lot better driving down."

Kelly returned Diane's clear gaze, still searching for some sign of evasion and seeing none. Kelly believed her. She couldn't explain why she believed Diane, but she did.

A wisp of an idea feathered in the back of Kelly's brain. Another question. "Tell me, did you notice anything that looked unusual while you were there at Derek's?" she asked. "Any sign of someone else having been there? Did he get any phone calls?"

Again, Diane closed her eyes as if recalling the scene. "No, he was alone and nobody called while I was there. Everything else looked the same, normal, I guess. The alpacas were in the barn, and Derek's car was parked in the usual spot, and . . . and . . ." Suddenly Diane's eyes popped open. "Wait a minute! I saw another car coming up the driveway as I left. I forgot about that until now."

Jennifer and Kelly exchanged glances. "Do you remember what it looked like?" Kelly asked.

Diane shook her head. "It was pitch-black outside, so all I really noticed were the headlights. But it might have been a dark color. And I think I remember another car parked on the side of the road as I drove off."

"Did you see anyone you recognized?" Jennifer pressed, leaning closer to her friend.

A disgusted expression passed over Diane's face. "No, I

didn't get a good look. I figured it was another one of Derek's girls."

Kelly leaned back in her chair and sipped her coffee, her brain sifting through the tantalizing information. There was another car coming up the driveway. Someone else was coming to see Derek that night. Who was it? Was it another girlfriend, or was it that angry guy from the bar, Gary? Apparently he had encouraged Diane to visit Derek that night. Did Gary recognize Diane's late-night visit as an opportunity to take revenge on the double-crossing Derek? Was Gary in the car that passed on the driveway? Maybe he figured Diane and Derek would be so engrossed in each other, they'd never hear his car approach. If so, he must have been surprised to see Diane drive past him.

Taking another deep drink, Kelly felt the caffeine rush in her veins while her brain buzzed with scenarios. Maybe Diane was set up by this Gary. Maybe he killed Derek, knowing he'd never be suspected because everyone knew Diane was going up there. Maybe, maybe. And maybe Diane was lying to throw Kelly off track. After all, Diane hadn't remembered a car until Kelly asked about someone else being at the ranch. Maybe Diane was a clever liar and was deceiving them.

Jennifer began asking Diane questions about the bar regulars. Was there anyone there who'd ever given her trouble? Any of the girls gotten jealous when their boyfriends paid too much attention to Diane?

Kelly let them talk while she sipped her coffee and let the buzzing thoughts settle. Yes, it was possible that Diane was lying, but Kelly didn't think so. Again, she had nothing substantial to account for that belief, except . . .

These last few months had taught Kelly to be careful about

jumping to conclusions when it came to murder. Since she'd returned to Fort Connor, Kelly had involved herself in three separate murder investigations—without police permission and despite Burt's warnings. All of those investigations had one startling fact in common. None of the "obvious suspects" turned out to be guilty. The real killers had each cleverly concealed his or her role in the crime. Now Diane Perkins was the obvious suspect in Derek Cooper's death. Was Diane being set up by a clever killer?

There was another question Kelly wanted to ask. Looking Diane in the eye, she said, "Your story makes sense, Diane. So I'm wondering why you lied to the police when they questioned you. Jennifer said you didn't tell them you went to Derek's ranch that night. You said you were at home asleep. Why did you lie?"

Diane's sea green gaze wavered, and she stared at the table once again. "I-I was scared," she whispered. "I was afraid they'd think I killed Derek. It was stupid, I know, but . . . but I couldn't think straight at the time."

"Had you been drinking?"

Her head dropped lower. "Yeah, I was still asleep on the couch that morning when they came. Their knocking woke me up."

Jennifer leaned closer to her friend and placed her hand on Diane's arm. "Diane, please listen to me. You need to get help with the drinking. That's the reason you're in this mess right now, you know that, don't you?"

"I know," Diane admitted, her voice so soft Kelly could barely hear her.

"I can check into some programs, if you'd like me to," Jennifer continued in a solicitous tone. "I'd even go over there with you."

Diane seemed to flinch. "I don't know, Jen . . . I don't know. They put you away, and . . ."

"Let me check, anyway. Meanwhile, promise me you'll stop drinking for now. Just for now, okay?" Jennifer pleaded. "The cops could show up anytime to question you again, you know that."

Diane looked up with a panicked expression. "Oh, God . . ."

If there was ever a time to strike a blow for sobriety, this was it. Kelly spoke up in a firm voice. "Diane, you lied to the police. They know you lied. They had plenty of witnesses at the bar tell them you were headed to Derek's ranch that night. You'd better believe the police will question you again. You have got to stay sober, or you won't have a prayer of convincing them you're innocent."

Diane blanched. Kelly figured either she was an excellent actress or had been in deep denial until now. "I'll try . . . I promise," she whispered.

"Good girl," Jennifer said, patting Diane's arm. "That's the first step."

Kelly pushed back her chair. This had been one intense lunch, and she was glad it was over. "I've got to go back to the computer, guys," she said as she rose. "Diane, I'm sorry if I was hard on you with all those questions, but I thought it might help you to go over your story again before . . . well, before the police come for another visit."

Diane looked up at Kelly with undeniable gratitude. "Thank you, Kelly. Thank you for believing me."

Kelly gave her a warm smile. "See you two later," she said as she turned to leave, wondering how she would explain all this to Burt.

* * *

Steve reached down to the gritty claylike surface of the indoor tennis courts and retrieved Kelly's racket cover. "How we managed to pull that one out of the toilet, I'll never know," he joked as he handed her the cover.

Standing on the sidelines, Kelly watched the next four players take the court and begin to warm up. The balls whizzed over the net, again and again, as the players rushed the net and raced across the court. "It had to be dumb luck," she said ruefully, watching the much better players charge the ball. "We happened to draw a couple that were worse than we are, that's all."

"That's happened twice," Steve said as he snatched their jackets from a nearby post. "I've got a feeling we're gonna get our butts kicked real soon."

"Oh, yeah," Kelly agreed as they headed toward the exit. Stopping for a second, she stretched high over her head and side to side. "Brother, every muscle in my back hurts. I'm heading straight for the tub after dinner."

"I give a mean back rub." Steve tempted with a sly grin.

She returned the grin. "I bet you do, but I'll take a rain check. I'm heading for the tub and an early night. I need to get up really early tomorrow so I can catch Burt."

"What's up? Jayleen need more help with the kids' party? I told you I'll be there, didn't I?" Steve helped Kelly slip into her winter jacket.

Wrapping her chunky wool scarf around her neck, Kelly snuggled into the warmth as they stepped outside and into the rapidly dropping temperatures. Below freezing tonight. Winter was definitely here to stay.

"Yes, you did, and Jayleen thanks you. But it's not that. I need some quiet time with Burt alone so I can ask him a few questions." She put her head down as they walked through the darkened parking lot toward Steve's truck. The chill wind whipped the colorful scarf so it flapped like a pennant beside her.

Steve halted in the middle of the parking lot. "Uh-oh," was all he said.

Kelly looked at him quizzically. They were only halfway to the truck. "What's wrong? Did you forget something?"

"Nope. I just figured out what you're doing. You're using Burt to find out about that alpaca rancher's murder, aren't you?"

"Uhhhh . . ." Kelly hesitated, caught off guard.

"That's a nondenial if I ever heard one," Steve said with a wry grin. Taking her arm, he headed them toward the truck. "What's up, Kelly? You told me that little spinner at the shop was dating this guy, but that doesn't strike me as enough reason for you to go nosing around. You didn't even know this guy."

"Well, something new came up," Kelly admitted, realizing she'd have to tell Steve the whole story or she'd never get dinner tonight. He'd park in front of the Jazz Bistro and idle the engine until she talked.

"Gotta do better than that," he said, opening her door and tossing both rackets behind the seat.

"Okay, it involves a friend of Jennifer's. I promise I'll tell you everything, but let's get to the restaurant first. I'm starving," she said as she climbed up into the seat.

Steve slammed her door and raced around to the other side of the truck. Climbing in, he started the engine, and a deep throaty rumble shook the vehicle. He revved the engine a couple of times before he backed out of the lot, then turned to Kelly. "Okay, what about Jennifer's friend? I don't want to wait until we drive across town."

Kelly stared into the December night. "It looks like Jennifer's friend—Diane—will be a suspect in Derek Cooper's murder," she said bluntly.

Steve turned his attention back to traffic. "Whoa," was all he said as they drove off into the darkened streets.

Nine

Burt shook the snowflakes off his jacket and slipped it behind a chair before he accepted the cup of coffee Kelly offered him.

"Cream and sugar, as usual," Kelly said with a smile as she led the way into the cottage living room.

"Okay, Kelly, what is so important that you needed to see me this morning?" he said as he settled into Kelly's black leather sofa.

"Well, I was wondering how the Derek Cooper investigation was going," she said, choosing the armchair for herself.

Burt smiled. "I figured it was something like that. All I can tell you is they're still investigating, still interviewing people who knew the victim. Friends, business associates. In other words, the investigation is proceeding." Burt sipped his coffee, watching Kelly from beneath his bushy gray eyebrows.

"Any suspects yet?" she probed. "Anyone look interesting?"

"There may be."

Kelly took a deep drink of coffee. Not as good as Eduardo's but it would have to do until she could get to the café.

"What's up, Kelly?" Burt queried. "I sense there's another reason you're asking. Is it about Lucy? I know she's still pretty shaken, but I think she's getting better. At least she hasn't broken down in class again."

"No, it's about someone else. Someone Jennifer asked me to meet. Someone who may have already appeared on the police radar screen."

Burt's bushy brows arched. "Oh, really?" was all he said, then he returned to his coffee.

"Yes, her name is Diane Perkins." Kelly waited for a sign of recognition from Burt. It came quickly.

"Do you know this Diane Perkins, Kelly?"

"Well, I'm beginning to." Kelly gave a good-natured shrug. "The three of us met for lunch yesterday so she could tell me about her, uh, her volatile relationship with Derek Cooper."

"Jennifer asked you to meet this woman?"

"Yes, Burt, she did. She's concerned about her friend. Apparently the police have already questioned her about Derek." Kelly released an exasperated sigh. "Diane did a stupid thing. She lied to the police when they questioned her. She didn't tell them she went up to his ranch that night."

"She told you this?" Burt's eyes narrowed.

"Yes, she did. Diane went up there to tell him off and end the relationship." Kelly watched skepticism flash through Burt's gaze. "I know what you're thinking, Burt. Yeah, she went up there to tell him off, they got into a fight, and she killed him. I admit, I was thinking the same thing until I spoke with her. Diane said she didn't kill Derek Cooper, and I believe her, Burt. She drove right out of the canyon, and—"

"Then why did she lie?" he interrupted.

Kelly took a deep breath and calmed the caffeine rush. She needed a cool head to convince Burt. "Because she was scared. Suddenly a policeman is knocking on her door one morning—"

"It was noon."

"Well, he was asking all sorts of questions. I'd be scared, too."

"No, you wouldn't, Kelly. You've already been in that situation with the very same detective. Lieutenant Peterson didn't scare you. He said you were cool as a cucumber."

Kelly searched for some plausible comparison. "Well, he wasn't waking me up and banging on my door, either. That would definitely get me out of sorts—"

"She was drunk, Kelly. Or sleeping it off. Peterson said her speech was slurred, she was disoriented, and empty vodka bottles were lying on the floor. Her friends at the bar say she does that regularly. Gets drunk and sleeps it off."

Kelly stared back at Burt, who was eyeing her over his coffee mug. She had no comeback to that comment. Kelly let out a sigh. "Yeah, she's got an alcohol problem, for sure. Jennifer and I did our best to convince her to stay sober. Peterson is bound to question her again."

"I'd say that's a strong possibility."

Kelly shook her head. "I know this sounds absolutely crazy, Burt, but I listened to that whole story, and I agree with Jennifer. Diane did not kill Derek Cooper."

"How can you be sure, Kelly?" Burt said, placing his mug on the table. "Maybe she doesn't even remember killing him.

There are witnesses at the bar who'll testify she's had black-outs before, when she doesn't remember what she's done. She's a drunk. And she threatened Derek Cooper in front of witnesses. Lots of witnesses."

"So I'm right, then," Kelly said ruefully. "Diane is smack-dab in the middle of Peterson's radar screen."

Burt smiled. "You'll have to ask Peterson that question. But, yeah, she's definitely a person of interest. She had motive and opportunity. Apparently Derek had been dumping on her for years. She finally got tired of it. Sounds like she was already drinking too much when she went to his ranch. Maybe they got into a fight, and *bam!* She let him have it."

Kelly remembered Diane's use of that same phrase, and a little shiver ran over her. Perhaps she and Jennifer were mistaken. Diane was definitely an alcoholic. Maybe she killed him in a drunken rage and couldn't even remember it. Maybe. Then how did she drive out of the canyon without running off the road? If she was so drunk she couldn't remember killing a man, she'd surely be too drunk to drive. Wouldn't she? Maybe. Maybe the murder itself sobered Diane on the spot. Hell, that would sober up anyone. Wouldn't it?

"Add to that, she has no alibi," Burt continued relentlessly. "She told Peterson she was at her apartment the night Cooper was killed, and there are plenty of witnesses who saw her drinking at the bar before heading to Cooper's ranch. On top of that, she lied to the police. That makes it look even worse." Burt wagged his head. "Not good. Not good at all."

Kelly felt the grimness of Diane's situation sink over her like a dark cloud. She could see her observations about Diane's story hadn't impressed Burt at all. Even so, Kelly felt obligated to pass along the other piece of information that might be relevant. "Yeah, it looks bad, that's for sure," she admitted. "There is one thing, though. Diane swears she saw another car driving up to Derek's ranch as she was leaving that night."

Burt's eyebrows arched again in obvious skepticism. "Really? Now, I wonder why she'd say that? Maybe she's trying to deflect suspicion from herself. Have you thought of that?"

Kelly gave a resigned sigh. She was getting nowhere, so it was time to throw in the towel. For now. "Okay, Burt, I know it sounds flimsy, but I'd like you to pass it along to Peterson anyway, okay?"

Burt looked at Kelly with that familiar fatherly expression she'd come to appreciate. "Sure, Kelly. I'll pass it along, for what it's worth. But I want you to promise you'll be more skeptical of this Diane from now on, okay?"

Skepticism was Kelly's second nature, so she could easily agree. "I promise," she said, crossing her heart.

Kelly tabbed through the spreadsheet, deftly adding numbers, transferring numbers. Numbers, numbers, numbers. Thank goodness for numbers in her life. Numbers were straightforward. Either right or wrong. Numbers didn't lie—unless someone made them. People could make numbers lie. Deliberately twisting numbers until they concealed the truth.

She drained the last of her coffee. Is that what Diane had been doing at lunch yesterday? she wondered. Twisting the truth, so that Kelly and Jennifer would believe her and maybe convince others? Had Diane killed in a drunken rage, then sobered up enough to realize what she'd done? Was she drinking herself into a stupor every night to escape her guilty conscience?

The cell phone jangled and she flipped it open while she continued entering figures. "Kelly here."

"Kelly, it's me. I'm over at Diane's apartment." Jennifer's voice was breathless. "She's going off the deep end. Her boss called this morning and fired her. And if that wasn't bad enough, who shows up at her door then? Peterson. And he brought another detective with him this time. She's a basket case, Kelly. She's crying and whimpering, almost hysterical. She has no money and no job, and now the police are after her. She's falling apart. I left Pete's as soon as she called me. But I don't know what to do now. I'm afraid to leave her alone."

"Is she sober, Jen?" Kelly asked, wondering if this was fear or a calculated response by Diane to get Jennifer's sympathy.

"Ohhhh, yeah. She's so sober she's shaking like a leaf. Says she hasn't had a drink since we had lunch together, and there's no liquor in the apartment."

"Well, thank God for that," Kelly breathed. "At least she was sober for Peterson's questions."

"Maybe so, but he scared her senseless. Told her not to leave town. Told her they knew she'd lied to them before. Stuff like that. I'm not sure she was too rational when she talked to them." Jennifer swore softly. "Damn it, Kelly, what do we do with her? We can't just abandon her, but . . . but I don't know what to do. Should we forcibly take her over and put her into a facility or something? I haven't had a chance to even ask how that works. She may freak out entirely if we take her there."

Kelly stared at the blinking cursor on the computer screen, her mind whirling. What should they do? How could they help Diane? Suddenly a face appeared in the back of Kelly's mind. A familiar face. Someone who'd been in this situation herself. Jayleen Swinson. Jayleen would know what to do.

"Jennifer, let me make a call," Kelly blurted. "Can you stay there with Diane for a while?"

"Yeah, for an hour or so, but I've got clients at two this afternoon. Who are you going to call?"

"Jayleen. She'll know what to do. I'll call her right now."

"Great idea, Kelly. Let me know as soon as you hear from her. I'll try and calm Diane," Jennifer said before clicking off.

Kelly found Jayleen's number and punched it into the phone, praying that voice mail didn't answer. Blessedly, Jayleen's voice came on instead. "Thank God you're there, Jayleen. Jennifer and I need your help."

"Hey, Kelly, are you all right?" Jayleen sounded alarmed. "Did you two have an accident or something? Tell me where you are, and I'll be right over."

"No, it's nothing like that, Jayleen. It's someone else who needs your help, a close friend of Jennifer's. She's in bad shape."

"My help? Is it someone from the shop? Anyone I know?"

"No, it's . . . it's one of Jennifer's girlfriends, a drinking buddy. She's, well, she's in real bad shape. Jennifer and I want to help her, but we don't know how to handle this. Right now, she's nearly hysterical. She's been trying to get sober, but this morning really pushed her over the edge. Her boss fired her, and the county police showed up at her door."

"Whoa . . ." Jayleen breathed. "A double whammy."

"Yeah, that's what we thought. We're the ones who encouraged her to stay off the booze, so we want to keep helping her, but I feel like the whole situation has been kicked up a notch."

"You're right, it has." Jayleen paused for several seconds. "Why don't you start at the beginning of this sorry tale and fill me in on how she got where she is now. What's her name?"

"Diane. Diane Perkins," Kelly said, then began to relate everything that had happened these last few weeks. Diane's drinking, her stormy shared relationship with Derek, her drunken threat at the bar, his death, lying to the police, bar stories, blackouts, Diane's story, and Burt's reaction. Kelly didn't leave out anything, and she did not varnish over anything either. Diane's behavior spoke for itself.

Jayleen was quiet for a full minute after Kelly finished. "I have to say, that brings back a lot of memories," she said at last.

"I hate to say it, but that's why I called," Kelly admitted. "I thought you'd know what to do. Should Jennifer take Diane somewhere? A treatment center or something?"

"Does Diane have family anywhere around?"

"No one, according to Jen."

"Well, then, it looks like it's up to us to pull this girl out of the cesspool she's fallen into. Better yet, give her a helping hand so she can pull herself out."

"Hey, Jayleen, Jennifer and I don't expect you to get involved. We simply needed some advice. We can handle it—"

"Begging your pardon, Kelly, no, you can't. Neither can Jennifer. Neither one of you has any experience with drunks, but I do. I was one. So I'm joining this rescue."

Feeling guilty now, Kelly tried again to dissuade goodhearted Jayleen's intentions. "Jayleen, you've got too much on your plate right now, you told me so the other day. We cannot impose on you."

"Trust me, Kelly, some things are more important than others. And this is one of them. Diane sounds like she's sinking fast. I remember when it was me, and my cousin Vickie was there to rescue me. I could never repay her when she was alive . . ." Jayleen's voice drifted off for a second.

"But maybe this is a way I can give back. By being there for someone else the way Vickie was for me."

Kelly had no response. Jayleen had told her how, after a lifetime of drinking, she'd turned her own life around with Vickie Claymore's help. If Jayleen wanted to make that kind of difference in someone else's life, who was Kelly to say no?

"All right, Jayleen." Kelly acquiesced. "But only if you'll let me help. I can at least do your clients' accounts. Take some of that burden off your shoulders."

"You don't have to do that, Kelly."

"Hey, you're not the only one who can give orders," Kelly said. "Now, what do you want us to do for Diane? Right now, I mean. Jennifer's babysitting her but has to leave soon."

"Have Jennifer bring her over to the shop until I can get over there. Will you be able to stay with Diane until later this afternoon when I can drive into town?"

"Sure," Kelly replied, mentally wiping her work schedule clean for the day. She could catch up tonight. "What do you plan to do when you get here? Take Diane somewhere? To a meeting or a counselor?"

"Not yet. I'll take her home tonight and stay with her, try to talk some sense into her if I can. She's gonna have a rough night, if I'm not mistaken. I'll take her to the AA meeting tomorrow night. But first, I'll put her to work helping me at the ranch. It'll be good for her. Is she tiny and weak or sturdy and strong?"

"She looks pretty sturdy to me, and she worked for a landscaper for years."

"*Great,*" Jayleen exclaimed. "Then she won't be lacking for work here. I've got tons of postponed projects around the barns and corrals. With any luck, she'll be exhausted."

Kelly's mind swam with the enormity of Jayleen's

commitment. "Whoa, Jayleen, you're taking on entirely too much. Please let Jennifer and me help. Please!"

"If I need help, I'll ask. And, matter of fact, I do think I'll take you up on that offer with the accounts. I was planning to tackle them tonight, so any help will be welcome."

Kelly wiped the night work schedule, too. Tomorrow would be good enough. "You've got it, Jayleen. See you here at the shop later this afternoon."

"I'll be there."

Kelly found herself saying a prayer of thanksgiving as she punched in Jennifer's cell phone number.

"Julie, could you do me a favor, please?" Kelly said as she gestured to one of the café's afternoon waitresses.

"Sure, Kelly. Do you want a refill?" Julie asked, reaching for the omnipresent coffee mug.

"Not yet, but would you make two big mugs of hot chocolate for my friend? We'll be over in the shop at the knitting table."

"Sure thing, Kelly. I'll bring it over in a minute."

Kelly headed down the hallway and found Diane Perkins exactly where she'd left her—standing in the main yarn room. Kelly had hoped that the surrounding color and texture would entice Diane to touch something. Anything.

Kelly had no experience babysitting adults, so she decided the best way to keep Diane occupied and distracted would be to plop her beside the knitting table and envelop her completely in colors, textures, cookies, and conversation. And hot chocolate. Kelly figured all that hot milk might calm Diane's nervousness.

Jumpy hardly described Diane Perkins at this moment.

Gone were the glimpses of humor or self-awareness that Kelly had seen two days ago. Now Diane radiated fear. She reeked with it. The tinkling doorbell gave her a start, and she jumped at a customer's squeal of delight at finding exactly the right yarn. Kelly had no idea if hot chocolate would help, but she figured it couldn't hurt. Hot chocolate and the warmth of the afternoon knitting circle could do the trick. A "double dose."

"I ordered you some hot chocolate, Diane," Kelly said, lifting her mug. "The waitress will bring it to the table."

Diane's gaze darted about the yarn room. "When's that woman, Jayleen, coming?"

"She'll be here soon, don't worry. Jayleen's a great gal. You'll like her." Kelly gave her a reassuring smile and gestured through the archway. "C'mon, let's wait for her in here. This is where we all meet, eat cookies, knit, and talk our heads off. It's a great group."

Diane held back. "Uh, I don't wanta meet anyone."

Ignoring Diane's hesitation, Kelly beckoned her into the room and pulled out two chairs. Kelly was relieved to see some familiar faces at the table. Lizzie and Hilda were deep in conversation with another knitter, a motherly sort that Kelly had spoken with countless times.

Thank goodness. If ever there was anyone needing maternal nurturing, it was Diane Perkins. Jayleen would provide the strong shoulder and the strong arm necessary to get Diane through this rough period, but some of Lizzie's motherly warmth would be welcome right now.

"Have a seat, Diane, and I'll introduce you to everyone," Kelly said loudly, hoping to catch the women's attention. Diane was hovering beside the chair, her eyes darting to the many smiling faces. "Folks, this is Diane Perkins. She's a

friend, and she's going to join us for a while this afternoon."
Diane sat gingerly on the chair, as if it might be hot. Kelly
continued smoothly. "Diane's going to help Jayleen at the
ranch. Jayleen's really swamped, especially with the kids'
party coming up."

Diane nodded at the friendly greetings sent her way,
mumbling a soft thanks as she ducked her head.

Hilda spoke up from the end of the table. "Lizzie and I
want to contribute to this charity event, Kelly. It sounds
like a worthy cause indeed. Tell us what we can donate. We
may not be sprightly enough to chase after children anymore, but we can help in other ways."

A pile of pastel yarn lay in Hilda's lap and was slowly turning into a baby sweater. How many nephews and nieces did
she and Lizzie have? Kelly wondered. "Let me ask Jayleen.
She's supposed to bring us a list," Kelly replied, reminding
herself to take another chore off Jayleen's plate tonight.

"Yes, dear, we'd love to help," Lizzie said, glancing up
from her busy needles. Kelly thought she recognized another baby blanket, this one multicolored, coming into
shape. "Can the children use some knitted sweaters? I have a
veritable collection of extras that I've knitted over the years.
That's why I've switched to blankets." She smiled, revealing
the deep dimples in her rosy cheeks.

"I'll check with Jayleen," Kelly said, moving her mug
aside so Julie could set two large paper cups of hot chocolate
in front of Diane.

Diane stared at the cups. "Two?"

"I thought the warm milk might be soothing," Kelly
said softly, as Lizzie and Hilda responded to questions from
another knitter. "Besides, it tastes good."

Diane's gaze darted Kelly's way for a split second before

it dropped. "Thanks," she whispered. Lifting one of the cups, she took a drink, then another and another.

Lizzie turned to Diane and beamed. "Do you knit, dear?"

Diane looked startled that someone had spoken to her. "Uhhhh, no." She shook her head, then drained the hot chocolate.

Watching Diane quickly finish the second chocolate, Kelly congratulated herself on the idea. Warm milk might not be much, but it was something. Who knows? Maybe Diane hadn't eaten anything all day.

"You must be the outdoor type, then," Lizzie continued. "You certainly look strong and fit and healthy."

Kelly let Lizzie chatter away, while Diane mumbled replies and drank hot chocolate. Meanwhile, Kelly dug in her bag for a forgotten knitting project that needed unraveling. Gesturing to one of Mimi's helpers, Kelly beckoned her closer and whispered, "Rosa, could you tell Julie in the café to keep those hot chocolates coming, please? Two at a time, every half hour, okay?" Rosa nodded, with a bemused grin, as she hurried off.

Eavesdropping on Lizzie's one-sided conversation with Diane, Kelly recognized a familiar line of questioning. Subjects were circling in on dating and male and female companions. Subjects of undeniable interest to a sheltered, spinster schoolteacher like Lizzie—especially one with a rather vivid imagination.

Kelly was about to head Lizzie off at the pass, when she noticed Lucy Adair approaching the other side of the table. Lucy settled into a chair and exchanged shy smiles with her fellow knitters. Thank goodness, Kelly thought. Lizzie's attention would be deflected from grilling Diane.

Lizzie beamed across the table. "Hello, dear, it's so good to see you looking so well."

Lucy blushed at Lizzie's compliment, glancing down shyly. "Thanks, Lizzie. You're sweet to say that."

"Lucy, I must say I have heard marvelous testimony about your spinning classes. In fact, I am tempted to try again to master the craft," Hilda proclaimed in a voice that could be heard all the way out to the entryway, no doubt. "I have failed miserably in every other attempt to learn to spin. Perhaps you will be able help me."

"Of course, Hilda. I'll be happy to help," Lucy said softly, removing a canary yellow yarn from her bag.

"Hilda is being much too hard on herself," Lizzie said. "She was coming along fine, but simply lost patience."

"My sister exaggerates my abilities," Hilda decreed. "I assure you, I was wretched at the wheel. Couldn't keep my hands and feet together."

"Well, from what I've observed in Lucy's classes, that sounds like par for the course," Kelly said. "Everyone in the class had trouble."

"Everyone except Megan. She's doing quite well," Lucy said, needles working the yellow yarn. Kelly thought she recognized a sweater sleeve.

Kelly was about to agree when she glanced toward Diane. Diane Perkins was staring across the table at Lucy, the empty paper cup squeezed tightly in her hand.

Uh-oh, Kelly thought, wondering if Diane recognized Lucy as one of Derek's other girlfriends. Kelly held her breath, waiting for Diane's reaction.

"Kelly, who is that girl?" Diane whispered.

Kelly hesitated, choosing her words carefully. Total honesty was out, given both women's past history with Derek Cooper. "She's one of the instructors here at the shop. She teaches spinning classes, why?"

Diane stared across the table again, ignoring the arrival of two more cups of hot chocolate, steam wafting from the tops of both. "Do you see that necklace she's wearing?"

Kelly nodded, noticing the gold chain around Lucy's neck for the first time.

Diane leaned closer, obviously wanting to keep their conversation from the others. "That's the same necklace Derek wore. It looks exactly like it."

Kelly stared back into Diane's sea green eyes, realizing that Diane didn't recognize Lucy, just the necklace.

"Uhhhh, really?" Kelly waffled, glancing to Lucy again. "It looks like a regular gold chain to me."

"There's a charm on it," Diane whispered. "I can see it. A spider on a web. Derek had a necklace exactly like that. He started wearing it several months ago and wouldn't take it off. Even when we were in bed together. He called it a good luck charm."

Kelly stared at the gold chain around Lucy's neck again. Was it possible that Lucy gave Derek a necklace like hers? Sort of a love token? Or was Diane's imagination on overload like the rest of her? Kelly pondered, wondering what to say to ease Diane's curiosity. She was about to ask Lucy when Lizzie did it for her.

"My, that's a lovely necklace, Lucy," Lizzie remarked. "Is that a charm I see?"

Lucy's busy needles paused while she touched the charm at her neck. Diane sat, riveted, holding her hot chocolate.

"Yes. It's a spider on a web. My spinning logo," Lucy said softly.

"That's sweet," Lizzie cooed.

Kelly released an inner sigh of relief. Leaning next to Diane, she said, "See, that's what it is. I told you she was a spinner."

Diane stared across the table for a few seconds more, then drained her third hot chocolate before turning to Kelly. "I want to see that logo up close."

Surprised at her persistence, Kelly countered the best she could. "Well, we can't go up and stare at her neck. Maybe there's a flyer or something with the logo on it." Deciding she needed to get Diane away from the table lest she come out and confront Lucy about the necklace, Kelly said. "Let's go find Mimi. She may have a flyer."

Kelly shoved the half-unraveled project back into her bag and headed for the main room, beckoning Diane to follow. Kelly fully intended to plop Diane at the front of the shop if necessary and put her to work. Unraveling was amazingly relaxing, Kelly had discovered. Maybe unraveling would keep Diane occupied and away from Lucy Adair until Jayleen arrived.

Kelly hustled around yarn-laden tables, past looms, and into the front of the shop, where holiday shoppers lined up at the register. "Why don't you save my place in line while I find Mimi," she suggested.

"She's running errands, Kelly," a voice called from the corner. "What do you need?"

Kelly hadn't even noticed Rosa, who knelt on the floor, digging through a bucket of bamboo knitting needles. "I wondered if you had a flyer or something with Lucy's spinning logo on it. You know, a web with a spider?"

Rosa peered up at Kelly, looking distracted. "I think they're in that cabinet behind the counter. I'd get it for you, but I have to find these needles for a customer. Ask Connie."

Kelly was about to join Diane in line when her cell phone rang. "Be back in a minute," she said as she hurried from the noisy sales room into an adjoining, quieter yarn room. Ellen looked up from a bin of lollipop yarns she was inspecting.

"Hey, Kelly." Jayleen's voice came over the line. "I'm driving through the north of town now. How's Diane doing?"

"Jumpy as hell," Kelly replied, giving Ellen a wave. "I'm drowning her in hot chocolate, hoping that will calm her down."

Jayleen chuckled. "Hot chocolate, huh? Can't hurt. I'll be there in a few minutes."

"What's this about hot chocolate?" Ellen asked as Kelly clicked off her phone.

"Oh, I'm just trying to calm down a friend who's strung pretty tight right now. I figured hot chocolate would be soothing," Kelly said, fondling the same bright fluff balls that Ellen was.

"What's wrong? Is someone in trouble?"

Kelly glanced toward the library table where Lucy was surrounded by nurturing knitters. Then she looked back at the line of shoppers where Diane was standing alone, consuming the fourth hot chocolate and not talking with anyone. "Actually, she's trying to get over Derek Cooper's death, just like Lucy. Unfortunately, Diane has some other problems mixed in as well. It's kind of complicated."

Ellen paused for a moment. "Sounds like Derek messed up lots of people's lives." Glancing around, she asked, "Where is she? Not with Lucy, I hope."

"Believe me, I got Diane away from the table as soon as I could. She's saving my place in line," Kelly said as her cell phone rang again. Recognizing a client's number, Kelly pointed to the front room. "Ellen, I've gotta take this call. Could you do me a favor and tell Diane I'll be there in a minute? She's wearing a denim jacket."

"Sure," Ellen said with a friendly smile.

Kelly sped through the foyer and stepped outside, only to see the phone screen read MISSED CALL. Brother, talk about impatient clients. Checking the number, she listened for messages as she peered through the large front window and noticed Diane was almost at the register.

Phone tag could wait for later, she decided as she hurried back into the shop. Right now, babysitting Diane was more important.

"Was that you outside? I thought you were in the other room," Diane said as she stepped to the counter. Their turn at last.

"Yeah, I had to talk to a client. Didn't someone—"

"Hey, Kelly, how can I help you?" a weary Connie asked.

"Hang in there, Connie, only a couple more hours to go." Kelly encouraged the normally exuberant clerk. "I just need a flyer with Lucy's spinning logo on it. My friend and I need to see one."

"Sure, let me get it." Connie opened a lower cabinet and began flipping through file folders. "Here's one," she said, handing a flyer to Kelly.

"Thanks, Connie, you're a jewel." Kelly stared at the logo at the top of the sheet, beside Lucy's name. A little spider was nestled in the middle of a delicate spiderweb. LUCY ADAIR, SPINNER AND TEACHER was printed beside the drawing. "See, it is her logo. That's why she wears the necklace," she said, handing the flyer to Diane.

Diane stared at the flyer for a minute. Whether she was picturing Derek or reading about Lucy, Kelly didn't know,

so she gave one last deflective comment. "It's just a coincidence, Diane, that's all."

Diane shook her head. "I don't know. It looks exactly the
same. That's what's so . . . so spooky."

Feeling a slight break in Diane's skepticism, Kelly ventured, "Well, when you think about it, wouldn't every drawing of a spider on a web look the same? I mean, it would have
to, right?"

Diane started to nod, when Jayleen Swinson's voice cut
through the shop noise. "There you are, Kelly," she said as
she strode past the customers. "Why don't you introduce
me to your friend?"

Kelly sent another silent prayer of gratitude out into the
heavens. "Jayleen Swinson, this is Diane Perkins," she said,
gesturing to both women.

Jayleen stepped forward, snowflakes on her denim jacket,
her hand outstretched to an obviously startled Diane. "Glad
to meet you, Diane. I hear you're looking for a lotta work
and a safe place to land. I can offer you both."

Ten

Kelly hurried across the driveway toward the shop entrance, the icy wind whipping her knitted scarf behind her. The light snowflakes had been chased away in the night by a frigid storm front that threatened to bring several inches of snow by this evening. As was typical in Colorado, the storm was being introduced by strong and blustery winds. Even Carl wanted to stay inside the cottage this morning.

Stomping both feet on the sheep-shaped mat, Kelly pushed through the entry door and into the warmth. "Brrrr," she said noisily, in case someone was nearby. Hearing no response, Kelly wiggled out of her winter jacket and left it and her bag on the knitting table in the main room. She paused for a moment to enjoy the peacefulness of the empty knitting shop, then grabbed her mug and headed toward the café and coffee.

Yawning as she rounded a corner, Kelly nearly bumped

into Mimi, who had her arms laden with skeins of colorful yarns.

"Oops," Mimi squeaked, jumping out of the way. "We've got to get mirrors for these corners."

"My fault, Mimi," Kelly apologized. "I wasn't paying attention. I'm still not awake yet. Didn't get much sleep last night."

Mimi made a sympathetic noise as she walked toward an antique cabinet in the corner of the main yarn room. "You're working too hard again," she chided as she deposited the yarns and arranged them in the cabinet. "I thought your consulting schedule was easier."

"Well, it wasn't my consulting that kept me up," Kelly said as she leaned against a bin that spilled over with red, white, and green striped yarns. Sock yarns, already imprinted with the colors so that, once knitted, they revealed a Fair Isle pattern. "I was at Jayleen's last night helping with her client accounts."

"Why? Is Jayleen sick?" Mimi asked, looking concerned.

"No, she was helping a friend of Jennifer's who's a friend of mine now, I guess." Kelly shrugged. "She's got a real drinking problem, and Jayleen was kind enough to volunteer to help her stay sober. She's up there at Jayleen's now, working at the ranch."

"What a wonderful thing for Jayleen to do. It's . . . it's exactly like Vickie helping her." She gave Kelly a maternal smile. "So, while Jayleen was helping this girl, you were helping Jayleen. How like you, Kelly."

Kelly felt a slight flush. "Well, it wasn't only me. Jennifer was there, too, finishing all the lists for the kids' party this Sunday. Jayleen had her hands full trying to keep Diane from panicking." She gave another big yawn. "Boy, I need some coffee, bad."

"How late did you stay?"

"Actually, all night. Both Jen and I fell asleep about two this morning, then woke up and came back into town early."

"Goodness, have you had breakfast yet? C'mon, I'll join you." Mimi didn't wait for Kelly to answer, taking her arm instead and escorting Kelly down the hallway and into Pete's café. They settled at a bay window table where they could watch the snowstorm approach over the mountains.

Jennifer walked over, coffeepot in hand. "You look as bad as I do," she joked as she filled Kelly's mug.

"Just keep this coming. I've got to catch up on my work today. This weekend is going to be super busy with the kids' party and decorating Curt's ranch house."

Jennifer took both their orders and hastened away, while Kelly indulged herself with Eduardo's rich brew, hoping to stay awake in front of the computer. Glancing across at Mimi, she decided to take a risk. Maybe it was sleep deprivation, whatever. Kelly decided it was time.

She leaned forward over the table and—in her customary go-for-it manner—jumped in. "You know, Mimi, I've noticed that you've been looking radiantly happy lately. And I think I know why."

Mimi looked at Kelly, obviously startled. "Wh-what do you mean?"

"Mimi, you and Burt make a great couple. Everyone thinks so. There's no reason to be shy about it."

Mimi's cheeks flushed a bright pink. "How—how did you guess?"

Kelly decided to fess up. "Well, I didn't notice at first.

Actually, Lisa and Jennifer figured it out first, then they told me."

"How did they know?" Mimi rasped, clearly clueless.

Kelly gave Mimi a wicked smile. "They saw you and Burt having lunch and dinner together. And laughing together. And gazing at each other with that special look."

This time, Mimi went crimson, her hands at her cheeks. "Oh, goodness! Does everyone know?"

"Pretty much," Kelly teased. "C'mon, Mimi. It's nothing to be embarrassed about. Burt's a great guy, a jewel. And you're an absolute sweetheart who's been alone too long. You two belong together. I can't think of a more perfect couple."

Mimi found her smile. "Thank you, Kelly. I was hoping you all would be pleased. You're my family, you know."

Kelly reached out and patted Mimi's hand. "You're family to me, too, Mimi. So take it from one of your 'Lambspun daughters,' it's time to tell the world that you and Burt are dating. In fact, you could announce it on Sunday at the party."

Mimi laughed softly. "Dating again at my age. Who would have thought?"

Kelly was about to say something reassuring to "Mother Mimi" when Jennifer approached with their breakfasts. The scent of bacon tickled Kelly's nose and swept away everything except hunger.

Her chin in her hand, Kelly closed her eyes as she sat in front of the computer screen. Two minutes. That's all. Maybe she could drift off for a couple of minutes. Kelly felt the warm fuzzy sleepy feeling close in around her—until her cell phone rang.

Startled awake, Kelly rasped into the phone, "Kelly here."

"Whoa, Kelly, you do sound sleepy." Burt's warm voice came over the line. "Mimi told me you and Jennifer were up at Jayleen's last night. How's Diane doing?"

"Well, she was pretty bad off, Burt." Kelly decided to be totally honest. Maybe it would strike some sympathetic chord. "She was shaking like a leaf, trying to stay sober, scared to death by Peterson, and on top of everything else, her boss fired her yesterday morning. Right before Peterson knocked on her door."

Burt paused. "That's too bad."

"Yeah, it sure is. Make sure you tell Peterson, would you? Apparently he really turned up the heat on Diane yesterday. That's why we called on Jayleen. She's been in this situation and pulled herself out."

"So now she's trying to help Diane Perkins?"

Kelly yawned. "Yeah. Jayleen's got her up at the ranch, working with her today. Tonight they're coming into town for an AA meeting."

"That's admirable of Jayleen to do that."

"I thought so, too, so that's why Jen and I went up there. We helped out with other chores so she could talk with Diane."

"Let's hope it takes," Burt said, his voice sounding a shade less judgmental than before, Kelly noticed. "I wanted to let you know that I passed along your comments about other people visiting Derek Cooper that night. Apparently, Diane told Peterson yesterday that she saw a car driving up when she left."

"Did they find out anything?"

"My friend said there were several voice messages from girls on Derek's cell phone. One of them was garbled and static-filled, but they could pick out a few words, like 'I need to see you,' then static again. They couldn't tell much. But there was another message that was clearer. Sounded like a jilted girlfriend who held a grudge."

"Could they trace either of the numbers?"

He shook his head. "Pay phones."

"Darn it. I was hoping that would lead somewhere. Jennifer learned Derek had a fight with another guy at the bar last month. Apparently this other guy, Gary something, had a business deal that Derek promised to invest in, then pulled out of it at the last minute. Jennifer said the bartender told her this Gary went after Derek in the bar when he found out."

"Did this Gary threaten Derek?"

"Not then, but two guys had to hold him back. Just like Diane," she couldn't resist adding. "But the bartender also said Gary came in a week later telling people, 'One of these days Derek Cooper will get payback.' " Kelly paused. "That sounds like a threat to me, Burt."

"I'll pass it along, Kelly. Does Jennifer know Gary's last name?"

"She's looking into it," Kelly said, then remembered something else. "By the way, Burt, could you check to see if Derek Cooper was wearing a gold chain when the police found him? The chain had a charm, too. A spider on a web."

"I'll ask, but I don't recall my friend saying anything about a chain. Anything else on that laundry list of yours?"

Kelly joined Burt's soft laughter, then decided to surprise him. "Yeah, matter of fact, there is. You and Mimi make a great couple. Just for the record."

Burt paused for several seconds. Kelly pictured him weighing his responses. "I figured you gals would catch on eventually," he said with a chuckle.

"Yeah, you can only fool us for so long."

"I'll remember that."

"Why don't you come clean at the party and tell everyone?"

"We'll think about it. By the way, Jayleen hasn't given me a list yet. What should I bring?"

"Jennifer's bringing the lists to the shop today. We've all got marching orders, and Jayleen is running this show, so we'd better stay in step," Kelly joked. Listening to Burt's laughter, Kelly added, "By the way, Jayleen will be bringing Diane Perkins with her. She'll be helping with the party, too, so promise me you won't scowl at the woman and scare her to death."

"I promise. It sounds like Jayleen is really babysitting her. I wonder what would happen if Diane got 'off-leash'?" he said, a touch of skepticism in his tone.

"Hey, Jayleen knows what she's doing with Diane. We're simply following her lead. If helping with a kids' party will help Diane, then it's doing double duty, in my book," Kelly said emphatically.

"I hope you're right. And for your sake, I'll give Diane Perkins the benefit of the doubt."

"That's all I ask, Burt."

"Hit me with your best shot, Pete," Kelly said, leaning her empty mug over the counter.

Pete glanced up from the refrigerator where he was storing homemade pies. "You're in bad shape today, Kelly. Both you and Jen are like walking zombies. You'd better get some sleep tonight."

Kelly tried to hide another huge yawn. No luck. "Believe me, that's on my to-do list. But I have to finish this client first." Watching Pete fill her mug, steam rising from the top, the vision of bourbon pecan pie flitted through her sleep-deprived brain. "Uhhhh, while you're at it, give me a slice of that wicked pecan pie of yours, too. I'll save it for a reward after these accounts."

Pete's genial face spread with a familiar grin. "Will do. Lots of brown sugar and alcohol. That'll do the trick," he said, chuckling. "One slice of pecan pie, coming up."

"Make that two." Curt Stackhouse's voice came from behind Kelly. "Sit for a spell, Kelly, and share that pie with me." Curt strode to a nearby table and claimed it with his gray Stetson.

"I'll watch you eat it, Curt," Kelly said as she joined him. "If I have that sugar and whiskey now, I'll be asleep on the keyboard the rest of the afternoon."

"What's the matter, Kelly? Steve keeping you up nights?" Curt teased, a twinkle in his eyes.

Kelly tried to give him a reproving scowl, but the slight blush she felt staining her cheeks defeated the effect. "Matter of fact, no. As if it were any of your business, which it's *not*, I might add."

Curt simply winked at her, then dove into the pecan pie that Pete placed before him. Kelly was about to chide her mentor, friend, and second-father figure, when Pete spoke up.

"Kelly and Jennifer spent most of the night up in the canyon at Jayleen's, helping out a friend. That's why they look wasted," Pete said.

"Thanks, Pete. I appreciate that." Kelly poked him in the arm before he retreated to the kitchen, laughing.

"What's happening at Jayleen's that she needs your help?" Curt asked between bites.

"It's kind of a long story," Kelly demurred, not wanting to invade Diane's privacy any more than she already had.

"It's a big piece of pie. I've got time."

Curt could be as determined as Steve when it came to wanting answers, so Kelly related the entire convoluted story of Diane Perkins and Derek Cooper. Curt concentrated on the pie until it was finished, then signaled to the waitress for coffee, before he turned his attention to Kelly.

"You know, that's real admirable of you and Jennifer wanting to help your friend. And I'm not at all surprised that Jayleen would go out of her way to help the girl, especially since she's walked that same road herself." He wagged his head slowly. "But did you and Jennifer consider the possibility that this Diane really is the killer? And if she is, you've put Jayleen in jeopardy."

Kelly felt Curt's stern gaze settle over her, bringing a chill. "Neither Jennifer nor I believe Diane killed Derek. I know the police think she killed him in a drunken rage and blacked it out, but I don't buy that, Curt."

"What if the police are right? This girl is a drunk, Kelly. She may have killed him and can't remember doing it."

"If she was that drunk, she wouldn't have been able to drive out of the canyon, then," Kelly retorted. "She'd have run off the road."

"Don't be so sure about that," Curt said solemnly. "People can do all sorts of amazing things when they're scared and trying to escape."

The image that Curt Stackhouse painted began to form in Kelly's mind. Diane, horrified at killing her lover and terrified of being caught. The chill spread, awakening all those similar thoughts she'd had about Diane from the start.

"I . . . I just don't believe that, Curt," was all she could think to say.

"Well, it doesn't matter what you or Jennifer believe, does it?" Curt continued. "Because she's up there with Jayleen now. What if she gets drunk again and attacks Jayleen?"

The chill ran right up Kelly's spine. Could that happen? Good Lord. Curt was right. If she and Jennifer were wrong about Diane, then Jayleen might be in danger.

"Jayleen's taking her to AA tonight," Kelly said. "Diane's really trying to stay sober. And you know Jayleen doesn't keep liquor around her house."

"All the same, I think I'll go on up there and take a little look-see," Curt announced, as he removed several dollar bills from his wallet and dropped them on the table. "Meet this Diane for myself. I take it Jayleen has her work right alongside her."

Kelly rose from the table with Curt, considering her next words. "You'll get a chance to meet her this Sunday, Curt. Jayleen's bringing Diane to help with the party. Unless you don't want her there, of course. We'd never do anything against your wishes."

Curt paused at the doorway, Stetson in his hand. Kelly watched his familiar smile return and felt herself relax. "That'll be fine, Kelly. In fact, that will work even better. Now, you go back to work, and I'll see you Sunday. And wear your boots. We've got tons of snow at the ranch. In fact, I may put some of those boys to work shoveling."

Eleven

"**Hey,** Kelly," Lisa called across the driveway.

Kelly barely heard her over the roar of the snowplow that was scraping the curved driveway, which skirted the knitting shop. "Be right there," Kelly yelled, trying to navigate through the foot-deep snow that had drifted from the golf course across her front yard overnight. Her boots sank into the dry, crunchy snow, bringing back childhood memories. Colorado powder. Squeaky snow.

"That's another reason I like living in a condo," Lisa said, watching Kelly maneuver through the depths. "No snow to shovel. They do it for you."

"I have to borrow Mimi's shovel. I tried three places last night, and they were sold out." Kelly joined Lisa on the front steps to Lambspun and stamped snow from her boots.

"Welcome back to Colorado," Lisa said as they escaped the frigid air into the warmth of the shop. "Remind Steve we're going skiing after the holidays, okay?"

"It's been so long, I hope I don't run into a tree," Kelly said as she shed her coat and dropped her things on the knitting table.

Lisa did the same and settled into a chair beside Kelly. "By the way, I did some checking at Social Services," she said, glancing around the empty room. "And I also checked with the therapist who worked with Lucy a couple of years ago. She suggested I encourage Lucy to come back to see her. We're both concerned. Do you know if Lucy's even seen a doctor about the baby yet?"

Kelly shook her head as she removed the nearly completed alpaca wool scarf from her bag. With a little luck, she could finish and have the scarf in the mail to Eugene Tolliver tomorrow. "I could ask her friend Ellen. She seems to know Lucy the best." Kelly checked her watch. "In fact, Lucy's spinning class should be over soon. Ellen and the others will be coming out. I'll ask her then."

"And I'll try to catch Lucy. That's why I'm here this morning. I actually rescheduled a client's therapy so I could talk with Lucy. I've been worrying about her ever since we spoke last week."

Kelly smiled at her friend, who was concentrating intensely on a red and green wool sweater. "You're a sweetheart, Lisa, you know that."

"Yeah, yeah, yeah."

Megan burst through the classroom doorway then, rushing up to Kelly and Lisa. "Oh, fantastic! I'm so glad to see you guys," she said, breathless. "I need your help right away!

My tennis partner, Sam, has to go to the hospital to be with his wife. She's gone into early labor."

Kelly grinned up at Megan. "I thought spinning was supposed to be calming. Why are you so excited? You're not having the baby."

Megan made a face. "That's true, but now I don't have a doubles partner, and we've got a big match after the weekend. Everybody I know is already teamed up, and I'm the president of the tennis club, for heaven's sake! Do you know anyone? Anyone at all?"

Kelly drew a blank. She'd been focused solely on softball and running since she'd returned to Fort Connor last spring. "Afraid not, Megan. Neither Steve nor I am anywhere near your level. We'd do more harm than good."

"Sorry, Megan," Lisa commiserated. "I can't help either. But I'll ask Greg. Does Bill play? You know, the guy you met last week?"

Megan shook her head. "Nope. He's a cyclist. No ball sports." She released a huge sigh. "It's mixed doubles, so I have to find a guy. And at this late date, he doesn't have to be good. I guess I'll have to keep looking." With that, Megan scooped up her knitting bag and hastened to the entrance, winter coat dangling over her arm.

"Boy, I hope she remembers to put her coat on when she gets outside," Kelly said.

Lisa laughed. "She will when she feels the cold."

The remaining spinning students tumbled through the doorway then, and Kelly spied Lucy talking with Ellen. "Class is over, here's your chance," she said to Lisa.

Lisa was already stuffing the half-finished sweater into her backpack. "Wish me luck."

Kelly chatted with the spinners who milled about the room as they fondled soft skeins of wools, alpaca, and silk. All the while, she kept an eye on Lisa, who was hovering beside Lucy and Ellen, clearly awaiting her turn.

At last Ellen gave a wave and approached the yarn bins, indulging herself like the other spinners. Kelly watched Lisa gesture Lucy toward the small alcove off the main room. Lucy's expression changed from curiosity to surprise to anxiety as she listened to Lisa. Her face paled, and her eyes became huge as she stared, not uttering a word.

Suddenly, tears. They burst forth like a dam had been breached, pouring down Lucy's face. "I can't . . . I can't," she cried out, then clapped her hand to her mouth and ran from the room. Kelly heard the familiar tinkle of the doorbell sounding after her.

Kelly glanced to Lisa in dismay. Lisa looked stunned, obviously unprepared for Lucy's emotional response to their conversation. Kelly beckoned her over, and Lisa collapsed into a nearby chair.

"Good Lord, I thought Lucy was getting better," Kelly said. "Apparently not."

Lisa shook her head, staring across the room. "I thought so, too. Believe me, I never would have approached her if I thought she would respond that way."

"Don't beat yourself up, Lisa. Her reaction was way over the top. I mean, you were suggesting counseling, for Pete's sake. And she's had that before."

"I know, that's what worries me, Kelly. I wasn't suggesting anything that she hasn't done before, so it wasn't strange to her. I'm concerned that she needs more care than a group counseling session can provide. And I'm worried about the baby." Lisa frowned. "We need to find a way to help her."

"I hope you have better luck than I did," Ellen commented from behind them, obviously having overheard their conversation. "I've tried every way I can to convince Lucy. But she won't go to therapy, and she hasn't seen a doctor for the baby yet." Ellen toyed with a skein of red and orange yarns. Burnt umber, pumpkin gold, and fire engine red.

"That's not good," Kelly said, turning to include Ellen in their conversation. "She's strung so tight she's going to break."

"I know, I've told her that myself, and she blames it on morning sickness." Ellen shook her head. "I've heard that there are medicines for that. I've even offered to go with Lucy to the doctor. Anything to get her some help."

"There has to be a way," Kelly insisted. "Maybe we can, uh, take her ourselves, you know—"

"You mean against her will?" Lisa countered. "Not a good idea, Kelly. In her present state, she'd be terrified out of her mind. That would make it worse."

"Yeah, you're probably right," Kelly admitted, watching Ellen nod bleakly.

"Let me talk to some more therapists. I'm way out of my league here, and I don't want to do any more damage than I may have already," Lisa said, pushing away from the table.

"C'mon, Lisa," Kelly objected, "you were only trying to help. Just like Ellen."

"Yeah, I know," Lisa said distractedly. "Listen, guys, I have to leave for the clinic. I'll see you later." With a quick wave, she was gone.

After a murmured goodbye Ellen also headed for the doorway, leaving Kelly alone once again. Even the main room was temporarily empty of holiday shoppers.

She let the comfortable relaxed feeling of knitting quietly settle over her. Meditative and peaceful, ordering her thoughts, freeing up new ideas. Even knotty accounting problems loosened as her fingers worked the yarn, moving through the familiar stitches. This time, however, Lucy's panicked expression interrupted the peaceful feeling.

Poor Lucy. Pregnant and alone. Just like Kelly's aunt Helen years ago. Helen had a family, true, but they practically disowned her when they discovered she was pregnant, particularly when Helen refused to reveal the father's name. Aunt Helen must have felt equally abandoned, until she went to Wyoming to stay with her cousin Martha's family. At least Helen had someone she could confide in there, someone who cared and supported her. Kelly watched the gray and white stitches gather on her needle as she imagined how her aunt would have felt in small-town Colorado being an unwed mother. Alone and unwanted, just like Lucy.

Lucy had found someone to confide in with Ellen, but clearly, Lucy needed more. She needed someone who could convince her she needed help. If Lucy's friends couldn't get through to her, who could?

The answer to Kelly's question appeared right before her eyes. Snowflakes glistening on her cherry red wool coat, Lizzie bustled into the room, settling herself in her usual place at the knitting table. "Good morning, Kelly," she said cheerfully. "How's that alpaca scarf coming? It appears you're nearly finished."

Kelly looked up at Lizzie and gave her a huge grin. Lizzie. *Yes.* Kind-hearted, solicitous, gentle Lizzie, who loved nothing better than to listen to other people's stories. Maybe Lizzie's warmth could penetrate the barrier Lucy had built around herself. "Matter of fact, Lizzie, I am," she said, holding up the scarf proudly. "Look how nicely it turned out."

Lizzie examined the scarf, making appropriate sounds of

approval. She beamed at Kelly. "It's lovely, dear. That gentleman at the gallery will wear it everywhere, I'm sure."

Kelly resumed her knitting, while Lizzie turned to her multicolored yarn. "Where's Hilda?" she asked, waiting for an opportunity to confide in Lizzie, and hoping they wouldn't be invaded by others in the meantime.

"Oh, she's checking the class schedules out front. Hilda has been inspired by Lucy's students, and she's convinced she can finally learn to spin." Lizzie's dimple showed in her round cheeks.

Ahhhh, Kelly exulted, as Lizzie provided the opening she was waiting for. "Speaking of Lucy, I was hoping you could help us, Lizzie," she said, in an attempt to catch Lizzie's considerable curiosity. "Several of her friends are concerned for her well-being."

Lizzie's attention left her knitting immediately. "Goodness, what's the matter? I thought she was slowly recovering from her grief over losing her lover so tragically."

"Well, we thought so, too, but we've learned it's, well, it's more complicated than that." Kelly deliberately dangled the vague comment.

"Oh, really?" Lizzie said, bright blue eyes widening as she leaned closer. "What are the, uh, complications, so to speak?"

Kelly let her needles drop to her lap and leaned closer. "You'll have to swear you won't repeat this to a soul, not even Hilda," Kelly said solemnly, trying to ignore the sting of her own conscience at invading Lucy's privacy again.

Lizzie's eyes grew huge. "I swear."

"Lucy is carrying Derek Cooper's child," Kelly announced in a hushed voice. "She was about to tell him, when Derek was murdered. So you can understand why she's been an emotional wreck since his death."

"Oh, my," Lizzie said, catching her breath.

"Apparently, she'd only told her friend Ellen, in class. Ellen confided in Megan and me because she was worried about Lucy. She needs to talk to a counseler. A grief counseler, at least. And she needs to see a doctor about the baby."

"Oh, goodness, yes! You mean she hasn't spoken with anyone?" Lizzie looked horrified. "Oh, she must, she must! That poor child! Bereft and alone . . . and with child. Oh, my, we must help her."

"Well, both Ellen and Lisa have suggested counseling, but Lucy refuses. In fact, she burst out in tears when Lisa offered to take her to see a therapist she'd used in the past."

Lizzie wagged her head. "Poor dear."

Kelly paused. "I thought maybe you could get through to her, Lizzie. I was sure that Lisa could reach Lucy, because Lisa had helped with Lucy's therapy years ago. But no. Lucy ran out of the room crying at the suggestion."

"How could I help, Kelly? I'm certainly not trained like Lisa."

"Actually, I think that might be better. You're a warm, caring, maternal woman, Lizzie." Kelly emphasized with an encouraging smile. "And if anyone is in need of some old-fashioned mothering right now, it's Lucy."

A small smile tweaked Lizzie's lips. "You're very sweet to say that, Kelly. And if you think I can help, I will gladly try my best to get through to the poor girl."

"See if you can convince her to see a counselor, someone, even a minister."

"Hmmmm, that's a thought. I'll do my best, dear. Oops, here comes Hilda. Not a word." She shushed dramatically.

"Good morning, Kelly," Hilda broadcast as she marched toward the knitting table and took her customary seat at the end. The better to teach class. "I have officially registered to resume my quest to learn to spin. Let us hope the old adage 'three's the charm' is correct." Hilda withdrew a delicate azure blue yarn from her bag and began to crochet, her hooked needle moving quickly. "I see you're nearly finished with that scarf for the Denver gentleman. Excellent. You'll have time to knit another gift."

Kelly did her best to look appalled. The better to tease Hilda. "Not a chance, Hilda. One gift per holiday is my limit. It takes too long."

Hilda eyed Kelly over her rimless glasses. "Then you should learn how to knit socks, my dear. They're much quicker."

Kelly laughed. "Quicker for you, maybe. All those little pointy needles . . . I don't think so."

"Nonsense, my dear," Hilda scoffed. "You're so adventurous in other ways. You must try socks."

Socks as an adventure. Now, there was a new concept. "I'll make you a deal, Hilda. I'll give socks a try when you learn how to spin. How's that?" Kelly challenged.

Twelve

Kelly's new boots sank into the melting snow as she walked through her front yard. Yesterday's snow was fast changing to slush. Turning her face toward the bright sunshine, Kelly had to stop and admire the snow-covered golf course, glistening—and melting at the same time.

Colorado weather. If you didn't like it, wait a minute. It was bound to change. Yesterday's frigid cold had thawed quickly that morning with the return of brilliant blue skies and bright sunshine. Temperatures were already in the forties, and it wasn't even noon yet.

Returning to the slush, Kelly trekked toward the Lambspun front porch, then stamped the mud from her boots. Reaching for the door, she nearly fell backward when Burt burst through the doorway.

"Whoa! Now I know what it feels like," Kelly exclaimed with a laugh.

"I'm sorry, Kelly," Burt said, hand outstretched. "Did I hit you?"

"No, no. Softball reflexes saved me. Besides, it serves me right for all the times I've rushed around corners and run into people. Where're you going in such a hurry?"

"Where aren't I going." Burt corrected with a good-natured smile. "Mimi gave me another list of stuff for Jayleen's party tomorrow."

"Oh, brother, that reminds me. I've got a bunch of things to buy, too. Including a frozen breakfast entrée."

"Anything but cooking, right?"

"You bet," Kelly agreed with a laugh. "Maybe I'll bring a platter of hearty sausage. I can microwave with the best of them."

"Sounds good to me, Kelly. See you tomorrow," he said, bounding down the stairs.

Kelly was about to enter the shop when she remembered something. "Hey, Burt, did you hear if a necklace was found on you-know-who?" she called after him, reticent to broadcast her curiosity to whomever might be nearby.

Burt barely slowed his stride as he answered over his shoulder. "I called yesterday, and nothing like that was found, Kelly. Not on the victim or at the scene." He gave a quick goodbye wave as he jumped into his car.

That was curious, Kelly thought as she entered the shop and headed toward the knitting table. Diane said Derek Cooper never took off the necklace, calling it a "good luck charm." Why then wasn't it found on his body? she wondered.

Shedding her coat and scarf, Kelly settled into a comfy chair beside the library table and retrieved the completed alpaca scarf. All that remained was to tuck the ends. If she was lucky, she could finish in time to drop the scarf in the mail today.

Kelly dug out her little plastic needle case and set about splitting each yarn tail into four sections, then meticulously weaving each one underneath and through the knitted stitches, concealing them completely. She was nearly finished when her cell phone jangled.

"Kelly, can you do me a huge favor?" Jayleen's excited voice came over the phone.

"Sure, what do you need?"

"Can you and Steve pick up some chocolate candy for the stocking gifts? You know, the loose kind that will rattle around inside."

Kelly laughed. "My favorite kind. We'll be glad to, Jayleen. By the way, how's Diane doing? You said she'd be helping tomorrow."

"Lord have mercy, I don't know what I would have done without the girl this week. She's been a lifesaver. Diane took care of all the livestock while I've been runnin' around town like that chicken without its head." Jayleen exhaled a long sigh.

"Well, that's good to hear," Kelly said. "I'm glad she's been useful. Sounds like you needed help."

"Boy, have I ever. Diane pitched right in, too. I mean, not everyone's cut out for ranch work, you know what I mean? But she's a strong girl."

"Has she, uh . . . has she been okay?" Kelly probed. "I mean, she hasn't tried to run into town to the bars or anything? I know you don't keep any liquor in your house."

Jayleen laughed her hearty laugh. "Nary a drop, Kelly, and no, Diane hasn't run off to the bars. Of course, the fact we're miles up a snowy mountain canyon helps, too. It'd be a long cold walk into town at night."

Kelly exhaled her own sigh of relief. "Thank God, Jayleen. I was half afraid you'd tell me she was climbing the walls at night or something."

"Well, don't get me wrong, Kelly. It hasn't been easy for Diane. Hell, no. She's been pacing at night and eating sweets. And drinking hot chocolate by the gallon. Matter of fact, you can add that to your list, if you would. She's nearly finished my huge can of chocolate mix," Jayleen said with a chuckle.

"Oops, I guess I got her hooked on that here at the shop," Kelly confessed. "It was the only thing I could think of that might calm her down when she was here the other day. I guess it worked."

"We may need a lot more of it, too," Jayleen added, her voice changing. "Diane had a call from one of her friends, saying that the police have visited the bar a second time, asking people questions. Diane got real nervous after that. You can understand why."

"Ohhhh, yeah," Kelly said, her good mood evaporating. "I hope that doesn't set her off."

"Well, we've got the party tomorrow, and she'll be plenty busy like the rest of us. Don't worry, Kelly, I'm keeping an eye on her. Gotta go. See ya tomorrow." She clicked off.

Maybe she should bring a whole tub of chocolate mix, Kelly thought as she returned to tucking the alpaca wool yarn. Both edges of the scarf were finished. Only the dangling yarn tails in the middle remained.

She glanced up at the sound of someone approaching the table and was surprised to see Lucy pulling out a chair on the opposite side of the table.

Lucy gave Kelly a quick smile. "Hi, Kelly," she said as she retrieved a fluffy mound of yellow yarn from her bag and began to knit.

Delighted to see Lucy actually trying to socialize once again, Kelly had to remind herself to restrain her enthusiasm. "Hey, Lucy, how're you doing?" she said in the gentlest voice she could manage.

"I'm okay," Lucy said softly, concentrating on the yellow wool.

Kelly decided not to venture another comment and returned to tucking alpaca yarn tails, hoping Lucy would relax in the peaceful setting. Several quiet moments passed, and Kelly sensed her strategy had worked. She glanced at Lucy and noticed her shoulders were no longer hunched, and she actually appeared more relaxed as she knitted silently.

Kelly also noticed something else. Lucy was wearing the gold necklace with her logo on it. A spider on its web. It really was a pretty design, Kelly thought.

Figuring the atmosphere was sufficiently comfortable, Kelly ventured a friendly comment. "That's a beautiful necklace, Lucy. It's your spinning logo, right?"

"Yes, a spider on a web," Lucy replied softly.

"It's really lovely."

Lucy reached up to touch the necklace before she returned to her knitting. "Thank you, Kelly. It's my good luck charm."

Lucy's reply caused a little buzz in the back of Kelly's brain. According to Diane Perkins, that was what Derek Cooper called the necklace. A good luck charm. Maybe this necklace was her way of keeping Derek close to her. Hopefully, the necklace would bring Lucy better luck than it did Derek Cooper.

"How wonderful to see you girls," Lizzie's voice interrupted as she walked into the room. "It's such a beautiful morning, isn't it? Bright sunshine melting all that snow, simply wonderful."

Lucy greeted Lizzie with a shy smile. "Hi, Lizzie."

"How's that baby blanket coming?" Kelly asked, glad to see Lizzie settle beside Lucy at the table. Perhaps it would be better to finish those yarn tails at home, she decided. That way, Lizzie could have some quiet time with Lucy.

"I'm nearly finished," Lizzie said, holding up the delicate creation.

Lucy reached over and touched the multicolored froth. "That's beautiful, Lizzie. Absolutely beautiful."

"Why, thank you, dear." Lizzie beamed. "But I've seen your work as well. You have an exquisite touch, Lucy, if I do say."

Lucy flushed at Lizzie's praise. "You're being kind."

"Not at all, my dear," Lizzie continued.

Kelly decided that was her cue to leave and quickly shoved her scarf into its bag, hastening away from the knitting table with a quick wave and murmured farewell. Pleased with being able to allow Lizzie some quiet time with Lucy, Kelly hoped the motherly knitter would be able to gradually reach through Lucy's defenses. Warmth could work wonders.

Heading toward the café and a coffee refill, Kelly noticed Ellen standing near the loom, staring up at the cones of novelty yarns. Shelf after colorful shelf, jammed with fat cones, in every hue and color combination imaginable.

Kelly sidled up beside her. "Hey, Ellen," she said in a lowered voice. "Stay away from the knitting table for a few minutes, would you? Lizzie's in there trying to talk with Lucy. I'm hoping some maternal nurturing can penetrate Lucy's shell."

Ellen turned quickly. "You think that'll work?"

Kelly crossed her fingers and held them up. "It can't hurt. Lizzie is the least threatening person I know. She exudes sweetness and warmth."

"Boy, I hope so. Something's got to reach Lucy."

"Do you have time for coffee?"

Ellen checked her watch. "I wish I did, but I'd better get back to work before I lose another hour to yarn lust."

"What do you do?"

"Medical transcription. Get to work out of my home, too. Like you, with your accounting."

Kelly laughed. "Working for yourself is a mixed blessing, isn't it? I'm still adjusting."

"Oh, yeah. Say, how's your friend doing? You know, the one you were drowning in hot chocolate."

Kelly paused. "Not too good, as a matter of fact."

"That's too bad."

Kelly was about to continue on her coffee quest when she remembered something. "Hey, Ellen, I'm curious about that necklace Lucy wears. She says it's her spinning logo. It's really pretty."

"It sure is. She just started wearing it, too. I guess she must have made one for herself. I remember her showing me the one she made for Derek several months ago," Ellen said as she wrapped a colorful wool scarf around her neck.

"Do you think she's wearing it in Derek's memory or something?"

Ellen shrugged. "Who knows? See you later, Kelly." She gave a goodbye wave as she left.

Kelly continued down the hallway toward Eduardo's coffee. The afternoon of holiday season errands lying ahead of her demanded a megadose of caffeine. Venturing into the shopping center on a Saturday afternoon in December wasn't for the fainthearted.

Thirteen

Kelly filched another piece of crispy bacon as she passed through the sunny Stackhouse kitchen. Enticing aromas of bacon and sausage, hot breads, and cheesy egg casseroles still floated in the air, tempting her.

"I love breakfast," she said, depositing several empty dishes next to the sink. "We should do this more often."

"Anytime you want breakfast, Kelly, give me a call," Mimi said as she loaded the dishwasher. "It's my favorite meal."

Eyeing the platter of bacon and sausage, Kelly couldn't resist. She snatched one of Megan's yummy biscuits, added a patty of sausage, and took a huge bite as she leaned against the wood-grained counter.

"You eating again?" Lisa asked as she brought another load of dishes to the sink.

"Ummmm," Kelly hummed in enjoyment. "Don't interrupt me."

"When you're finished, come on out and help us. Steve and Greg brought the boxes down from the attic. I can't believe how many decorations there are," Lisa said, disappearing through the doorway again.

"You go with them, Kelly. I don't need any help," Mimi said, rinsing a juice glass. "Besides, it's fun working in such a beautiful kitchen. So sunny and bright. I swear, I can feel Ruth here."

"Can't fool me. You're pushing me out so I won't steal any more sausage," Kelly said as she followed after Lisa.

"I'll make coffee," Mimi called after her.

Kelly walked through the sprawling high-ceilinged living room, where Curt had put a huge evergreen tree in front of the windows. It looked at least eleven feet tall to Kelly. A big difference from the small townhouse-sized trees she usually bought in the East. Kelly could smell the fresh evergreen scent. Inhaling deeply, she let memories from Christmases past rush in. Aunt Helen. Uncle Jim. Her dad. Wonderful family-filled memories from years ago. Nostalgia tinged with sadness. All of her family was gone now.

"Careful, careful," Megan's voice came from the adjacent family room.

Steve and Greg were stacking boxes on the floor, on chairs, on tables—wherever Megan directed. Meanwhile, Jennifer and Lisa removed the contents of each box and placed them gently on the dining room table, where Megan was arranging them carefully.

"Oh, my gosh," Lisa exclaimed, holding up several glass balls and sparkly garlands. "These look handmade. How beautiful."

Watching her friends admire what was obviously a box filled with Stackhouse family treasures, Kelly smiled. She had a new family now. Everyone here was part of her family. She'd not only created a new life for herself in Colorado, but she'd also created a new family as well. A much bigger family, too. In fact, it seemed to get bigger all the time, she noticed as Jayleen strode through the room.

"Look out, comin' through," Jayleen warned as she wove a path through the others, Diane Perkins right behind. Both women's arms were filled with bulging grocery bags. "If anyone needs something to do, come see me. Diane and I have nearly fifty stockings to stuff. And that doesn't count toys."

"I can help with that, Jayleen," Curt offered from the entryway, as he stomped snow from his boots. "Let me finish clearing the walkway, and I'll lend a hand."

"That's okay, Curt. We've got a lot of extra hands in here," Jayleen called out.

"Here are the lights," Megan said, excitement in her voice. "Oh, wow, look how many there are."

"I'll handle the lights," Burt announced. "That was always my job."

"Be my guest, Burt," Steve said as he lifted a large grapevine wreath from a box. "Untangling lights isn't my idea of decorating."

"Ahh, but it's really detective work," Burt said as he took the twisted strands of lights and sat down on the rug, plopping the huge pile beside him.

"A job requiring higher-order skills, right?" Kelly said, joining her friends.

"Absolutely," Burt said, loosening knots. "Lots of concentration. I'm good at that."

"Kelly, help Jennifer and me put up these homemade decorations. Megan's organizing all the ornaments so we'll be ready after we put the lights on the tree. You can grab another box," Lisa ordered, heading toward the living room, her hands filled with boxes.

"Aye, aye, captain," Kelly teased as she followed after, box in hand.

"Hey, Burt, these look like outside lights to me," Greg announced, holding up an amazingly untangled string of lights. "Why don't Steve and I put these up outside? Curt can show us where."

"Sounds good." Burt gave the lights a quick once-over before he returned to his untangling.

"Mimi, save us some of Megan's biscuits, would you? We'll be outside for a while," Steve called as he grabbed his jacket and followed Greg through the front door.

"Will do," Mimi's voice sang from the kitchen.

"Ohhhh, look at these handmade stockings," Kelly exclaimed as she opened a box. "Ruth must have made these. Satin and lace and velvet, wow." She stroked the soft velvet, admiring the various patterns and combinations of colors Ruth had used in her creations. Crimson red satin, emerald velvet, and sapphire blue silk.

"Now those definitely belong over the fireplace," Jennifer said as she strung sparkly garlands around the old-fashioned fireplace. "Look, I see tiny hooks wedged in the brick."

Kelly set about hanging the stockings while Lisa and Jennifer arranged yarn angels, beaded candles, nutcrackers, toy soldiers, Raggedy Ann and Andy dolls, and teddy bears. There were even faded and worn paper decorations. The elementary school glue had loosened over the years, but amazingly, the wreaths, Santas, and angels were still intact. Kelly figured they had been made by Ruth and Curt's children years ago and watched Lisa carefully tuck them into safe corners on bookshelves.

"Coffee's ready," Mimi announced, leaning around the kitchen doorway. "Kelly, I've already poured you a mug."

Kelly made a beeline for the kitchen, following her nose. Before she'd crossed the living room, however, a mini hurricane blew through the front door.

Curt tumbled into the house, three small children in tow, all squealing loudly with holiday excitement. A tall young man with curly red hair followed after them, joining the noisy cluster as they stamped snow from their boots.

"Now, kids, you've gotta stay out of the kitchen, okay? The ladies are making surprises for the party," Curt warned, wagging a finger at the giggling children.

"Okay, Grandpa," the taller girl said with a solemn nod. "Don't worry, I'll look after them."

Kelly had to smile. The matronly little girl didn't look more than seven years old. "These are all your grandchildren, Curt?"

"So far," Curt said with a wink. "This is Natalie, Matt, and Joseph. Kids, say hi to the folks before you run off to the family room. I've got your toys out already." All three children gave quick hellos and waves before scampering from the room. "And stay out of the kitchen," Curt called after them. "The ladies are busy."

Jayleen appeared beside Mimi in the kitchen doorway. "I don't know about Mimi and Diane, but it's been a long time since anyone's called me a lady," she said with a genial laugh. Mimi gave her a playful swat with the kitchen towel.

Curt grinned. "And this is my nephew Martin," he continued, gesturing to the tall redhead beside him. "He's my sister's boy. Say hi to the nice folks, Marty, while I get the kids settled." Curt shed his rough suede coat on the way out of the room.

"Hi, nice folks," Marty said with a good-natured grin as everyone called out greetings. "I brought something for breakfast. Hope I'm not too late."

"Oh, we've got plenty left, Marty," Mimi said as she beckoned him into the kitchen.

"Great, I've brought lots of orange juice," he said, lifting two large bottles from a grocery bag.

Following them into the kitchen, Kelly grabbed her waiting mug of coffee while Mimi introduced Marty to Jayleen and Diane. "And this is Kelly," Mimi added.

"Glad to meet you," Kelly said with a friendly wave as Jennifer joined them.

"Hey, Marty, I'm Jennifer, and I've come for that juice."

"Sure thing," Marty said, pouring her a glass. "Would you like me to make that a screwdriver? I know Uncle Curt has some vodka around here."

Jennifer gave a crooked smile. "No, thanks, just straight OJ is fine."

"Why don't you dig in to those breakfast leftovers?" Jayleen suggested. "We've got plenty, and you look like you're hungry."

"Hey, I'm always hungry," Marty said with a grin.

"Well, then, grab a plate and fill up," Mimi said. "Just make sure to leave a couple of biscuits for the guys outside."

"Wow, where do I start?" Marty surveyed the breakfast dishes spread out on the counter. "Decisions, decisions."

Kelly watched him enthusiastically fill his plate. "Do you live in town, Marty?"

He gobbled two slices of bacon before answering. "No, I live in Loveland, not far from my office." He added three of Megan's biscuits to his plate. "I'm a lawyer."

Kelly took a sip of Mimi's coffee, grateful that it was

stronger than usual. "What type of law, civil or criminal?" she asked, surprised that someone in Curt's family had a career that kept him indoors most of the time. Curt's daughter was in ranching, and his son flew Navy fighter jets. Everyone else Kelly had heard Curt mention was also in ranching or land development.

"A little bit of both, actually . . . whoa! Are those burritos?" Marty said, pointing toward a baking dish.

"Help yourself," Mimi invited.

"Smothered in green chili, too. My favorite," he said, heaping burritos onto his already full plate.

Mimi beamed. "Enjoy. We've got plenty."

"It's a good thing Megan made three pies," Jennifer whispered beside Kelly. "It looks like Marty can really put it away."

Kelly laughed softly as she sipped her coffee and watched Marty pull out a counter stool and dig in.

"Wow," he said, closing his eyes in obvious enjoyment. "This is delicious."

Jayleen chuckled. "Now that's what I call a good healthy appetite. You've come to the right place, Marty."

"Boy, I haven't eaten like this since Aunt Ruthie was still alive," Marty said, then downed the orange juice Mimi poured for him.

"You know, Marty, back in my old bar-crawling days, those screwdrivers were what we called 'sissy drinks,'" Jayleen said with a devilish smile.

Diane snickered but kept her eyes on the stocking she was filling with candy. Kelly recognized Jayleen's teasing when she heard it, but wondered how Marty would react. It came quickly. His boyish face spread wide with a grin as he hunched over his almost empty plate.

"I'm not sure, but I think my manhood was just maligned," he said. "Let me finish this biscuit, then I'll go outside and wrestle a sheep or something."

"Stay away from my sheep, boy." Curt's voice sounded from the doorway. "You left the gate open the last time, and they went every which way."

"Hey, Uncle Curt, give me a break. I was only ten," Marty said after he devoured his fifth biscuit.

"Twelve, as I recollect." Curt gave Kelly a wink as he poured himself a mug of coffee.

"I'm never gonna live that down, am I?" Marty grinned as he spun the counter stool around.

Unfortunately, when he did, Marty's hand accidentally knocked over the refilled juice glass, and a rivulet of orange juice spilled across the counter.

"Oops, I'm sorry." Marty sprang from the stool, grabbing for a nearby napkin—and in the process knocked over the juice pitcher.

Mimi, who stood gazing at the scene in amazement, quickly sprang into action, mopping up orange juice with a dish towel. Kelly and Jennifer joined in the cleanup, grabbing paper towels and wiping the floor. Marty was already down on his hands and knees, wiping along with them.

"Here we go," Curt muttered to Kelly with an ironic smile as she tossed the soggy towels into the trash. "The boy is a walking accident. Always has been. Whenever he's around, things literally jump off the table."

Kelly poured herself another mug of coffee. "Good thing you brought extra juice, Marty."

"Oh, yeah," Marty said as he grabbed the last two biscuits, then added sausage and bacon as well, placing them on another full plate.

"Hoooweee, boy. That's one healthy appetite you've got there."

Marty simply grinned as he settled onto the counter stool once again. He was clearly getting his second wind.

Just then, Steve's voice came from the doorway. "Hold it right there, guy," he commanded, finger pointing right at Marty, who was hovering over his plate, Megan's biscuit halfway to his mouth. "I don't know who you are, but if that's the last biscuit, you and I are gonna have a serious talk outside."

Kelly had to turn away to hide her smile. Steve was using his "worksite command voice" in hopes of wresting control over the baked goods.

Greg appeared behind Steve and slipped off his jacket. "Yeah, that other biscuit is mine, too. So step away from the biscuits, now."

Marty stared at both men. "You guys are gonna beat me up over biscuits?"

"That's up to you," Steve said, standing his ground, arms folded.

"Sounds like a threat to me, son," Curt advised. "I'd take it serious, if I was you."

A mischievous grin danced across Marty's face. "Gotta catch me, though, and I'm a helluva fast runner."

"But you have to get past us first," Steve warned.

"Good point," Marty conceded and placed the biscuit on the counter. "Boy, you guys take your food seriously."

"Damn right," Steve said, snatching the biscuit before Marty could change his mind.

"They only get that serious when it's Megan's biscuits," Jennifer said, pouring a glass of juice. "Ah declare, what men won't do for hot bread." She tossed her head, à la Scarlett.

"Megan's biscuits, huh? Where can I buy them? I'll order a case," Marty said, leaning out of Steve and Greg's way as they cruised the breakfast entrées.

"You can't buy them, they're—" Kelly started to say before she was interrupted by Greg's shout.

"Dude, who the *hell* are you?" Greg cried as he surveyed the empty breakfast dishes. "You've eaten all the food!"

Mimi giggled. "Greg, you sound like Papa Bear in the nursery tale. 'Who's been eating my porridge?' "

"Greg's right," Steve said, scraping the last of the scrambled eggs from the glass dish. "There's nothing left."

"Steve, Greg . . . this is Curt's nephew Marty." Jennifer introduced them with a devilish smile. "Marty, say hi to the big, tough, hungry guys who've been putting up lights outside in the freezing cold while you've been chowing down in here."

"Oooops," Marty said, shamefaced. "Sorry, tough hungry guys. Listen, just tell me where I can buy those biscuits, and I'll skulk away to the corner."

This time, Curt spoke up. "You can't buy 'em, son. They're homemade. Their friend Megan made them. She made the pies, too. Closest thing to Ruthie's I've ever tasted."

"Whoa, you're kidding," Marty said. "Now you're talking." He sprang from the counter stool, homing in on the pies like a heat-seeking missile.

Jennifer quickly stepped between Marty and the pies. "Hold it right there, Marty. You get one piece of pie," she announced as she slipped a slice of Megan's blueberry pie onto a plate and handed it to him. "If you want seconds, you gotta go through these guys." She winked.

"You guys are cruel, you know that?" he said as he took the plate.

"Give it up, Marty, you had ten biscuits—at least," Jayleen teased from across the room, still filling stockings.

"Naw, it was only eight," he retorted.

"Ten!" Greg cried. "Now I know I'm gonna pound him. After the pie, Marty. You and me, outside."

"Then, it'll be my turn," Steve said, reaching for a slice of pie. "After I finish the pie, that is."

"Like I said, gotta catch me fir—," Marty started, until the forkful of pie entered his mouth. Then, all speech ceased. Marty closed his eyes, clearly savoring Megan's masterpiece.

"I told you it was good, boy," Curt said, sipping his coffee.

"Mmmmmmmm," was all Marty uttered.

"Curt, we're gonna need your shotgun. I'll take the first pie watch," Steve said, watching Marty's reaction.

"Mmmmmmmm."

Curt laughed softly. "I'd better bring the dogs, too. When that boy has his mind set on food, it's hard to stop him."

"Okay, okay, let me have a slice," Kelly said, salivating as she watched her friends.

Once again, Ruth's recipe and Megan's mastery did not disappoint. The delectable mix of blueberry and flaky pastry melted on her tongue. Even without vanilla ice cream, it was delicious.

"Okay, okay, where is this Megan friend of yours?" Marty asked when he'd literally licked his plate clean. "I wanta propose. Right now."

"She was in the family room last time I looked," Curt said with a sly smile.

Kelly shot Jennifer a sharp glance and received a raised-eyebrow response. *Oh, yeah. Let's see what happens,* Kelly's matchmaking instincts said.

Marty headed for the family room, Kelly and Jennifer right behind. Kelly placed her finger to her lips and beckoned for Steve and Greg to follow. Curt was already grinning like an oversized Cheshire cat.

"It's about time you folks showed up," Lisa chided as they entered.

"Finished, at last!" Burt crowed from his spot on the floor, where he held up a large and neatly coiled string of tree lights. "Now we can start the tree."

"Before we start, I've got to find out who Megan is," Marty said. "Megan of the biscuits and Aunt Ruthie's blueberry pie."

Megan stared at Marty in surprise. "That's me. Don't tell me you've started eating the pie already? That's for later."

"I couldn't help myself. After I tasted those biscuits, it was love at first bite," Marty said with a big grin as he strode toward Megan. "I wanta propose—"

Unfortunately, that was as far as Marty got before his feet became caught in the newly untangled string of tree lights. Marty pitched forward, losing his balance, and crashed to the floor.

Kelly didn't know whether to laugh or cry at the sight of Marty, decorated in tree lights, in the middle of the floor, looking amazingly calm while chaos erupted all around.

"Oh, my God!" Megan screamed.

Burt stared, a stunned expression on his face, then sank his head in his hand.

"I say we keep the lights on and electrocute Marty before he causes any more trouble," Greg advised, sinking into a chair. "Let's string him up outside, Steve."

Steve couldn't answer. He was bent over double laughing. Mimi was right beside him, holding her sides. Jennifer was collapsed against the wall with laughter.

"Hooooweeee, boy, you are nothin' but trouble," Jayleen cackled from the kitchen doorway, Diane laughing over her shoulder.

Lisa marched over to Marty like an irate schoolteacher about to chastise a playground misfit. "*Who* are you, again?" she demanded.

"He's my bad-news nephew," Curt replied, shaking his head with a rueful smile. "Whenever he's around, things like this happen."

"Get him out of here!" Megan yelled, pointing at Marty.

"Hey, give me a minute, and they'll be okay," Marty said, slipping green strands over his head.

Kelly and Lisa sank to their knees beside Burt, helping him untangle Marty. "First the kitchen, now the lights," Kelly teased. "You're oh for two, Marty."

"Hey, I can explain—" Marty began before Megan shushed him.

"*You!* Not a word," she commanded, pointing right at him, her face flushed. Kelly had never seen Megan so mad.

"Uhhh, does that mean I can't propose?" Marty looked up at her innocently.

"Propose *what*?" Megan demanded.

"Marriage?" Marty suggested, devilish smile returned, clearly unfazed by hostility. "Or maybe biscuits first, then marriage."

Megan's eyes widened, and her mouth dropped open. All color drained from her face. She didn't say a word. She simply stared at Marty.

Marty observed her reaction and glanced at the others. "Uh, guys . . . is that her happy expression?"

"More like appalled," Steve said with a wicked grin.

"Give it up, Marty," Jennifer teased. "You're gonna have to buy those biscuits in a can from now on."

"Yeah, no biscuits for you!" Kelly cried, pointing at him in mock vengeful fashion. The rest of her friends joined in the playful chant—"No biscuits for you!"—before they collapsed in laughter.

Marty, to his credit, hung his head and played along, peeking playfully at Megan. Then pouting.

"Just get him out of here before I really get mad," Megan directed, gesturing to Marty before she picked up a pile of ornament hangers that had slipped off the dining table in the ruckus.

"What happens if she really gets mad?" Marty asked Kelly as she helped him extricate his foot from a green strand.

"No one knows," Burt replied. "Megan doesn't get mad. She's a sweetheart. But if anyone can do it, you're probably the one." He unwound the last of the strands from around Marty. "Now, let's see what the damage is."

"We'll help you, Burt," Kelly offered as she and Lisa untangled strands.

"I can help, too," Marty suggested.

"Nope," Lisa countered, hands in front of his face. "You've got to go before you mess up anything else."

"Okaaaay," Marty agreed amiably as he stood up. "But there's got to be something I can do."

"You can go sit in the corner and be quiet," Megan instructed, pointing to the far end of the family room.

"At least let me help you pick up the stuff I knocked over," Marty offered, approaching the table. "I mean, you've got all those decorations—"

Megan spun about and raised her crossed fingers in the

familiar horror-movie signal to ward off evil. "Back! Get away!"

Instead of being thwarted by Megan's angry reaction, however, Marty looked positively encouraged. He grinned at her. "Hey, give me another chance. Let me help with some of these." And he reached out for the table, filled with rows of neatly aligned glass ornaments.

"Don't even think about it," Megan said, swatting his hand away.

"But I just want to help," Marty said, continuing his approach. Megan swatted at him again, but this time, Marty dodged the blow. Then—he tripped over a hassock.

Marty pitched forward, grabbing onto the dining room table as he hit the floor again. But this time, he wasn't alone. The neat rows of colorful ornaments began to drop to the floor beside him as, one by one, they rolled and slid off the table.

Megan clapped her hands to her face and screamed.

"Dude, you're a disaster," Greg crowed when the noise died down.

"Wow, I'm sorry, Megan. I can help pick 'em up," Marty offered apologetically as he rose from the floor.

Megan stared at him. Not in horror this time, Kelly noticed. Megan didn't look appalled, either. Thunderclouds stormed across her delicate face. She glared at Marty.

"I take it you're really mad this time, huh?" Marty observed. "Uh, guys? Is this really mad?" He glanced over at the others.

"Ohhhh, yeah."

"Clueless, totally clueless."

"Back away while you can."

Marty didn't get the chance. Megan's hands snaked out,

grabbing Marty's shirt as she yanked him toward her. "*You!* You're a *disaster*!" she hissed into his face. "You've ruined everything! The lights, the ornaments, *everything*!"

"Well, not everything, there're some balls over there," Marty said, pointing.

"Guys! Get him out of my sight before I hit him with something! *Now!*"

Marty glanced to the others. "Is she usually this violent?"

"Megan's a pussycat. You must bring out her bad side," Steve said as he and Greg answered Megan's summons.

"Hell, I didn't even know Megan had a bad side," Greg said as they escorted Marty to the edge of the living room, where Curt watched with a baleful eye. "I told you we should have strung him up outside."

Fourteen

"I'll get the broom and dustpan so we can sweep up the broken glass," Kelly offered, watching everyone help Megan pick up broken ornaments.

"We'll need this," Mimi said as she approached, trash can in hand.

Kelly headed toward the kitchen, but came to a halt as she rounded the corner. She spotted Diane reaching into a cabinet and withdrawing a bottle of vodka. Kelly stepped back from the doorway, out of sight, while she watched Diane glance over her shoulder as she opened the bottle then splashed vodka into a glass of orange juice. The bottle was whisked back into the cabinet in seconds.

Kelly felt a knot form in her stomach. *Damn*. Diane was falling off the wagon. And right in the middle of the police investigation, too. Maybe Diane shouldn't have come today.

Maybe it was too soon. None of that really mattered, though. Kelly knew what she had to do right now.

"Hey, Diane," she said as she burst into the kitchen. "Could you take the broom and dustpan and help Megan and the others clean up the ornaments? I think I got a piece of glass in my hand." Kelly poked at her palm. "Those kids will be coming any minute."

"Sure thing," Diane agreed amiably. She drained the juice glass and grabbed the broom and dustpan from the wall rack, while Kelly labored over the invisible sliver in her palm.

Once Diane left the kitchen, Kelly retrieved the vodka from the cabinet, opened the bottle, and upended it into the sink.

"Thank goodness all those stockings are finished and safe in here," Jayleen said as she strode into the kitchen, nodding toward the table. Red and green stockings were stacked high, candy canes poking from the ends.

"Better keep Marty out of the kitchen," Kelly warned as she shook the last drop of vodka down the sink.

"Whoa, what's that all about?" Jayleen said as she approached.

"I spotted Diane taking a drink when I turned the corner. She didn't see me." Kelly caught Jayleen's disappointed gaze. "So I sent her to clean up while I remove temptation, so to speak." She dropped the empty bottle into the trash can and covered it with paper towels.

Jayleen shook her head. "Lord, Lord, I was hoping that wouldn't happen. But if it had to, it's good that it happened here. I'll explain to Curt what happened to his liquor."

Lisa poked her head around the corner then. "Kelly,

Jayleen, you two can drink coffee later. We've gotta finish the tree. Unless you want to see Megan go ballistic again, you'd better get out here right now. Those kids will be here soon."

Kelly and Jayleen hurried from the kitchen to join the others who were busy adding ornaments to the tree. The tall evergreen's branches were filled with twinkling lights, glass ornaments, strings of glistening beads, and paper chains.

"Wow, you guys work fast. It looks beautiful," Kelly said as she approached the armchair where Steve was seated, drinking coffee. She sat on the chair arm and leaned closer. "Did you see what I saw a few minutes ago? Between Megan and Marty, I mean," she whispered.

"Ohhhh, yeah," Steve observed with a grin. "Megan never saw it coming."

"Nope. He showed up in her blind spot. This is going to be fun to watch."

The doorbell rang then, and the deluge began as children piled into the foyer.

"Whoa, heads up, guys," Lisa advised. "The party is starting already."

"Good thing we're all rested, right?" Jennifer said.

Megan collapsed into a chair at the dining room table. "I'm exhausted," she croaked, her head falling backward. "Are the kids gone yet?"

"The last stragglers are leaving now," Kelly said, glancing toward the entryway, where Curt and Jayleen, Mimi and Burt were busy stuffing tired children into winter coats and handing them over to waiting parents outside.

"I think we'll head home, too. Before that snowstorm

hits," Lisa said. "We're supposed to get another three or four inches tonight."

"Good idea," Greg agreed, draining his coffee mug before he rose from the table. "Maybe I can run a few miles before it hits."

"Ooooh, that run will have to wait until tomorrow morning for me," Kelly groaned from behind her mug.

"Coffee, I need coffee." Megan leaned on the table, forehead nearly touching the surface.

"Waitress to the rescue," Jennifer said, reaching for the coffeepot beside her elbow. "I swear, I don't know how any of us would have gotten through this afternoon if Kelly hadn't made the coffee. Black as tar, I swear."

"I may not sleep for a week. How do you do it, Kelly?" Lisa said as she slipped into the coat Greg held for her.

"The only civilized way to drink it," Kelly replied.

"That's what keeps her going. Caffeine," Steve added, resting his hand on Kelly's shoulder as he sat beside her.

Megan took a deep drink, closing her eyes. "Ahhhh," she said at last. "I may still live."

"Hey, anybody sitting there?" Marty pointed to the chair beside Megan.

"He's baa-aack," teased Jennifer.

Megan looked up at Marty, clearly horrified at the suggestion. "No way! Go sit at the end of the table."

Marty complied, after claiming yet another slice of pie from the buffet server. "Hey, I need a break, too. I just spent two hours playing Shaggy, the dog, with the kids. I'm beat."

"Serves you right. Now sit there and be quiet," Megan ordered.

"Sure thing," Marty agreed aimiably before turning his attention to the pie.

"I'll believe that when I see it," Greg said, ushering a grinning Lisa from the room. "See you later, guys."

Curt and Jayleen joined them at the table, Burt and Mimi close behind. "I sure hope you left some pie for us, Shaggy," Burt teased as he headed for the kitchen. "If not, I'm taking you to the pound. Turn you in as a stray."

"Please do," Megan suggested.

"How many pieces does that make, boy?" Curt prodded.

"Uhhh, I lost count," Marty replied with his infectious grin. "Can't control myself around Megan's cooking, I guess."

Megan scowled at him. "Don't go there." Marty simply grinned in reply, but amazingly, didn't say a word.

"All I know is I'll have to run an extra two miles to work off Megan's biscuits and pie, not to mention all the other great food," Kelly said. "In fact, I may need to run tonight after all."

"Oh, no! I forgot about tonight," Megan groaned, dropping her head in her hands. "I was going to go over to the tennis club and see if I could pick up a partner. But I just can't. I'm exhausted."

"You picking up guys, Megan?" Steve teased. "I've got some friends you'd like. Really nice guys."

Megan wrinkled her nose at Steve. "You know what I mean. I still haven't found a tennis partner, and the match is Tuesday night." She exhaled an exhausted sigh.

"Wish I could help you, Megan." Mimi commiserated as she pulled out a chair beside Jayleen. "I asked everyone at the shop if they knew someone who could play at your level, but I couldn't find anyone."

Diane spoke up from the other end of the table. "Sorry, Megan, that's not my game."

Jayleen reached for the pot of coffee, offering it around

before pouring herself a cup. "I tried playing tennis once. Years ago. Hit the damn ball outta the park, as I recall." She gave Megan a wink. "So I wouldn't be any good to you."

"Thanks, everybody, but it's got to be a guy. Mixed doubles." Megan heaved another sigh.

A comfortable silence descended upon the table for a moment, with only the sound of silverware clinking against china plates as Megan's pie disappeared.

"I play tennis," Marty said before he licked his fork.

Megan cast a scornful glance his way, not even responding.

Marty licked the fork again. "No, really. I'm pretty good, actually."

"Rii-iight," Jennifer teased.

"We've seen you in action, Marty, and it's not pretty," Steve said with a laugh.

"Pretty good at making a mess, you mean," Burt added, chuckling.

"No, really." Marty leaned back in his chair, good-natured smile intact despite the verbal abuse. "I only screw up inside the house. Get me outside with a ball, and I'm poetry in motion." He winked.

The entire table erupted in laughter at that comment, even Megan, Kelly noticed. Meanwhile, Marty kept smiling and drinking his coffee. After the hilarity and varied catcalls had died down, Curt spoke up.

"The boy's telling the truth. He was a star athlete all through high school and college. Got a tennis scholarship, too. Get him outside with a ball, and he's fine. Inside the house, that's another story." Curt grinned at his nephew.

"I rest my case," Marty said, arms behind his head as he tipped the chair back even farther.

Kelly observed Megan's skeptical expression and decided

to up the ante. "Actually, I think he may be right. Marty had little Joseph on his shoulders when he transformed into Shaggy. On all fours, yet. Marty still managed a one-handed catch," she said, giving Marty a nod. Marty grinned but didn't say a word.

"Well, then, your search is over, Megan," Jennifer chimed in, gesturing toward Marty. "Not only have you found a tennis partner, you've found a star player."

Kelly almost laughed out loud at the expression of pure horror on Megan's face at Jennifer's clever and sneaky suggestion.

"You've got to be kidding," Megan rasped.

"No, I'm not. If Marty's that good, then you two may take the championship. We all know what a killer you are." Jennifer leaned back in her chair and sipped her coffee, clearly waiting for Megan's response.

Megan stared at Marty with a mixture of distaste and disbelief for a second, then shook her head. "No, no, no. No way."

"Sounds like you don't have much choice, Megan," Steve said, a resigned tone in his voice. "You can't find anyone else at this late date."

"No, no, never, not on your life, no," Megan chanted, eyes closed.

"He's right, Megan," Jennifer added.

Megan sank her head in her hands, still chanting, "No, no, no, no, no . . ."

Marty, meanwhile, sat smiling, twirling the fork, and tipping his chair back farther and farther. Kelly fervently hoped Marty wouldn't follow earlier behavior and crash to the floor. Megan was on the edge, Kelly could tell. But if Marty tipped over first . . .

Kelly chimed in again. "Megan, it's either Shaggy or throw in the towel. You can always quit," she said, giving Steve a wink. Megan's competitive streak was her Achilles' heel.

Megan looked up and grimaced, then looked over to Marty—and flinched. She collapsed on the table. "No, not him, anybody but him," she chanted, eyes squeezed shut as she pounded the table.

"You won't regret it," Marty promised.

"Please, God. Somebody, anybody . . ."

"Hey, Megan, why don't you let Kelly and me help you out?" Steve suggested. "We can meet tomorrow and hit for a while. Give Marty a test drive. If he's a total klutz, we'll escort him off the court and hand him over to Burt. Burt can take him to the pound. How's that?"

"Sounds like a plan, Megan." Kelly followed Steve's clever lead.

Megan lay there silently for a few seconds, then raised herself, eyes still closed.

"A killer, huh?" Marty toyed with the fork.

"Don't go there. You're at the top of the list," Megan warned.

Marty sipped his coffee, then glanced at the knowing smiles around the table. All except Megan, of course. "Poetry in motion, I promise," he said, then winked while laughter rippled throughout the room.

Fifteen

Kelly slipped through the front door of her cottage and stamped the snow from her running shoes. "You were smart to stay inside, Carl. It's brutal out there."

Carl gave her his humans-are-crazy, brown-eyed doggie stare. Even chasing after squirrels in this weather was curtailed.

Peeling off her jacket and scarf, Kelly headed toward the bedroom and a hot shower. The cell phone's jangle stopped her.

Burt's voice came over the line. "Kelly, I know it's early, but I wanted to let you know. I spoke with my friend with the county police, and he said several of Diane Perkins's bar buddies gave statements to Peterson about her actions that night. So I'm afraid that Diane has definitely moved to number one on Peterson's list. I'd be surprised if he didn't ask her to come down to the department for more questions this week."

Kelly felt even colder. "Oh, brother. I hope she holds up better this time."

"Yeah, I feel kind of bad, too," Burt admitted. "She seemed like a nice girl when I met her this weekend. It's too bad. But, you know, Kelly, she did lie to the police."

"Because she was afraid," Kelly found herself replying.

"Or she was drunk. I know she looks okay now, but remember, she was known to drink so much she had blackouts."

"I know," Kelly agreed reluctantly. "But those barflies aren't Diane's friends. They're gossipmongers, that's all."

"Maybe so, Kelly, but Peterson will sort it out. Listen, I'll see you later at the shop, okay?" Burt said before hanging up.

Kelly tossed the little phone to her bed then stripped and stepped into the shower. Hot water. That's what she needed. Hot water and lots of it. She turned the handles and steaming water poured into her face. Kelly closed her eyes and pictured Lieutenant Peterson. Peterson, the pit bull. He was relentless. Would another interview push Diane off the wagon again?

"**More,** Eduardo, more. Here's a second cup," Kelly instructed, handing an empty cup across the counter.

"Kelly, we're going to have to cut you off," Pete teased, as Eduardo obligingly filled both mug and coffee cup. "You're addicted. Have you thought about joining Coffee Drinkers Anonymous?"

"Stop, Pete, you don't know what she's like without caffeine," Jennifer intervened, slipping into her winter jacket. She beckoned Kelly to walk with her. "Listen, Kelly, I'm off to the office now, but I've got a lead on this Gary guy. You remember, he's the one at the bar I talked about?"

"Yeah, he's the guy who did a deal with Derek, right?"

"Right, and Derek screwed him, too," Jennifer said as she wrapped a peacock blue and mint green knitted wool scarf around her neck. "I've been trying to track him down, but it's like looking for a needle in a haystack. I mean, I wasn't sure if he was a real estate agent or a developer or what."

They wove around and through the customers milling about the knitting shop. Less than two weeks before Christmas. Last chance for help with projects.

"You could ask Steve," Kelly suggested as they reached the entryway, only to step aside for more customers who were escaping from the cold into the shop's inviting warmth.

"I was going to, but there was a message on my cell this morning. Another agent returned my call, and she thinks she knows him. I'm going to talk with her this afternoon." Jennifer pulled a matching wool knit hat over her lustrous auburn hair. She looked at Kelly with concern. "Wish me luck. It may be a straw in the wind, but I don't know anything else to do to help Diane."

Kelly hesitated, not wanting to add to her friend's concern, but she had to. "I had a call from Burt this morning. He said several of those barflies gave Peterson statements about Diane and her behavior and her threats to Derek. He says it doesn't look good. Peterson will want to interview her again."

Jennifer closed her eyes. "Damn, damn, *damn*," she whispered. "They're jackels! All of them at that bar. I swear, I'm never going back there."

Kelly took a deep breath, hoping Jennifer was serious. Maybe something good would come from this tragedy. "I told Burt that, too, not in the same words, of course." She gave Jennifer a smile.

"I've got to go," Jennifer said, checking her watch. "Listen, I'll let you know what I find out from that agent, okay? I'm not ready to throw in the towel."

As she watched her friend exit into the blustery cold, three other customers entered, snowflakes glistening on their winter coats. Kelly stepped out of their way and headed toward the library table, hoping there was a seat left in the holiday crush. Spying two empty chairs, Kelly made a beeline for the one closest to Lizzie, who was instructing a fellow knitter beside her.

"Hello, Lizzie," Kelly greeted, then pointed to the colorful red and green bows adorning Lizzie's silver hair. "You're looking all Christmasy. Very pretty."

Lizzie dimpled, cheeks flushing rosy. "Why, thank you, dear. How sweet of you to notice. Tell me, did you finally send that scarf to the gentleman in Denver? How did he like it?"

Kelly pulled out another skein of alpaca wool from her bag, this one black and white and gray, resembling a tweed. "I sent it on Saturday, so he should be receiving it soon." She started casting the tweed alpaca onto her knitting needles. "I sure hope he doesn't hold mine up next to Jennifer's. She knitted a scarf for his partner, Ronnie. I'm afraid mine won't do well by comparison. I mean, I could still see little mistakes and stuff."

Lizzie gave a dismissing wave of her hand. "Don't worry, dear. We all find those mistakes, especially when we're starting out."

"I'll bet you and Hilda never made mistakes."

The other knitter beside Lizzie giggled as she rose from the table, shoving her yarn into a large purse. "I'll bet they didn't, either. Lizzie and Hilda went straight to master level."

"Oh, bosh." Lizzie blushed, waving at the departing knitter. "You two exaggerate so."

Kelly returned to her casting on, counting until she had the required amount, then she began the knit stitch once again.

"Are you doing another scarf, dear?" Lizzie inquired, looking up over her eyeglasses, her fingers working a peach mohair yarn.

"I decided that I deserved a warm alpaca scarf, too, so this is my Christmas present to myself." Her fingers picked up speed as she settled into the knitting rhythm. The holiday hubbub swirled around them and others chattered away at the table, while Kelly and Lizzie knitted quietly.

Finally, Lizzie broke the meditative spell. "I've made it a point to spend some time every day with Lucy," Lizzie said, leaning closer. "I've been trying to gain her confidence."

"That's wonderful, Lizzie." Kelly gave her a huge grin. "See? I told you she needed mothering."

Lizzie knitted silently for a few minutes more, then spoke up. "I fear she may need more than that, dear. I couldn't help myself, I had to say something. She looked so anxious and sorrowful since that dreadful incident. So I told her I was worried about her and asked if there was something bothering her. I promised she could tell me anything. I was hoping to inspire a healing conversation. Well, the poor thing burst into tears. I took her aside and tried to comfort her. And when I asked if there was anything I could help her with, well, she blurted the whole sorrowful story to me." Lizzie shook her head, clearly saddened by what she heard.

"She told you about the baby?" Kelly asked, relieved that Lucy had opened up at last.

"Yes, she did. And just as we feared, she hasn't been to a

doctor yet. I told her I'd be happy to take her, but she acted like she didn't hear me." Lizzie looked up at Kelly with a worried frown. "Instead of accepting my offer to take her to the doctor, she asked me about my church and the priests. She wanted to know if the priests listened to people and tried to help them. I told her that they did, and she immediately begged me to take her to see the priest. I was so taken aback, that I agreed. I called Father Riley to explain the situation, and he said he'll gladly spend some time with Lucy." Lizzie shook her head again. "Poor little thing. Perhaps he can get through to her."

"When are you taking her?"

"This afternoon. I declare, it was the only way I could calm her down."

Kelly mulled over what Lizzie said, glad that Lucy had responded to Lizzie's nurturing, but wondering why Lucy was so adamant about wanting to see a priest. The stitches added row upon row as Kelly knitted, tweed alpaca piled in her lap.

"She worries me, Kelly," Lizzie said softly. "There's something else bothering Lucy, I fear. Something else that's haunting the poor child."

Kelly let Lizzie's concerns sift through her, letting them resonate with her own worries about Lucy, as she added row upon row of tweed stitches. Lucy's reactions were so extreme. Or were they? A stray wisp of a thought drifted from the back of Kelly's mind. *Why would Lucy want to see a priest? What did she want to confess?*

Was something else simmering inside Lucy? Something other than being pregnant and abandoned and alone? Kelly knitted on those thoughts for several minutes, but no answers came. Not a one.

* * *

Whrrrr! The tennis ball whizzed past Kelly as she raced to the sideline. Too late. Once again, Marty's skillfully placed shot landed right inside the baseline, kicking up a puff of gray dust.

"Man, you've got one wicked backhand, Marty," she yelled as she retrieved the ball. "I thought you said you hadn't played in months."

"Haven't played since September," he called across the net, where he danced along the baseline.

"I'm glad we don't have to actually play you guys," Steve said as he strolled toward the net, beckoning Kelly.

Kelly was only too eager to join him. This might have been a friendly practice session, but she and Steve were getting their butts kicked. Megan's and Marty's shots were a passing blur. She didn't have a prayer getting to most of them in time. Even when she did, it was all Kelly could do to pull off a stroke. Placement was out of the question. Steve hadn't fared much better, she noticed. Talk about being outclassed.

"I think Steve and I have seen enough," Kelly said with a smile as Megan and Marty approached the net. "Megan, you'd be nuts not to take Marty as your partner."

"Hey, thanks, guys," Marty said, grinning as he bounced a tennis ball on his racket. Perfect control, Kelly noticed. How did he do that? she wondered.

Megan gave a dramatic sigh, glancing first at her friends then to her partner. "Yeah, I have to admit, he's good."

"Told you," Marty teased. "Poetry in motion." He danced about, still bouncing the tennis ball.

"I wouldn't go that far," Megan countered. "But I confess, you surprised me. You're good. Real good."

Steve snorted. "Marty's better than good, Megan. I expect you two to take that championship." He reached over and touseled Kelly's hair. "Kelly and I will be washed out tomorrow night."

"Ohhhh, yeah," she agreed. "I've seen our opponents play. We're gonna get our heads handed to us. Hopefully, it'll be merciful and quick."

"Listen, guys, we hate to rush off, but Kelly and I have reservations at the Jazz Bistro for dinner. So we've gotta run." Steve's arm dropped around Kelly's waist, urging her off the court.

Kelly took the hint and waved goodbye to a surprised Megan and a grinning Marty. "See you later, guys."

"You want to hit some more?" Marty asked Megan as Kelly and Steve headed for their warm-up suits at the edge of the court.

"Smart move," Kelly whispered to Steve as she pulled on her warm-up, watching Marty effortlessly jump over the net to the other side of the court.

"Just doing my part to move things along," Steve said with a wicked grin.

"Refresh my memory. Do we actually have reservations for tonight?" Kelly asked as she slipped on her winter jacket.

"We will as soon as I call from the truck," Steve said with a wink.

Sixteen

The stoplight turned green, and Kelly moved ahead in traffic. Everyone seemed to be doing holiday shopping at the same time she was today. Cars clogged the streets, intersections, parking lots. Everywhere that Kelly went, the shoppers were sure to go. She'd resigned herself to completing only half of her holiday gift list today.

Her stomach growled. Food would help. At least it would get her off the crowded streets for a while. Spying her favorite "boutique" coffeehouse up ahead, Kelly assumed she'd never find a parking spot at the busy shop, until—wonder of wonders—a car backed out of a spot right in front of her. She grabbed it. Parking good fortune! Clicking the car lock, Kelly wound her chunky wool scarf tighter around her neck and walked toward the popular coffeehouse.

Her cell phone jangled, and Jennifer's anxious voice came across the line. "Hey, where are you? I thought you'd be at the shop this morning, and you haven't answered your phone."

"I'm out in the holiday crush, shopping," Kelly replied, noticing the cheerful expressions on the faces of the people who filled the streets of Old Town. Holiday mood. "I suddenly realized the Lambspun shop party is this Sunday, and I hadn't bought a thing. So I'm playing hooky from work today."

"And tonight, too, I hope," Jennifer said. "I found out all about that Gary. His name's Gary Livingston, and he's really making my antennae buzz. He's been involved in some shady deals. So I was hoping you could come with me to the bar tonight so we can grill the bartender. Maybe learn something that will help Diane."

Kelly sighed inwardly. She really didn't want to go out tonight, especially to that bar. Listening to the description of the patrons, Kelly doubted she'd fit in. But . . . she'd promised Jennifer.

"Okay, but it'll have to be later this evening, and only for an hour. Steve and I have to show up at the tennis arena and get our butts whipped for charity. So it'll be nine before I can join you."

"Why don't I pick you up at your house?" Jennifer suggested. "One hour max, I promise. We'll go in and flirt with the bartender, Ted, and see what we learn. It can't hurt."

"Oh, yeah, it can," Kelly countered as she paused in front of the coffeehouse door, stepping aside for customers entering and leaving the busy place. "You know I don't flirt well. I'll probably scowl at him instead, and he'll clam up."

"Oh, you know how to flirt, all right. You do it all the time with Steve."

Even though she heard the tease in Jennifer's voice, Kelly couldn't resist taking the bait. "I do not," she protested.

"Yeah, you do. You smile and act coy and shy all the time."

Coy? Kelly cringed at the word. *"Coy!"* she snapped. "I've never been coy in my life!"

"Ahhhh, I think I hit a nerve."

"You did not!" Kelly continued to spew, even though people's heads turned as they walked by. She moved to the edge of the pavement, near the cars. The better to straighten out Jennifer's thinking. "I'm . . . I'm just annoyed that my natural hesitation is being misconstrued. That's all."

"Hesitation?" Jennifer's voice turned incredulous. "What the hell are you hesitating about? Steve's a great guy and he's obviously crazy about you. Why hesitate?"

"I . . . I . . ."

Jennifer didn't wait for the answer. "You're just scared of taking it to the next level, that's all."

"I am not," Kelly said, not as vehemently as before.

"Yes, you are, but we'll have to talk about that later. Right now, I'm pulling into the office parking lot. Call me when you finish the tennis game, all right?"

"Why should I?" Kelly complained petulantly, still smarting from Jennifer's arrows. "Maybe I won't come. You can go flirt alone."

"Yes, you will. You promised, remember?"

"You are so annoying."

"I know. It's one of my finer traits. See you tonight." Jennifer clicked off.

Kelly frowned at the little phone, forming the rest of her well-rehearsed arguments. She'd give Jennifer an earful tonight. She didn't like being teased. Never had. Why did everyone tease her? Kelly wondered. What was it about her?

All annoyance fled, however, the moment Kelly entered the coffeehouse. The aroma of coffee enveloped her, heavy and redolent. Dark. Rich. Seductive. Black gold. She inhaled deeply and headed for the counter.

A woman vacated an inviting stuffed armchair along the wall, and Kelly claimed the prize, tossing down her coat and scarf. First, parking good fortune, now, comfy chair luck. Clearly she was meant to stay in the inviting environment and relax for a while. Holiday shopping and crowds could wait.

Without even perusing the extensive menu board above, Kelly recited her familiar and healthy order. "I'll have the chicken and walnut salad and a large black coffee to—"

She paused. Her gaze fell on the glass display case, where sinfully rich, decadent desserts beckoned. Normally she could withstand their siren calls, but not today. She was tired of crowded streets and stores and . . . and annoying friends who loved to tease. Nope. No healthy salad today. If there was ever a time for decadence and chocolate, this was it.

"Cancel that. I'll have the Black Forest chocolate cherry thing," she ordered, pointing at the dessert. "I need some chocolate."

"Chocolate coming up," the young barista said with a genial smile, obviously used to patrons losing all willpower in her presence. "And coffee, right?"

Kelly nodded, until . . . she spotted the holiday beverage menu overhead, decorated like the rest of the old-fashioned shop, with draped greens and tinsel. "Does that really say chocolate mint hot chocolate?"

"Oh, yeah. We sell a lot of that during the holidays. As well as the gingerbread spiced latte. It's got cinnamon and cloves and allspice and—"

"Stop," Kelly said with a laugh, holding up her hand as she handed over her credit card. "I'm sold. I'll have the hot chocolate now and the spiced latte later."

Awaiting her order, Kelly checked her cell to see if she really had missed calls. Indeed there were two in addition to Jennifer's. Jayleen and Steve had also called earlier, when the noise of shopping obviously drowned out the cell phone's ring—especially buried in her purse.

Waiting for Steve to answer, Kelly scribbled her signature and managed to balance hot chocolate, dessert, and cell phone through the crowded coffeehouse to her comfy chair.

"Hey, there. I called earlier, but missed you."

"That's because I was out shopping for presents. We have the Lambspun holiday party next Sunday, remember? I totally forgot and hadn't bought a thing." Kelly took a bite of the Black Forest wonder. The chocolate melted on her tongue.

"Me, either. Thanks for the heads-up."

"Plus, I needed a break from the crowds, so I'm at the coffeehouse," she said, admiring the huge version of Van Gogh's *Starry Night* adorning the wall in front of her.

"You're eating, I can tell."

"Yep. Some decadent dessert. The shoppers made me do it. Too many of them. And the traffic." She took another bite and hummed loudly into the phone.

Steve laughed. "Sounds like chocolate. You only make that noise when you're eating chocolate."

Kelly stared at the blues and yellows in front of her. Chocolate noises? She didn't know she had chocolate noises. "You're right. Good guess."

"I don't guess. I pay attention."

Well, he did, she had to admit. She took another bite of decadence then a sip of the rich mint hot chocolate. "Oh, did I mention the mint chocolate hot chocolate?" she tempted.

Steve chuckled. "That traffic must really be bad, from the sound of it. Why don't we grab some of that good stuff after dinner tonight? I thought we could try out that new Indian restaurant."

Now Kelly was really sorry she had to join Jennifer tonight. Maybe she'd let annoying Jennifer fend for herself. But, then . . . she'd promised.

"Darn it, that sounds wonderful, but I can't tonight. As soon as we get thrashed at the courts, I have to go barhopping with Jennifer."

"Excuse me?"

"I know, I know. Believe me, I'd much rather be having Indian food with you, but I promised her," Kelly added before she consoled herself with the last Black Forest bite.

"We really do have to restrict your caffeine. You're starting to hallucinate."

"No, really. Jennifer wants to grill the bartender about some guy who threatened Derek Cooper in the bar one night. I know it sounds crazy, but she's trying to do everything she can to help Diane."

"Yeah, it does sound crazy. Why does she need you?"

"To keep her company, I guess. Help her flirt with the bartender, whatever." She took another sip of hot chocolate. The sugar had kicked in and a general lethargy seeped into her veins now. The shop was so cozy and comfortable and filled with tempting goodies, just like the knitting shop. Except there was food, not yarn, tempting her here.

"Since when does Jennifer need help flirting? Never mind, I don't want to go there," Steve said with a sigh. "In fact, I think I'll go holiday shopping after the match. With luck, I can get something for everyone before the stores close."

"Men. I don't understand how you can shop like that."

"It's called efficiency."

"Yeah, yeah, yeah."

"You'd better have some coffee. You're getting drunk on that chocolate. We've gotta play a few hours from now."

"I'll get coffee after this. Uh, after the spiced latte, that is. I'm taking that to go." Kelly drained the cup, licking the rim.

"Sugar high, if I ever heard one. We'd better forfeit tonight."

"Naw, I'll be fine," she promised, wondering again how Steve could tell so much from the sound of her voice. He really did pay attention. A stray thought swam through the sugar to the surface. "Hey, Steve, let me ask you something. Am I coy?"

"How's that again?"

"Jennifer says I'm coy with you. She says I flirt by being coy. I told her she was nuts, but I wanted to check with you."

"Coy, huh?"

"Yeah. I don't think I'd know how to be coy if I tried. But, you know Jennifer."

"Yeah, I know Jennifer. Coy, hmmmm. Let me think."

He was teasing her, Kelly could tell. But she was so mellow with chocolate, she didn't even care. "C'mon, stop teasing. Tell the truth. Am I coy?"

Steve laughed softly. "No. You're Kelly. You're you. You're unique."

Kelly pondered that. She wasn't coy. She was unique. She liked that. See? Steve knew her. Jennifer was off base.

"Unique, huh? Good. I like that," Kelly said, admiring the imitation Van Gogh.

"Listen, forget that latte and order some espresso right now, or you'll still be sitting there looking at *Starry Night* when we're supposed to be playing."

Whoa. Kelly sat up. "How'd you know I was looking at the painting?"

"I told you, I pay attention. Go get some espresso, and I'll see you at the courts later," he said amiably before clicking off.

Kelly stared at the phone. Boy, he really did pay attention. Glancing toward the counter, she was just about to get up and order the espresso when her cell phone rang again. She sank back down in the comfy chair's embrace. Clearly, she was meant to be here for a while.

Eugene Tolliver's voice came on the line. "Kelly, your scarf arrived yesterday, and it's lovely. In fact I'm wearing it now. How thoughtful of you to make that for me. And with your own little hands."

Kelly heard the sound of laughter and responded in kind. "You're welcome, Eugene. Even though my own little hands aren't as adept as Jennifer's. I do hope you didn't compare your scarf to Ronnie's."

"Don't be silly. Your scarf is absolutely beautiful. My scarf, now, thank you very much. And that's the other reason I'm calling. Ronnie and I will be driving up to Fort Connor this weekend, and we'd love to take you and Jennifer to lunch. That way we can thank you in person."

"Eugene, you don't have to drive all the way here in that awful holiday traffic to thank us."

"It is awful, isn't it? I swear, it gets worse every year. It almost makes me yearn for those earlier days when Denver was still dusty and undiscovered. Ah, well, we cannot impede progress, I suppose."

"Well, you can certainly stay out of it. No need to drive in for lunch—"

"Actually, my dear, lunch would only be part of the reason we're coming. Ronnie was absolutely captivated by the yarns Jennifer used in the scarf, and now he's simply consumed with fiber fever, I believe you called it. He's intent upon taking a class with your mentor and shop owner, Mimi."

"Really? That's great," Kelly enthused. "Mimi's a wonderful teacher. Sounds like Ronnie got hooked like I did."

Eugene gave a dramatic sigh. "Hooked doesn't begin to describe it, my dear. He's been fixated ever since Jennifer's scarf arrived. He must have bought at least a dozen books with instructions, but nothing has captured his fancy. Until I suggested we visit the shop. I recalled how Jennifer had raved about the teachers."

"A wise decision, Eugene. Mimi is the best."

"I certainly hope so, because there'll be no living with him if not. You and Jennifer will be available for luncheon then? I do recall mention of a café attached to the shop. It sounds intriguing."

"As a matter of fact, Eugene, we won't need to have lunch at all," Kelly said, remembering. "The Lambspun holiday party is this Sunday. The shop will be open, and there will be plenty of food. Lots of people will be there. All the Lambspun regulars."

"Regulars? Hmmmm," Eugene pondered aloud. "Including that interesting young man you mentioned?"

Kelly smiled, hearing the tease in Eugene's tone. "Jennifer mentioned him, I didn't, and yes, he'll be there. Steve's his name. Along with lots of others."

"How can we resist, then? We'll be there. Ahhh, another call is coming in, Kelly. I simply must take this one. A pushy gallery owner I've been avoiding. Take care," he said, clicking off.

Remembering that she'd missed an earlier call from Jayleen, Kelly checked through her message directory. Indeed, there was one. Unfortunately, Kelly could barely make out what Jayleen was saying because of static and noise. Outside interference, Kelly surmised, as she nodded a thank-you to the barista, who brought a gingerbread spiced latte to go.

Taking that as her cue to leave, Kelly grabbed her coat and scarf and relinquished the comfy chair to someone else. Heading toward the counter, she flipped through her cell directory for Jayleen's phone number, only to watch the cell phone choose that moment to die.

Damn, Kelly thought in aggravation. That always happened when she was super busy. She'd have to call Jayleen later, after she charged her phone. Catching the young blonde barista's attention, she handed over her credit card. "An espresso to go," she said, then took a sip of the spiced latte. Another rush of sugar, spicy and sweet, raced through her. "Uhhh, better make that a double espresso."

"**So** you and Steve left Megan with Marty yesterday?" Jennifer asked as she steered around a corner. "Good thinking. Let's see what happens."

"Yeah, Marty's been real clever so far. Let's hope he doesn't blow it."

"Or trip over the tennis net," Jennifer joked.

Kelly shook her head, watching the headlights of oncoming traffic. "I don't think there's much chance of that as long as he stays out of the house. I swear, he really was poetry in motion on the court. He played the baseline like a pro. It looked like he was dancing out there. And when he rushed the net, look out. You never saw it coming. And his serve? Forget about it. It blew right past you."

"Whoa, that's high praise coming from a jock like you."

"Well, he's that good. Steve's thinking of trying to recruit him for his softball team."

"Oh, yeah, I wanted to tell you something before we get to the bar—"

"I know, I know. Don't snarl. Don't bark. And don't bite," Kelly quipped. "No promises."

"Actually, that wasn't what I was about to say, but it is good advice. Seriously, I wanted to tell you something I heard at the office today. Geri Norbert's canyon property is going back on the market. In fact, it came on this afternoon. The woman who bought it is selling it again. Dumping it, from what her agent whispered to me."

Kelly stared at Jennifer's profile in the darkened car. "You're kidding. Really?"

"Really," Jennifer said with a solemn nod. "I dunno, Kelly. I'm telling you because I'm your agent, and I promised to let you know whenever canyon property comes on the market. But I swear, there's something going on with this place. Two owners have both dumped it back on the market after buying it. All within the last two months, too. Something's up with this property. I can feel it. Maybe it's haunted."

Kelly laughed. "More likely their financing fell through. That doesn't mean there's anything wrong with the property."

"I hear you, but my antennae are buzzing. Let me check into it tomorrow and get back to you, okay?"

The image of Geri Norbert's beautiful canyon ranch shimmered in Kelly's brain. "Jennifer, if that ranch is back on the market, I want to make another offer. A higher one, if necessary. I don't want to miss out again."

Jennifer sighed. "I know you do. But let me ask some questions first, okay? I'll draw up the contract tomorrow afternoon, and I'll bring it over to your place tomorrow night. How's that? By then, I should have learned something."

"Sounds good."

"Okay, real estate business over, bar business begins," Jennifer said as she pulled into a parking lot. The bar anchored the end of a shopping mall, beside a popular restaurant.

"Let's make this quick, Jen," Kelly instructed as she slammed her door. "I want to get back and check my bank accounts again. The mortgage lender will want another statement."

"One hour, no more, I promise," Jennifer said as she held the door open for Kelly.

Kelly was actually surprised when she stepped inside. She'd pictured Diane's favorite drinking establishment as a rowdy, slightly disreputable sort of place. Instead, she found an upscale, vintage décor. Warm golden light from the hanging chandeliers and brass fixtures reflected off the long expanse of polished wood bar. Burgundy leather chairs and bar stools clustered around tables along dark wood-paneled walls. Kelly reminded herself that it was the people, not the establishment, that set the tone.

Alcohol did different things to different people. Some became boisterous and loud. Some used it as an excuse to release all inhibitions. Others turned belligerent and surly. Some simply fell asleep.

"Hey, Jennifer, where you been?" a guy called from the end of the bar. "We missed you."

"My ass," Jennifer muttered to Kelly before sending the guy a bright smile. "Been super busy, Chuck," she said, steering Kelly to the other end of the bar and two empty chairs. She signaled the handsome, blond bartender and said

to Kelly, "Okay, you're my new client, and we've been look-
ing at canyon properties. Bellevue Canyon in particular.
That will give us the opening to talk about Derek's place.
Then we'll take it from there. Just follow my lead."

"Gotcha," Kelly said, watching the bartender approach,
blond ponytail hanging down his back. He looked to be in
his late twenties. White shirtsleeves rolled up.

"What's up, Jennifer?" he asked as he leaned on the polished wooden bar. "We haven't seen you for a while."

"Well, Ted, you can blame it all on Kelly here," Jennifer
said with an engaging smile. "She's been keeping me super
busy looking for mountain properties. Especially canyon
places."

"Lucky you," Ted said to Kelly. "I'd like one of those
myself, but my bank account says not yet."

"Well, I'm not sure my bank account is in better shape,
either," Kelly joked. "But I've got an insane streak."

Ted laughed as he poured a glass of Kelly's favorite
mountain amber ale. "What can I get for you ladies?"

Kelly pointed to the glass in his hand. "I'll have one of
those, thanks."

"You got it, Kelly. How about you, Jennifer? The usual,
extra-strong margarita, double shot?"

Jennifer paused. "No, I'll take the same as Kelly."

Kelly couldn't help but notice Ted's look of surprise at
Jennifer's order. He placed the tall glasses on coasters in
front of them. "Diane hasn't been around for a while. How's
she doing? Is she all right?"

Jennifer sipped her beer. "Yeah, she's okay. She's just
keeping a low profile since Derek's death. Besides, she's not
really comfortable coming here anymore, and you can't really

blame her. I mean, with the police interviewing everyone at the bar, asking questions about her." Jennifer frowned.

"Friend of yours?" Kelly asked, playing along.

"Yeah, and she's in a lot of trouble."

"Sounds like it. I mean, if the police are involved," Kelly continued. "What happened?"

"Her boyfriend was murdered up at his ranch in the canyon. You know, the canyon you like so much. Bellevue."

Kelly deliberately affected a surprised look. "Whoa! That's scary."

"Got that right," Ted agreed, wiping a glass with his white towel.

"Now, that property has everything you want, Kelly." Jennifer cleverly changed direction. "Stables, corrals, plenty of pasture. He even had alpaca, like you. And the house looks gorgeous."

"You been up there with Derek?" Ted teased.

Jennifer shot him an exquisite look of scorn. "In his dreams. Hell, no. I wouldn't cross the street with that bastard."

"Whoa! Strong words. The guy's dead."

"Yeah, and he was a scumbag when he was alive." She shook her head. "No, Diane told me all about his place."

Ted kept wiping. "Damn shame about Diane. Everybody here gave statements. I swear, the police must have taken ten statements. They came back twice." He wagged his head. "I like Diane, I really do, Jennifer, but I don't know . . . it doesn't look good."

Jennifer took another leisurely sip. "Diane couldn't kill Derek. I know she couldn't." She paused. "Did the police take a statement from that guy, Gary? You know, the one that nearly attacked Derek here in the bar one night? He lost a lot of money in some business deal with Derek. Got burned pretty bad, to hear him tell it."

Ted glanced up. "No, he wasn't here when the police came. Matter of fact, I haven't seen Gary around much for a while."

"Neither have I," a woman's voice announced.

A pretty, slightly plump brunette slipped into the chair beside Kelly, sipping a strawberry-colored concoction Kelly took to be a margarita. Her flushed cheeks indicated it might not be her first of the evening.

"Hey, Nina, how are you?" Jennifer smiled. "You been looking for that Gary guy or something?"

Nina gave a disgusted snort. "Not anymore, I'm not. He runs hot and cold. I've had it with him. He calls up, almost panting on the phone, I swear to God. We hook up, then I don't hear a word for weeks."

"That's just normal for a guy," Jennifer said. "You know guys don't call back when we want them to."

Nina screwed up her pretty features. "I don't understand guys. I mean, if you like someone, you're gonna want to be with them, right? I mean, like, why don't they call?"

"They do call. When they think of it," Jennifer continued sagely. "You've gotta understand guys. The next day, when you're thinking about him, he's thinking about food. Or what game's on television that night. Whatever. It has nothing to do with you. In fact, he may actually be crazy about you."

"You think?" Nina stared at Jennifer incredulously.

"Who knows?" Jennifer shrugged. "Give it a little more time."

"The doctor is *in*," Ted said with a chuckle as he moved toward another customer. "Damn, Jennifer, I've missed you. Come back more often."

"Doctor of Love, huh?" Kelly teased, sipping her ale.

"Okay, doc, if you say so," Nina said.

"How long's it been, anyway? Since you two were to-gether?" Jennifer asked.

Nina closed her eyes as if counting. "Uh, it's been about two weeks or so." She nodded. "For a while I thought he'd stayed away because the cops were all over here, asking questions. You know, about Derek Cooper and all. And, you know, he hated Derek's guts. I thought maybe he didn't want to take the chance of the cops asking him questions."

Kelly sat up straighter at that. She glanced at Jennifer, but Jennifer had already zeroed in on Nina's comment.

"You mean because he had a fight with Derek here in the bar?" Jennifer asked.

Nina nodded. "Yeah, I guess. I don't know why that would bother Gary, though. After all, he and I were together the night that Derek was killed. He called me from the bar and asked if he could come over. So it's not like he had any-thing to hide."

Jennifer's shock was evident. She sat back and stared at Nina with wide eyes. It wasn't hard for Kelly to read the disappointment in her friend's expression.

"You were with Gary the rest of the night?" Jennifer asked, voice subdued.

Again, Nina nodded. "Yep, the rest of the night and into the morning." She gave a devilish grin. "Believe me, I kept him busy."

Kelly drained her glass, then toyed with the coaster while Nina chattered away and Jennifer made halfhearted comments. Might as well throw in the towel, she thought, purposely glancing at her watch. "I'd better go, Jen. Early day at work," she said, hoping to make a speedy exit.

"Me, too." Jennifer followed her lead, placing some bills on the bar top. "I'll get this, Kelly."

"Hey, thanks," Kelly said as she eagerly relinquished the bar stool. Jennifer was already donning her coat.

"See you, Nina," Jennifer said over her shoulder as she and Kelly waved their goodbyes and headed out. Nina gave a distracted wave, scanning a new male arrival already.

Kelly slipped on her winter jacket. "I'm sorry, Jen," she said as they pushed through the exit door.

"Damn," was all Jennifer said before they stepped out into the cold night.

Seventeen

"Tell Eduardo I want his Breakfast Supreme. Scrambled eggs, bacon, pancakes, the works," Kelly said to Jennifer as she sat at a window table. "I ran double distance this morning. Not only am I starving, I'm exhausted. I need fuel."

"I don't know how you run outside in this weather," Jennifer said as she poured coffee into Kelly's waiting mug. "It's all I can do to race from my condo to the car each morning. Brrrr!" She gave an exaggerated shudder.

Kelly took a sip, then another. Ahhhh. Warmth began flooding through her. "Actually, it's invigorating," she said with a mischievous grin. "And it feels so good when you come inside and jump into a hot shower."

Jennifer made a face before she returned to the kitchen. Kelly relaxed at the cozy corner table and drank her coffee as she stared outside at the brilliant Colorado sun doing its best to raise the frigid temperature. The bare tree limbs allowed an unobstructed view of the frosted foothills, snow-covered Rockies rising behind.

Maybe she could find time to drive out to the canyon today, she mused. Roads were cleared. If she went in the early afternoon, the sun would still be out. The image of Geri Norbert's canyon ranch beckoned. Kelly closed her eyes. She could picture those gorgeous mountain views now. Snow-capped high peaks glistening in the distance, evergreens coated with snow. Would the roads still be icy? she wondered. Perhaps she should take a drive up there. See how tricky those roads could be. She needed to know if the canyon roads were as treacherous as she'd heard tell.

"Jennifer, bring that whole pot of coffee over here and leave it, would you, please?" Jayleen's tired voice chased away Kelly's mountain dreaming.

"Been working late?" Kelly asked when Jayleen sank into the chair across from her. She noticed Jayleen lacked her usual spark today. She was moving in uncharacteristically slow motion.

"Lordy, I wish I had been working." Jayleen rubbed her hand across her face. Dark shadows rimmed her eyes.

"I'm sorry I forgot to return your call, Jayleen," Kelly apologized, suddenly remembering. "My phone ran out right as I was dialing yesterday, and I was going nonstop all night."

"That's okay, I figured I'd better come in and talk to you folks anyway," Jayleen said.

"Boy, you look as tired as I feel, Jayleen. What's up?" Jennifer asked as she poured a dark stream of coffee into Jayleen's cup then set the pot on the table.

Jayleen raised the cup and drank deep, several times. "Okay, that's better. Now, I think I've got the strength to tell you gals what's happened."

Jennifer shot Kelly a concerned glance and sank into a chair beside them. "What is it, Jayleen? Is it Diane?"

"Yeah, I spent all last night at the hospital."

Kelly leaned forward over the table. "Did Diane fall off the wagon again? I told Jen what happened Sunday at Curt's. Did she slip out and head to town or something?"

Jayleen shook her head. "Naw. If she had, then I could have handled it. But this time, I needed help."

"God, Jayleen, what happened?" Jennifer pressed.

Jayleen took another big gulp of coffee. "Lieutenant Peterson called yesterday. He told Diane they wanted her to come to the police department and answer some more questions. He also told her she could bring an attorney with her if she wanted."

Jennifer closed her eyes. "I knew it, I knew it. Did Diane freak out? Start yelling and screaming like she did when I was with her?"

"Nope, not at all," Jayleen said, draining the last of her coffee. "In fact, she got real quiet and scared-looking. I told her I'd go with her to the police station. But maybe it would be a good idea to talk to a lawyer. Just in case."

"What'd she say to that?" Kelly asked.

Jayleen shook her head. "Nothing. She just sat and stared out the window, looking scared. I figured she needed some time alone, so I went back out to the stables and barns, thinking maybe she'd join me. After an hour passed and she didn't come out, I went back inside the ranch house, and that's when I found her. She was lying in the bathroom with pills scattered all around the floor—"

"Oh, God, no," Jennifer whispered.

"I tell you, it scared the hell out of me. I thought she was dead," Jayleen continued. "But she was just groggy. Couldn't stand up or anything. That's when I knew she needed more help than I could give her. So I loaded her into the truck and tore out of the canyon like a bat outta hell. The hospital emergency room was able to pump her stomach or whatever they do with overdoses nowadays."

"Were they sleeping pills or something?"

Jayleen shrugged. "I don't know, Kelly. I'd never seen them. They're sure not mine. I don't need anything to put me to sleep at night." She gave a good-natured smile. "Maybe they were hers. Who knows."

Jennifer shook her head. "Stupid, stupid, stupid. Now the police will be certain that Diane killed Derek. I mean, she's just attempted suicide and is in the hospital treatment center. It almost screams 'I'm guilty.' It can't look any worse than that."

"I know," Jayleen said with a sad nod. "But she clearly needs a lot of help. The counselors and psychologists will be talking with her today. Diane will stay there for a couple of days, they told me."

"Have you had a chance to talk with her?" Kelly asked.

Jayleen nodded. "Yeah, I told her don't worry about anything except getting healthy. Straightening out. They've got a good group of people at the treatment center there. I've heard from others that it's excellent. Diane will get the help she needs. I told her again that I couldn't have straightened out without help from folks like that. And AA, of course." She shook her head as she poured more coffee for herself. "Lord, I hope she pays attention to them."

"Maybe this was good that it happened, Jayleen," Kelly volunteered. "I mean, some people have to hit bottom to make a change, right?"

Jayleen nodded. "Oh, yeah."

Eduardo appeared then and set Kelly's huge breakfast platter in the midst of the somber table. "Enjoy," he said with a smile.

"Hey, Eduardo, that looks pretty good," Jayleen spoke up. "Could you rustle up one of those breakfasts for me, too?"

"Sure thing," he said, heading back to the kitchen. "Oh, Jennifer, your table around the corner is looking for you."

Jennifer jerked up, as if awakening. "Oh, my gosh, all this made me forget my customers. Talk to you later, guys."

"Later, Jen," Kelly said, watching her friend hurry away. Kelly stared at her breakfast. Suddenly, she'd lost her appetite.

"**Hi,** Kelly, how are you?" Mimi asked as Kelly meandered through the yarn room, touching and feeling as she went along. "Are you looking for another project?"

"No, I'm still working on my own alpaca scarf." Kelly trailed her fingers across the soft skeins as she slowly made her way to the library table. After hearing Jayleen's disturbing news, Kelly felt like she was moving in slow motion, too.

"What's the matter?" Mimi asked as she draped two knitted sweaters over the antique cupboard. "You look worried."

Kelly set her bag and mug on the table and sat down. "Well, I guess I am, Mimi. The police asked Diane Perkins to come in for questioning again, and this time, she may need a lawyer."

"Oh, no," Mimi exclaimed. "I'm so sorry. I was hoping things would clear up for her. She's such a nice person."

"I know." Kelly sighed, pulling out the alpaca yarn. "I wish there was something we could do, but Jennifer and I keep running into brick walls. Last night, we went to that favorite bar of hers and Diane's, asking questions. Jennifer was convinced some guy over there might be the culprit because he attacked Derek one night. Derek cheated him in some business deal. Jennifer was there when it happened and said the guy looked like he could kill Derek, he was so mad."

"Really?" Mimi asked, clearly concerned. "Did you learn anything?"

Kelly gave a rueful shake of her head. "Yeah, we did. We learned the guy, Gary, spent the whole night with some girl from the bar, so he definitely couldn't be guilty. Jennifer was so disappointed. She's trying hard to find something that'll prove Diane's innocent."

"That's hard to do, Kelly. Proving someone's innocence. It's often perception," Mimi said in a thoughtful voice. "At least, that's what Burt tells me."

Kelly smiled. "Burt giving you detective lessons, Mimi?" She wondered what other lessons Burt and Mimi might be engaged in.

Mimi's cheeks tinged pink. "Of course not." She gave a disparaging wave. "He simply tells me about some of the cases he's worked. It sounds awfully complicated to me. And to think, people's lives hang in the balance, depending on what evidence the police detectives find."

Rosa popped around the corner and beckoned to Mimi. "I finally reached that vendor, Mimi. Do you want to talk with her now or later?"

"Right now. I've been trying to reach her for days," Mimi said, dashing from the room. "Talk to you later, Kelly."

Kelly welcomed the quiet that settled over the room now, December morning sun shining through the windows. Kelly couldn't shake the melancholy feeling that had clung to her ever since Jayleen brought her the sad news. They had tried so hard to find something, anything that could help Diane, and failed. And if that wasn't bad enough, Diane chose this time to "freak out," as Jennifer put it, and attempt suicide. It didn't look good. Not good at all.

"Ah, Kelly, I'm so glad to find you here alone," Lizzie's voice announced as she bustled into the room. "I looked for you all day yesterday, I was so anxious to speak with you." She slipped off her cherry red winter coat with the fur collar, then plopped her oversized knitting bag on the table and sat in the chair beside Kelly.

"I'm sorry, Lizzie, I was out yesterday doing holiday shopping. What did you want to tell me?"

Lizzie leaned closer. "I wanted to talk to you about Lucy. I took her to see Father Riley on Monday, remember?"

In the hectic last couple of days, Kelly had forgotten. "Oh, yes, yes, how did that go?"

Lizzie's eyes widened like saucers. "Kelly, I'm concerned about Lucy, I truly am. I took her in and introduced her to Father Riley. He's such a dear, kind man. He invited Lucy to sit with him and talk in his office. He even brought her a cup of tea. I waited in the outer offices, of course."

Kelly watched Lizzie pause before continuing. "Did Lucy seem comfortable talking with him? Did she look scared? I mean, she runs like a rabbit whenever any of us tries to talk with her."

"Actually, Kelly, she seemed anxious to talk to Father Riley. She was asking me all sorts of questions about him and the church all the way over in the car. And she was quiet as a mouse when we entered the rectory. She simply stared about with those huge blue eyes of hers. Then, she went docile as a lamb following after Father Riley into his office."

"Lizzie, that sounds good. I mean, we were all hoping

Lucy would find someone to talk to, and it looks like this Father Riley is the one. So what's got you so concerned?"

"Well, dear, it's what happened next that bothered me. After Lucy finished talking with Father, she came out of his office, face all streaked with tears, red from weeping. And Father, well, he was standing in the doorway of his office with such a worried expression, it took me by surprise. I caught his gaze for a second, and he shook his head, the way he does when he's deeply concerned about something. That captured my attention, Kelly."

She fixed Kelly with a solemn gaze. "Lucy was more upset after talking with Father Riley than before. That and Father's reaction made me very curious. It made me wonder what on earth the poor child told Father that had him looking so concerned and sent Lucy into tears. She did not say one word on the way home. She simply sat, crying softly into tissues, despite my efforts to console her."

Kelly didn't respond, letting all of Lizzie's concerns and observations sift through her mind. Lucy was determined to see Lizzie's priest and insisted on an appointment. If she was so anxious to speak with him, why then was she so distraught afterward?

"I admit, Lizzie, that does sound strange. Not that I'm an expert on confessional behavior," Kelly admitted with a wry smile. "Do you think Father Riley came on too strong and rebuked or scolded Lucy? I mean, he wouldn't have reprimanded her for having a child out of wedlock, would he?"

Lizzie stared at Kelly with a shocked expression. "Good heavens, no! Father would never do that. Why, he's a veritable pussycat of a man. Kind and gentle. It's more likely he would offer to take her to the weekly meetings of the young mothers' group."

"Forgive me, Lizzie, but I was simply trying to find a reason for Lucy's reaction. Do you think he made her feel guilty because she hasn't been to see the doctor? Maybe that's what upset her so."

"No, Kelly, he wouldn't have done that either. And I had already offered to take her to the doctor this week." Lizzie frowned as she pulled the pale peach yarn from her bag and began to knit. "No, no, it's nothing simple like that. I sense there's something else bothering Lucy. And it's something very painful, judging from the expression on her face. I've seen the ravages of guilt before. It is unmistakable, and that's what bothers me, Kelly. The guilt and shame I saw on Lucy's face as she ran weeping from Father Riley's office."

Kelly pondered everything Lizzie had just said while they both knitted in silence. She didn't doubt Lizzie's veracity for a moment. Lizzie had a keen eye.

What on earth would Lucy be feeling guilty about? Perhaps she came from a very strict family where bearing a child out of wedlock was considered a shameful and terrible stain upon a family's reputation. Ellen had mentioned that Lucy's mother had died and her father remarried, and Lucy had been estranged from them for several years. So it didn't make sense that she would be scared of an absent family's judgment of her, did it? What, then? Certainly not her friends' opinions. Everyone at the shop loved Lucy and had been nothing but supportive of her since Derek's death. Kelly had no doubt they would be even more kind and solicitous when they learned that Lucy was pregnant. What, then?

Kelly pondered and came up with nothing. She continued knitting, the tweed alpaca scarf lengthening slowly as she sorted through possibilities. Shame. Was Lucy ashamed to tell her friends about the baby? That didn't seem likely either. What then? Stitches continued, row upon row, meditative. Lizzie had ceased speaking as well, quietly working her frothy yarn, worried frown still in place.

Why did people feel guilty? Because they'd done something to make them feel ashamed? What could sweet inoffensive Lucy ever do that would make her feel guilty? What could she possibly do?

A fragmented memory floated by, elusive. Something Lucy's friend Ellen had said when they were in the knitting shop talking about Derek's death. What was it? Something about Lucy. Lucy was expecting Derek's child . . . and she hadn't told him yet.

Suddenly the elusive fragment surfaced in Kelly's mind. She remembered now. Ellen said Lucy had planned to tell Derek that night, the very night he was killed. She tried to call him but couldn't get through. She couldn't tell him . . . or so she said. What if Lucy was lying? What if she really did go see Derek that night? What if it was Lucy in the car Diane saw driving up to Derek's?

Another wisp floated by. Burt's mention of a lot of messages from women on Derek's cell phone. One of the messages was garbled, but police made out the words "need to see you." What if that was Lucy calling? What if she drove up to see Derek that night and told him about the baby? What if he rejected her? Spurned her and the baby. Derek Cooper certainly didn't sound like a man who was ready to settle down and be a father.

Kelly let all the disparate thoughts swirl around her mind, jumbling into one another. Did Lucy kill Derek? Was that possible? Was she crazy to even imagine it? Kelly wondered. How could sweet, shy, quiet Lucy kill Derek Cooper?

How was that possible? It didn't make sense, did it? *No,* a little voice whispered from the back of her mind.

Then another part of Kelly's brain spoke up, louder this time, joining the argument raging inside her head. *Not necessarily. Remember how Derek Cooper was killed.*

The killer waited until his back was turned then swung a shovel, slamming it into the side of Derek's head. A shovel wasn't too heavy, even for someone like Lucy. She could have swung the shovel, especially if Derek Cooper had just spurned her and her baby. For someone as troubled as Lucy Adair appeared to be, that final rejection might have literally been the straw that broke the camel's back. And Derek Cooper's head.

Kelly finished one row, then turned the scarf and began the next row. Stitches neatly forming one after another, row by row, building on one another, like her thoughts. Thought by thought, idea by idea, slowly building scenes in her mind. Kelly sat knitting, quietly turning over motive and opportunity in her mind, picturing sweet, shy Lucy killing her faithless lover, Derek.

Would Derek's rejection of Lucy and her child cause her to strike out in rage? The heat of such rage and passion often brought with it a superhuman strength. Perhaps that was what happened, and now Lucy could not live with the guilt of what she'd done. Perhaps that was the root of the intense emotion Father Riley and Lizzie both witnessed. If Lucy did kill Derek Cooper, then that would explain the guilt.

Another tweed row, then another, and all the while Kelly kept sorting through her thoughts, becoming more and more certain she'd found the answer. Why else would Lucy be consumed with guilt? Had Lucy confessed to Father Riley? Was that why the priest looked so worried? Father Riley was bound by his priestly vows not to reveal what was heard in the confessional.

How could anyone learn the truth then? Kelly wondered. Maybe she could speak with Lucy. No, that wouldn't work. Lucy would run like a rabbit. Should she try to talk to her with Lizzie? No, Lizzie had done her part. Besides, if Lucy started crying again, Lizzie's motherly instincts would take over her skeptical side.

Another row, then another. Then Lisa's face appeared in her mind. That's it, Kelly decided. She and Lisa could talk with Lucy. It had to be someone Lucy felt safe with, or Lucy would be terrified and run away again. Lucy knew and trusted Lisa. Now all Kelly had to do was convince Lisa. Would she agree with Kelly's plan? After all, Lisa's last attempt to counsel Lucy had resulted in Lucy's tearful escape from the knitting shop.

Kelly finished knitting the row she was on, then shoved the alpaca wool and needles back into her bag. Lisa needed to be convinced that Lucy was hiding something. Something that was causing all the pain and stress they'd witnessed. Kelly wouldn't be able to convince Lisa. Her reputation for sleuthing would damn her. Lisa would know Kelly was on a fishing expedition. But Lizzie could convince her.

She grabbed her coat and knitting bag as she rose from the table. "Lizzie, I have some errands to run, but I was wondering if you'd be willing to speak with Lisa on the phone. I think if anyone can get through to Lucy, it will be Lisa. That's why I'd like you to tell her everything you told me about Lucy, if you would, please."

"Certainly, dear, if you think it will help," Lizzie replied.

"It's the only thing I can think of, Lizzie. Someone needs

to convince Lucy she needs professional help," Kelly said as she headed for the door, zipping her winter coat.

Kelly pulled into the gravel driveway, steering around an iced-over puddle. Halfway down the driveway, she stopped and turned off the ignition. A gust of wind rocked her car. Spitting snow flew sideways in sheets. Despite that, Kelly wrapped her chunky wool scarf around her neck, pulled her knit hat down over her ears, and jumped out of the car. The lure of Geri Norbert's canyon property was stronger than freezing cold, bitter winds that roared, and icy snow that stung her cheeks. Even the slippery canyon road hadn't stopped her.

None of it mattered. The sight of evergreens coated with snow, branches laden down, touching the ground, pastures and fence posts draped in white made the entire drive worthwhile. Snow stretched to the horizon. Thirty minutes before, Kelly had glimpsed her favorite view of the Rockies in the distance, glacier peaks, coated with winter. Then the clouds changed, merged with one another, and filled the sky overhead until it was solid white. Snow sky. Unmistakable.

A wind gust blew Kelly back several inches as she stood beside the fence. This high up, the wind howled. Not seeing the alpacas, she figured they had sought shelter in the barn, since the doors were open. Another gust blew her scarf around her face, whipping the scarf ends. She nestled into her jacket as she took in the wintry scene. Even though Kelly loved summer and the lush green of the canyon, winter was beautiful, too. Somehow the run-down ranch house and barns looked picturesque in the snow. Yes, the roads were scary to drive in these conditions, but she'd get used to them. Kelly was sure of it.

That familiar feeling returned to Kelly full force. The feeling that came over her whenever she saw this gorgeous canyon property. Desire. She wanted this ranch. It didn't matter if two other buyers dumped it. It didn't matter that Jennifer was convinced something was wrong with it. Heck, it didn't matter if there really were ghosts. Kelly didn't care. She wanted it. And she wasn't about to let it slip through her fingers again. She'd tell Jennifer to up the offer, if necessary.

A blast of wind blew icy snow-sleet into her face, stinging Kelly's eyes. Another blast pushed her into the fence, scarf ends flapping like ships' pennants. Kelly wiped her eyes, took one last panoramic look, and raced to her car. Jumping in, she revved the engine and turned the heater to high. Better not linger up here too long. After all, the trip out of the canyon was all downhill and icy.

"**Hey,** Kelly, you staying warm?" Jayleen asked.

Kelly nestled her cell phone between her neck and shoulders while she rinsed her dinner dishes. "Trying to. Particularly since I drove up to Geri Norbert's ranch today. Brother, that road is nasty when it's snowing."

"Whoa, girl, you picked a bad day to drive up here. What were you doing?"

"Taking another look. Jennifer told me yesterday that the ranch is back on the market again. The second buyer dumped it like the first one did. Jennifer thinks it's haunted." Kelly wiped her hands on a dish towel and retrieved the phone, which was about to slip off her shoulder.

"You're kidding," Jayleen said, clearly surprised. "What

is going on with that place? It's a great property. Maybe those folks weren't meant to live in the mountains. I'll bet that last buyer from back east got a taste of winter here and decided no thanks."

"Who knows, Jayleen." Kelly poured a dark stream of coffee into her mug, then wandered over to the patio door. She peered into the darkened backyard, spotting Carl galumphing through the snow. "I don't care why she dumped it, I'm just glad she did. Maybe I'll have a chance to grab it this time. Jennifer's coming over in a few minutes with a new purchase offer. Wish me luck."

"You know I do, Kelly," Jayleen said. "Three's the charm, you know. This'll be the third time you offered on it."

Kelly laughed. "I'll remember that. By the way, did you visit Diane this afternoon? How's she doing?"

"I sure did. She's doing okay, I guess. Kind of subdued. Both the alcohol counselor and the psychologist spoke with her this morning, so she's got plenty to think about. She's a smart girl. She'll figure it out. I hope." Jayleen let out a long sigh. "Oh, and I remembered to ask her that question you told me."

"Good, good." Kelly set down her mug. "Does she still remember seeing a car when she left Derek's that night? I was wondering if she'd imagined it, maybe."

"Nope, she says she remembers it clear as day. There was a small car driving up to Derek's as she was driving away."

The anxious voice inside her head exulted. "Okay, that means there was someone else coming to see Derek that night after Diane left," Kelly said.

"Providing Diane's telling the truth."

Kelly paused. Jayleen's tone had turned somber. "Do you think she's lying to us?"

"I dunno, Kelly," Jayleen said with a sigh. "She lied to me the other day. When we were driving back to the ranch Sunday night, I asked her flat out if she'd taken a drink while we were at the party. Told her someone had seen her with the vodka. She denied it right to my face."

Kelly winced. "Damn, Jayleen, do you think she's been lying to us all along?" All those earlier doubts about Diane crept out of the corners of Kelly's mind. They hadn't gone far.

"Hard to say, Kelly. I know I did my share of lying in my drinking days. Usually to cover my butt. So I don't know what to say. Maybe Diane only lies about her drinking. Then again, maybe it goes deeper than that. I'm hoping to hell this time at the hospital will clear up her thinking and set her straight."

Kelly pondered what Jayleen said. If Diane lied about her drinking, what else has she lied about? Kelly wanted to believe Diane, but . . .

"Listen, Kelly, I've gotta get back to work. I'm finally unpacking those boxes in the barn. Promise me you won't be driving into this canyon again until the roads are cleared. You don't have a truck or a four-by-four, so that makes it trickier."

"I promise. Today was icy enough for me. I'll talk with you tomorrow. I think I hear Jennifer at my door now."

Kelly was halfway to her front door when Jennifer pushed it open, escaping inside. "Whoooo! It's frigid out there," she said, stamping her feet.

"Come on in." Kelly beckoned. "I've got coffee and hot chocolate ready."

Jennifer shed her coat and gloves and shivered, rubbing her sweater-clad arms. "Hot chocolate. Why don't we sit at the kitchen table?" She retrieved a legal-sized black vinyl folder and followed Kelly into the cozy cottage kitchen.

Kelly poured hot chocolate into a large ceramic mug as Jennifer settled at the table. "Okay, tell me everything you found out. But you know, it won't change my mind. I drove up there this afternoon in the snow and ice, and I still want that ranch." She gave her friend a wink before taking a deep drink of coffee.

"You drove up into that canyon in this weather?" Jennifer exclaimed, clearly shocked. "Now I know you're crazy."

"No, I wanted to see if I still felt the same way about the place in the winter as I did in the summer and fall. And I do. It's beautiful. Snow-covered evergreens, Rockies glistening in the distance, even the barn looked pretty."

"Okay, okay, I know how much you love the place. But I have to tell you what I found out today. My conscience demands it." She took a big sip of chocolate, then another. "The first two buyers dumped the property because they got spooked. Strange things started happening. I never could get a straight answer from the agent for the second buyer, but the first buyer's agent finally answered my questions. His client, the developer, was going to build some mega mountain home up in the canyon. Then, two weeks after he brings a builder out there, one of his condo developments at the east of town was torched, remember?"

"I remember." Kelly raised a skeptical brow. "But maybe it was faulty wiring. Steve's told me things like that happen."

"Yeah, well, apparently he thought so at first, until the investigators discovered a gas can at the scene. A strange, old-fashioned gas can, not like one you'd normally find. Investigators also found evidence that the fire had been deliberately set with, you guessed it, gasoline."

"That's too bad, but arson happens. You know that."

"Yeah, I do. And the agent said that's what the developer chalked it up to until two weeks later when a gas can exactly like the first one appeared in the canyon property's driveway. Close enough to the road so you could see it, the agent said. And there was another can exactly like it on the front porch of the ranch house." Jennifer gazed solemnly at Kelly.

"Hmmmm," Kelly pondered out loud.

"Yeah, that's what I said. It also made the hair on my neck stand on end, Kelly. That was a direct message to that developer. The other agent thought so, too."

"That's why he sold it?"

"Yep." Jennifer nodded. "The agent told me his client decided he wasn't about to play games with some sicko, so he put the property right back on the market. And he got even more for it, too. That woman from out of state made an above-price offer and he snapped it up, the agent said."

Kelly considered everything Jennifer told her, turning it over in her mind. "You know, Jen, it sounds like that developer has made some enemies over the years. And one of them decided to target him, that's all. At least that's what it sounds like to me."

Jennifer sighed. "You could be right, Kelly. But my instinct tells me there's something else happening here. I don't know what, but I can feel it. I wish I could have talked with the agent for the second buyer. But I could never reach her, so I had to pump the assistant, and all she'd ever say was the client got 'spooked.' That's all, no details."

Kelly smiled at her well-meaning friend. "Well, Jen, you know I don't spook easily."

"Don't I know it," Jennifer said with a resigned sigh.

"So unless you've got photos of Marie Antoinette's ghost walking through the kitchen with her head under her arm, I want to proceed. Did you bring the new offer?"

"Right here." Jennifer unzipped the portfolio. "By now, you're familiar with the verbiage, so we'll go straight to the signature lines."

"What about price? How much above market should I offer?"

"Actually, considering the circumstances, I think you'll get it at market. Word's out now about this place, plus the holidays are upon us. No one's paying attention. There's only been one offer since yesterday, and it's from that weird guy in Denver."

"Weird guy from Denver?" Kelly grinned. "Please tell me you're joking."

Jennifer leaned back in the chair, sipping hot chocolate. "Nope. He works alone, dresses like an overage Gothboy, all in black. And he always, always underbids. Sometimes insultingly so. All of his clients are from out of town, too. Who knows how they find him. On the Web, probably, under 'Strange People.' Maybe they threw darts at a website. Who knows?"

Kelly laughed. "Overage Gothboy. Okay, that is strange. Sure he won't change tactics?"

Jennifer shook her head. "Nope. I've checked with other agents. That's his standard operating procedure. He tries to pick up Colorado properties for rock-bottom prices. Trouble is, there aren't many in that category anymore. So I think we'll be safe offering at market. Especially since I sense this second buyer wants to sell as quickly as possible. Even the agent's assistant sounded spooked."

"Well, overage Gothboys won't spook me, either. Let's do it." She pulled out the chair across the table. "Will you still be able to submit this tonight?"

Jennifer nodded with a smile. "Oh, yeah. I called the agent's assistant and told her I might be bringing an offer tonight. She promised she'd stay awake till midnight."

Eighteen

Kelly tabbed through the spreadsheet columns, checking the amounts calculated, entering revenues and expenses methodically as the cursor moved across the screen. Only a scratch at the patio door penetrated her concentration. Carl pressed his nose against the glass, clearly asking to come in.

Kelly escaped the computer and slid open the glass door. Both Carl and a wintry blast of cold air surged inside the cottage. "I told you snow doesn't slow down squirrels," Kelly admonished her dog as he shook snowflakes from his smooth black coat. "You've been out five times this morning, Carl. Why don't you curl up and take a nap inside where it's warm and cozy?"

Carl rubbed his head against Kelly's leg, then lifted it for a pat. "Silly boy." She rubbed his soft ears.

Her cell phone jangled then, and Kelly grabbed her mug before settling into the leather sofa. The better to watch the snow flurries outside. "Kelly Flynn," she said, then took another sip of coffee.

"Hi, Kelly," Lisa's voice said. "I talked to Lizzie this morning. She's really worried about Lucy, and I can't say I blame her, judging from what she told me."

"I'm glad to hear you say that, Lisa. I felt the same way after I spoke with Lizzie yesterday. Lucy sounds like she's getting worse."

"Yeah, I think you're right," Lisa said with an audible sigh.

Kelly deliberately paused, taking another sip of coffee, giving Lisa time to think. "So do you think you'd like to try talking with her again? It sounds like the priest made some progress. Maybe he kind of broke the ice, so to speak."

"Yeah, but according to Lizzie, Lucy was weeping and distraught all the way home. Exactly the way she was when I mentioned therapy."

Kelly could hear the reticence in Lisa's voice, so she gambled and voiced her real concerns. "You know, Lisa, I sense there's something else behind Lucy's emotional outbursts."

"You mean other than being pregnant, alone, and abandoned?" Lisa barbed. "That would do it for most women."

"I agree, but I sense there's something else bothering Lucy, and it has to do with Derek."

Lisa was silent for a minute. "Kelly, you're fishing for something, I can tell. You're looking for clues to that Derek Cooper murder, aren't you?"

"Kind of." Kelly hedged. "I think Lucy knows something that she hasn't told anyone yet, and it's eating her up inside. Maybe she told the priest, and that's why she was so upset. Who knows?"

"Damn, Kelly," Lisa protested. "You can't go interrogating

Lucy. She's too fragile right now. I won't let you, I swear I won't."

Kelly decided to use her friend's protective instincts to advantage. "I understand that, Lisa, that's why I'm asking you to take the lead. Lucy needs help badly. We both know it. She's starting to self-destruct right in front of our eyes. Someone has to take the initiative."

Lisa exhaled another sigh of exasperation. "I know, I know, I just don't want to push Lucy over the edge, that's all. It has to be done the right way. Lucy needs to feel safe before she'll talk. I know it."

Thank God, Kelly thought. "Exactly. That's why I'm asking you, Lisa, instead of trying to talk to Lucy myself—"

"In your usual Rottweiler-style, right?"

Kelly grinned. "I promise, I'll be a pussycat. I'll sit quietly while you two talk—"

"That'll be the day."

"If anyone can get Lucy to open up and talk about Derek, you can."

"I hope so. But there's someone else who could help, too. Someone who will make Lucy feel absolutely safe. Mimi."

Kelly sat up. That was a brilliant suggestion. No one was as warm and reassuring and comforting as Mother Mimi. "Lisa, that's positively brilliant!" Kelly enthused. "See why I asked you to take the lead?"

"Yeah, well, let's hope this works. I'll call Mimi right now. She can call Lucy and ask her to come to the shop this afternoon. Mimi will have a better chance of getting Lucy to show up. I'm also going to check with some doctors and counselors to get information I can share with Lucy. I want to be able to take her to see someone immediately if she'll let me."

"Lisa, you're wonderful."

"Yeah, yeah, yeah. Listen, I'll call you back. Talk to you later." Lisa hung up before Kelly could even say goodbye.

"Thanks, Lisa," Kelly said out loud as she watched wind-whipped snowflakes swirl outside.

"Go ahead and sit down. We want to look relaxed when Lucy comes in," Lisa said, pointing Kelly toward one of the two leather armchairs tucked in Mimi's cozy corner office.

Kelly did as she was directed. This was Lisa's show, and she was going to let Lisa run it. Kelly knew her dictatorial friend would toss her out if she noticed any interference. "Yes, ma'am," she said and sank into the comfy leather, afternoon sunshine pouring over her shoulder.

"Got your coffee, right?" Lisa asked as she sat in the other armchair. "We don't want you having a caffeine attack in the midst of everything."

"I'm fine, don't worry about me." Kelly gave her friend a sardonic smile. "I'll disappear into the upholstery."

Lisa gave a skeptical look, then pointed to the doorway. "Shhhh, here they come."

Kelly relaxed into the chair, even though she felt anything but relaxed as she heard Mimi and Lucy's voices drift toward the office. Her heart was racing, and she felt anxious, wondering if Lucy would respond to Mimi and Lisa and open up at last. Whatever was festering inside Lucy needed to be brought out into the light for healing.

Shapes were starting to come into focus. She sensed Lucy would provide key pieces to this puzzle. If Diane was telling the truth about seeing a car, then Lucy had to be the one driving up to Derek's that night. Kelly was convinced of it.

"Why don't we sit in my office and relax for a few minutes?" Mimi said as she held the office door open for Lucy. "We can have a nice cup of tea."

"Thank you, Mimi, that would be nice—," Lucy said as she entered. Her smile quickly disappeared, however, when she spotted Kelly and Lisa already seated.

"Hello, girls," Mimi said nonchalantly as she ushered Lucy inside the office, then closed the door.

"Hey, Lucy, how are you?" Lisa greeted warmly.

Kelly raised her mug and gave Lucy her friendliest grin. "Lucy, I've got some bags of wool in a barn in Wyoming that need spinning. I'm hoping you can help me after the holidays."

"Lisa, why don't you pour Lucy a nice cup of tea? And add some milk to cool it down," Mimi suggested.

Lucy looked at Lisa and Kelly, blue eyes widening in obvious concern. "You already have visitors, Mimi. I can come back later."

"Nonsense, dear, Lisa and Kelly are part of our Lambspun family, too. Just like you are." Mimi gestured to the love seat against the windows. "Come, sit beside me, why don't you?" Mimi settled into the love seat and patted the leather beside her.

Lucy hesitated for a few seconds then sank into the love seat, placing her extra-large yarn bag on the floor at her feet. She glanced around apprehensively once more.

Mimi reached over and patted Lucy's arm, her voice warm and soothing. "Lucy, you know how much I care about you, don't you?"

Lucy nodded, eyes getting wider.

"Well, Lisa and Kelly and everyone here in the Lambspun family love and care about you, too. And we're worried about you. You've been keeping this grief to yourself for too long. We think you need some help. You need to talk to someone. Someone who can help, like a counselor."

A panicked look darted across Lucy's delicate features. "I-I-I spoke with a priest Monday," she said in a breathy voice. "Lizzie took me. I've already talked to someone."

Mimi leaned closer, still patting Lucy's arm. "Lisa knows several wonderful counselors and therapists who could help. She used to be in a group with you, remember? Lisa can help you find the right person, Lucy."

"I'll stay with you, Lucy, as long as you need me," Lisa offered in a soothing voice. "If you don't like the first counselor you meet, then we'll try the next one, and the next, until you find exactly the right one for *you*."

Lucy's gaze dropped to her lap, her hands clasped tightly. "I'm okay, I really am," she whispered. "I don't need to see anyone else."

Mimi bent down, clearly attempting to catch Lucy's eye. "Lucy, we know about the baby. You need to think about what's best for the baby, too. All this turmoil has tied you in knots inside. That's not good. Not for you. Not for the baby."

Lucy's head jerked up, and Kelly saw real panic in her eyes. "How—how—"

"Ellen told us, dear. Out of concern for you. Don't be upset with her. She was worried sick for you and for the baby. She said you haven't seen a doctor yet—is that true?"

Tears welled in Lucy's eyes now and spilled down her pale cheeks. "No . . . not yet," she whispered.

"I can take you to the doctor, dear. And Lizzie can come, too, if you'd like. She's so worried about you." Mimi's rhythmic patting continued.

Lisa leaned forward, offering the teacup. Mimi took it

from her and handed it to Lucy. Lucy unclenched her hands long enough to grasp the cup and bring it to her lips.

"Don't worry about expenses, Lucy," Lisa continued softly. "I've checked with my doctor, and she sees patients on a sliding scale. I've already spoken with her, and she'll make room in her schedule whenever you want."

"You see, dear?" Mimi comforted. "Everything will work out. You're not alone, you know. We're your family, and we'll take care of you. I promise." She took the empty cup from Lucy's shaking hands.

Kelly watched the tears run down Lucy's cheeks, sensing the dam was about to break.

"I know you must feel alone, what with Derek gone. Losing him was an awful shock. I know how much you loved him, and how he loved you and—"

"But he *didn't*!" Lucy burst out suddenly. "He didn't love me! He lied! He lied! He didn't want me at all!"

The dam broke at last, and a deluge of tears burst forth. Lucy sank her head in her hands and wept, shoulders shaking. Kelly reached for a nearby box of tissues and handed them to Mimi, who was trying her best to soothe Lucy's anguish.

"There, now, I'm sure that isn't true. . ."

Lucy refused to be consoled. Shaking her head, she wailed, "He didn't want me or . . . or the baby. He cursed at me! And then he threw money on the ground! He said that's all I'd ever get from him." Another high-pitched wail emerged, as she collapsed in tears again.

Lisa glanced over to Kelly and nodded slightly. Kelly took that as Lisa's acknowledgment that Kelly had guessed right. Lisa left her chair and sank to the floor beside Mimi and Lucy.

"It'll be okay, Lucy, it'll be okay . . ." Lisa crooned, patting

Lucy's other arm. Mimi had never ceased her stroking. "Did you go to Derek's to tell him about the baby?" she asked after a moment.

Lucy nodded her head, face still buried in her hands. "He—he didn't answer his phone, so . . . so I drove up there."

"Maybe he was simply surprised when you told him about the baby, dear. Maybe that's why he was so . . . so . . . ." Mimi was clearly straining to come up with a reason for Derek's cruelty.

Lucy's hands slid away from her blotchy, wet face. She shook her head again. "No, no. He laughed when I told him about the baby and about us getting married. He laughed." Her mouth trembled. "He said he wasn't about to be trapped into marriage by some dumb little chick who . . . who was too stupid to keep from getting pregnant. Then he threw money on the barn floor . . . in the dirt . . . and told me to take care of it." Her head sank again as the tears flowed.

Kelly sat spellbound, listening to Lucy's tale of rejection. Jennifer was right. Derek Cooper was a scumbag. Or he was when alive. It was impossible not to be affected by Lucy's anguish. It was truly heart-wrenching. To be rejected so cruelly and callously was unconscionable.

But had it driven Lucy to take revenge? Had Derek's rejection of her and the baby enraged Lucy to the point of murder?

"There, there, now," Mimi soothed, offering Lucy another cup of tea. Lucy grasped the cup and drank deeply, tea sloshing over the edge this time.

Lisa took the empty cup and offered a huge handful of tissues. Lucy took them and swiped at her face. "Did you leave then?" Lisa asked softly.

Lucy's mouth trembled. "He—he pushed me out. He

grabbed the money and shoved it down my shirt and told me he never wanted to see me again. Then . . . then he yanked off the necklace I made for him and threw it in my face." She bent her head and pressed wads of tissues to her face.

"There, there, now, Lucy, you're better off without that awful man," Mimi said, a judgmental tone creeping into her voice as she patted.

"But—I *took* it," Lucy cried out again, shoulders shaking. "I took the money like . . . like a whore." She buried her face in the tissues with an anguished cry.

"You're no such thing, Lucy, you're a wonderful girl," Mimi said defiantly, slipping her arm around Lucy's shaking shoulders and drawing her closer. "And you'll be a wonderful mother, too."

"And you'll have plenty of help, Lucy. I found where all the child care services are in town, and I'll take you to register," Lisa said. "It will be okay."

Kelly sat watching, not saying a word, but her mind was spinning a mile a minute. Lucy's tale of her confrontation with Derek Cooper did not resemble the version Kelly had scripted in her imagination. Lucy's grief and anguish were real. There was no doubt. Kelly could feel it in her gut. Lucy's words rang true.

Peering at Lucy, Kelly forced her skeptical side to weigh in, but it had nothing to say. All the well-rehearsed scenes Kelly had allowed her imagination to create collapsed now, like punctured balloons. They'd all been created out of thin air, and the air rushed out of them just as quickly. Lucy didn't kill Derek Cooper.

"Thank goodness you left before that wretched man became violent," Mimi said. "I'm surprised you could drive out of the canyon in that state. Was it still daytime?"

Lucy shook her head. "No, it was night. But I—I drove slowly."

Kelly leaned forward and asked in a soft voice, "Lucy, do you recall seeing any other cars when you went to Derek's?"

She nodded, sniffling. "When I was going up the drive-way, someone else was leaving," she said, wiping her nose. "Probably another one of Derek's girlfriends."

"That's okay, dear," Mimi soothed. "It's better forgotten."

"And when I left, I saw a car parked at the bottom, too. On the side of the road."

Kelly sat up. Diane said she'd seen a parked car that night. "Did you see anyone in the car?"

"No, it was dark, and the headlights were off."

Kelly stared at Lucy without saying a word. Diane had lied before. Was she lying again? Maybe it was actually Diane in the parked car. Had she driven away from Derek's ranch only to return? Did she come back to fight with her old lover one more time or to kill him?

It had to be Diane. There was no one else who hated Derek Cooper enough to kill him. And she lied. She lied to Jayleen. She lied to them all.

Suddenly all the small things that had bothered Kelly about Diane's version of events crept out of hiding. Why hadn't she paid attention before? Kelly already knew the answer. She *wanted* to believe Diane.

"Here, Lucy, drink some more tea, and then you and I can go visit my doctor. She's really nice, and I think you'll like her," Lisa suggested as she offered Lucy another cup.

Lucy accepted and drained the cup in a few seconds, clearly thirsty after all the tears.

"I'd like to come, too, if that's all right, Lucy," Mimi

offered, reaching for Lucy's oversized yarn bag. "Here, let me carry this for you."

Lucy looked up, gratitude glistening in her wet blue eyes. "Thank you, Mimi, I'd like that. And thank you, Lisa."

"That's what families are for, Lucy," Lisa said, helping Lucy from her chair and guiding her to the door.

Mimi started after them then glanced to Kelly. "Kelly, would you please tell Rosa that I won't be coming back the rest of today? She can close up."

"Sure thing, Mimi. And you'd better call Burt while you're at the doctor's office. Lucy will need to give a statement to the police about all of this."

Mimi nodded. "Yes, I know. And don't worry. Burt and I will stay with her the entire time."

Nineteen

Kelly absentmindedly dragged her hand across the candy-colored fibers as she walked through the yarn room, not paying attention to the softness beneath her fingers. She barely noticed the bustle of customers jostling each other around the bins. She was oblivious to the color and commotion surrounding her. Oblivious to it all. Her mind was still back in Mimi's office.

She needed to talk with Jennifer. Kelly knew Jennifer had been wrestling with her own doubts about Diane. They needed to talk. But not yet. Kelly wanted to fortify herself first. She wondered if there was enough caffeine in the world for this conversation.

"Hey, Kelly, Jayleen dropped off an envelope for you," Rosa said as she hurried through the room. "You were in Mimi's office, so she wrote a note and left. I put it on the library table."

Kelly wound through the shoppers, retrieved the envelope, and retreated to Pete's café and out of the holiday crush. Welcoming the midafternoon quiet, she signaled the waitress as she found a corner table. Eduardo's strong brew appeared and Kelly indulged herself, drinking deeply for a few moments before she picked up the manila envelope.

Jayleen's note was taped to the front. *I found this picture when I was sorting through some of those boxes in my barn. It was taken at an alpaca breeders' dinner. Take a look at who's sitting next to Derek.*

Curious, Kelly opened the envelope and pulled out an eight-by-ten black-and-white photo. It seemed like a typical banquet photo. Smiling faces around a table. Jayleen had drawn an arrow to Derek Cooper. Blond, handsome, grinning. His arm was draped around the woman beside him. Kelly stared at the woman and caught her breath.

It was Ellen Hunter. Or, it looked like Ellen Hunter. She had the same smile, the same wavy blonde hair. And she was snuggled close to Derek. Was Ellen Hunter one of Derek Cooper's old girlfriends, too?

Kelly sat back, staring at the photo while she sipped her coffee. Ellen had never let on. Never indicated she knew Derek. Not a word, not a gesture, nothing. She talked like she didn't know him. Why? Why would she keep it a secret? It didn't make sense.

Maybe it wasn't really Ellen in the photo, she thought. Well, if it wasn't, then it was her twin. How could that be, though? Ellen was Lucy's best friend, her constant companion, watching over Lucy, worrying about her. And Lucy was Derek's girlfriend. Or one of them, at least. It didn't make sense.

Kelly continued to stare at the photo while she sipped

her coffee. A stray thought drifted through the others churning through her mind. Ellen said she and Lucy met several months ago at a neighborhood coffeehouse. Several months ago. Lucy met Derek several months ago at the alpaca banquet. Coincidence? Probably. It didn't make sense . . . or did it?

Signaling to the waitress for more coffee, Kelly punched Jennifer's number into her cell phone. An idea had surfaced suddenly. It was a crazy idea, but she was going to follow it up anyway.

"Hey, Jen, are you going to see Diane today?" she asked when Jennifer answered.

"Actually, I'm picking her up at the hospital. She's checking out right now. And she wants to drop by the shop before I take her to Jayleen's ranch."

"How's she doing?"

"Real subdued. Calm, almost. I confess I've never seen her like this before." Jennifer's voice turned somber. "I guess the doctors and counselors must have gotten through. At least, I hope they did."

"Let's hope so, Jen. Listen, could you ask Diane a question while you're driving over? Ask her if she remembers if Derek ever had a girlfriend named Ellen. Blonde, wavy hair."

"Blonde with wavy hair? That sounds like Ellen at the shop—you know, Lucy's friend. She never let on that she knew Derek."

"Well, I'm looking at a photo Jayleen found of Derek sitting at an alpaca breeders' banquet with his arm around Ellen Hunter. It's either her or her twin."

Jennifer took in her breath. "Damn."

"That's what I say." Kelly flipped over the photo to see the photographer's stamp and date. "It would have been two years ago."

"We'll be over in a few minutes."

Diane Perkins stared at the black-and-white photo, frowning. "You know, I'm not sure, but I think that's her. Derek called her Elly. Can't remember the last name."

Kelly glanced to Jennifer, who was seated at the library table with them. The late afternoon crowd of shoppers had thinned considerably, so they were momentarily alone in the room.

"So she did go with Derek," Kelly said.

"Ohhh, yeah. And he dumped her like he did every girl." Diane shook her head. "But apparently this Elly didn't want to stay dumped. She kept coming back to his ranch. Showing up when he had other girls there. Leaving ugly messages on his answering machine. Stuff like that. At least, that's what Derek said. I wasn't around his place all the time."

"Sounds like she was stalking him," Jennifer suggested.

Diane shrugged. "According to Derek, she was. I didn't see her more than once or twice, but I do remember her coming up to us outside a restaurant one night. She started cussing him out until Derek threatened to call the cops."

"Wow, she sounds worse than a stalker. Sounds like she had it in for him," Kelly said.

"Yeah, she did. She bashed in his windshield one night when we were in a club. She left a note, too. So he'd know it was her."

"Didn't Derek call the cops?" Jennifer asked. "He had a

pretty short fuse himself. I can't believe he would just let her get away with that."

"Yeah, I was surprised he waited so long to do something. But I guess he finally called somebody. Someone must have talked to her, because she stopped showing up after that."

"You never saw her, Jen?"

Jennifer shook her head. "Nope. But I remember Ted talking about some woman coming to the bar a couple of times looking for Derek."

Kelly gazed out into the winter sunset darkening the sky. Were Ellen Hunter and Elly the same woman? Elly sounded almost deranged. Ellen acted normal. They couldn't be the same person, could they?

"Kelly, do you know if Lucy's all right?" Ellen's voice came from the adjoining room. "I called her cell and Mimi picked up. She said they took Lucy to the doctor. What's happening?"

Kelly looked up to see Ellen Hunter stride into the room, winter coat and scarf dangling, as if she were rushing somewhere.

"Hey, Ellen, uhhhh . . . yes, Mimi and Lisa took Lucy to the doctor," she said, momentarily taken aback at Ellen's sudden appearance.

"Is she all right? Is the baby all right? I was—" Ellen's gaze settled on Diane, who had turned in her chair and was staring back at Ellen.

"It *is* you," Diane said as she stood up. "Elly, right? What are you doing here?"

The brief look of surprise Kelly had glimpsed in Ellen's eyes disappeared. Her gaze hardened. "You're mistaken. My name's Ellen, not Elly."

A wry smile twitched Diane's mouth. "Well, you used to

be Elly. Back when you were giving Derek Cooper hell. I remember you."

"You're crazy. Either that or you're drunk. I don't know who you are," Ellen snapped.

Both Kelly and Jennifer stood at that, flanking Diane. "Hey, Ellen, calm down," Kelly said. "No need to talk like that."

"Well, she's talking crazy, she must be drunk. I've never seen her before," Ellen replied, face flushed, staring daggers at Diane.

Diane returned her stare, then replied in a quiet voice, "It's true, I've been drunk a lot. But right now, I'm sober as a judge. And I do remember you, Elly. You were one of Derek's girls."

Ellen's face darkened as she glared at Diane for several seconds. "Kelly, I'll call you later, and you can tell me about Lucy," she said in a cold voice, before she stalked out of the knitting shop.

"Whoa . . . what was that all about?" Jennifer said.

Kelly stared out into the early evening, her thoughts racing. She'd never mentioned Diane's drinking to Ellen. So why would Ellen call Diane a drunk, unless . . .

Ellen Hunter was lying. Kelly was sure of it. Ellen knew Diane Perkins, all right. And she hated her. Kelly was sure of that, too.

"**Lucy's** doing pretty well, considering." Burt's voice came over Kelly's cell phone. "She did good at the station. Didn't break down once giving her statement."

Kelly watched Carl sniff his way around the frozen back-yard. "That's great. Where's she now? At home?"

"Yep. Mimi is going to stay with her tonight. Lisa will take her to the counselor's appointment tomorrow. I think she's going to be all right."

"Sounds like she'll be getting the help she needs at last," Kelly said, then paused. "I know you're probably tired, Burt, but I was wondering if I could ask you to do me a favor."

"Sure, Kelly. What do you need?"

"I need you to ask some questions of your buddies on the Derek Cooper case."

The sound of beeping came on the line, signaling another call was coming through. Kelly didn't recognize the number, and let it go to voice mail.

Burt gave a tired sigh. "Kelly, I know you and Jennifer want to believe Diane Perkins is innocent, but let's look at the facts that we know—"

"It's not about Diane. It's about someone else. Something has come up, and I'm curious."

"Kelly, if you're curious, then I'm curious. What's up?"

"First, could you check one of those voice messages on Derek's phone? You said there was a message from some woman with a grudge. Could you find out what she said?"

"I'll ask. What next?"

"Could you check to see if there were any cops who patrol Bellevue Canyon? If so, could you find out if any of them noticed a car parked near the bottom of Derek Cooper's driveway that night? Pulled off to the side of the road. Lucy confirmed what Diane said about a car being parked there. Lucy saw it, too. She told us this afternoon."

Burt's sigh was audible. "I thought you said this had nothing to do with Diane. It looks like you're still chasing shadows, Kelly. I think you know who was in that car at the bottom of the road."

"That's what I thought, Burt, until this afternoon. Jayleen gave me a photo that shows Ellen Hunter and Derek Cooper together as a couple. Until he dumped her, that is."

"You mean Ellen from the spinning class?"

"The same. Apparently she started stalking Derek after he dumped her. He may have reported her to the police. Maybe there's a report. It was a couple of years ago, I think."

"Wait a minute, wait a minute, I've got to write this down," Burt said. "You're saying that Ellen Hunter was stalking Derek Cooper two years ago, right?"

"That's what I'm told."

"Okay, who told you all this?"

Kelly paused. Burt wasn't going to like her answer. "Diane told me. She was with Derek one night when Ellen came up to them. She recognized her."

"Kelly, Kelly, Kelly . . . you are grasping at straws, I swear you are." Burt's disbelief was audible.

"I know what you're thinking, Burt, but could you please check out everything? For me. Forget it was Diane for a minute, please, and just check it out."

"Okay, Kelly," Burt said with a huge sigh. "If you think something's there, I'll check into it for you. I'll get back to you as soon as I hear something."

"Thanks, Burt. You're a sweetheart," she said before clicking off.

Finding Jennifer's number, Kelly punched that in next, while she slid the patio door open. Carl galumphed inside the kitchen. "Cold enough for you, Carl?" she asked as she rubbed his shiny black head. "Too cold for me." Carl responded by slurping her hand.

Jennifer's voice came on the line. "Hey, Kelly, what's up?"

"Is Diane all safe and sound back with Jayleen?"

"Yeah, I'm driving away now. Man, these roads are tricky at night."

"Well, take it slow and easy. Drive over to my place when you get into town, okay? We're going out."

"What? Where're we going?"

"Back to the bar. Does Ted work tonight?"

"Ted? Yeah, he works nights. May I ask why? You weren't crazy about the bar, as I recall."

"We're going to show Ted that photo of Derek and Ellen. Let's hope Ted has a good memory."

"I'll be there as soon as I can."

Twenty

"**Hey,** Burt, I was hoping it was you," Kelly said, answering her cell with one hand while she steered through holiday traffic with the other.

Last Saturday before Christmas, and the roads were gridlock. Parking lots were a nightmare. Kelly swore she would shop earlier next year. But then, she said that every year.

"I'll bet you're out shopping, right?"

"Ohhhh, yeah. Me and thousands of others, bumping into each other."

"Well, don't bump into anyone. I've got a few answers for you. Still waiting on the others."

Kelly held her breath, feeling her pulse race. "Hold it, Burt. I've gotta pull out of this traffic so I can pay attention. Otherwise I'll run into someone for sure." Spotting an entrance for a discount store ahead, Kelly steered into an illegal parking place and idled her engine. She took a deep breath. "Okay, tell me what you found."

"Well, I checked on that voice message first. My friend said the message was short but the woman really sounded angry. She called Derek a 'bastard' and said something like 'you've done it again, but you won't get away with it this time.' Something like that. Then she hung up."

"Interesting," Kelly said, wondering what Derek had "done again." Was the woman talking about herself or Lucy? Had Derek hurt Ellen in some way other than dumping her?

"I can tell you're thinking that caller might be Ellen."

"Yeah, I am, and I'm wondering what Derek did to her to make her so mad she'd stalk him. Clearly, it sounds like she was trying to hurt Derek in some way, don't you think?"

"Well, if she did stalk him or go to his ranch, there's no record of it. No reports filed, not even for the broken windshield, nothing. So Diane was either mistaken or lying. Maybe Ellen was just another dumped girlfriend, and Diane exaggerated."

Kelly stared out at the volunteer bell-ringer standing in the cold beside the store entrance. Shoppers piled through the doors and piled out of them. Many of them dropped something into the red kettle, Kelly noticed. Spreading holiday blessings.

"I don't think so, Burt. Jennifer and I verified Diane's account. We went to the bar last night and showed the photo to Ted, the bartender. He identified Ellen Hunter as the woman who used to come to the bar pestering Derek a couple of years ago." She waited for Burt's reaction to her news. It came quickly.

"You're kidding."

"Nope. Ted said Ellen came in several times, and Derek

laughed about her 'stalking' him. Derek made a joke of it, of course. But Ted remembers her."

"Well, I'll be damned. You've got my instincts buzzing on this now. Wait a minute . . . there's another call coming in. I'll get back to you, Kelly."

Kelly clicked off her phone and tossed it to the seat, wondering if she should venture out into the traffic nightmare again or wait for Burt's call. One look at the bumper-to-bumper traffic made her decision for her.

Spying a car backing out of a nearby parking space, Kelly swiftly pulled her car into the empty spot. If she was going to wait for Burt's call, she might as well get more shopping done. A chill breeze whipped the knitted scarf around her neck as she trekked through the melted snow-slush in the parking lot. Brilliant blue sky, bright sun, cold as hell.

She dropped some dollar bills into the bell-ringer's kettle and was about to join the throngs crowding into the store when her cell phone rang. Kelly stepped away from the shoppers and their noise before she answered. Burt's number flashed on the phone screen. "Hey, Burt, what's up?"

"Kelly, can you call Ellen and ask her to come to the shop this afternoon? We need to talk to her."

Kelly felt her pulse speed up. "What did you find, Burt?"

"Yesterday I called and asked the deputy sheriff who patrols Bellevue Canyon to check his records to see if any unidentified cars were spotted on the road near Derek's that night. He said he didn't remember any, but he'd check again. That was him calling back. Dispatchers received a neighborhood nuisance complaint that night. Someone parked a car partially blocking a canyon resident's driveway. Seems the old man didn't like that, so he took down the license plate and called it in." Burt paused to take a breath.

Kelly couldn't hold hers any longer. "And . . . ?"

"The car is registered to Ellen Hunter of Fort Connor."

Kelly held absolutely still while her mind raced, puzzle pieces sorting in her head, fitting together at last. *Ellen.* It was Ellen waiting in the car. Why? She must have followed Lucy to Derek's that night. Did she wait in the car? No. No, she couldn't have. The canyon resident would have seen her. Ellen must have left the car and walked up the driveway. Was she spying on Lucy and Derek?

"I'll call Ellen while I drive to the shop, Burt. I'm heading there now."

Kelly signaled a waitress as Ellen shed her coat and settled across from her at a corner table in Pete's café. This late in the afternoon, only a few customers were scattered about. "Coffee?" she asked Ellen as the waitress refilled Kelly's mug.

"No, I'm good," Ellen said, digging into her briefcase and opening a notepad. "Now, who is this client of yours again? I know a lot of doctors in town, and most of them are with group practices of some sort. They may have their own transcription people."

"I think this guy is on his own," Kelly said, willing the lie to her lips. "And he said he was looking for someone." She glanced to the doorway where Burt was hovering and beckoned him over. "Hey, Burt, come over and join us."

"Thanks, Kelly. I could use some coffee," Burt said with a friendly smile as he joined them. He reached for the carafe the waitress had left and poured a dark stream into his cup. "How're you doing, Ellen?"

"I'm fine," she replied, looking at Burt with surprise. "Do you have a class today? You're usually not here this late."

"No, Ellen, I don't," Burt said, leaning his arms on the table. "Kelly and I are here to speak with you. We think you need some help."

Ellen peered at them both, clearly surprised by the turn of conversation. "Help with a client?"

Kelly leaned forward then, cupping her hands around her mug, and spoke in a soft voice. "Ellen, we need to talk with you about Derek Cooper."

Ellen sat back, glancing from Kelly to Burt then back again. Kelly glimpsed fear in her eyes before anger swept it away. "Why? I didn't know Derek Cooper. He was Lucy's boyfriend."

Kelly reached into the folder at her elbow and withdrew the photo of Ellen and Derek, handing it to her. "Jayleen said she remembers seeing you at several alpaca banquets with Derek a couple of years ago. And the bartender at Derek's favorite bar identified you as well. He remembered you kept coming into the bar looking for Derek. Did Derek dump you, Ellen? Is that why you started stalking him?"

Ellen's face flushed as she stared at the photo, her mouth tightening. She tossed the photo to the table. "I wasn't stalking him. I went there to tell him what a piece of trash he was, that's all." She bit off the words.

"Is that why you broke his windshield one night? Diane remembers you yelling at him and calling him names," Kelly continued, keeping her voice calm. She didn't want to stoke Ellen's anger any more than she had to. Ellen blazed with it already. Kelly could feel the heat.

The mention of Diane's name brought a fiery glare. "That drunk! Are you going to believe *her*?"

Kelly let the flames die down while she switched her approach. "Derek sounds like a bastard—"

"Damn right!"

"Apparently he dumped every girl he ever went with. I can understand your being hurt when he left you, Ellen. Is that why you've been so solicitous with Lucy? You've been taking care of her like a big sister, almost. Were you trying to keep her from being hurt by Derek?"

Ellen's expression changed swiftly. The flames disappeared from her gaze, replaced with concern. "I didn't want Derek to hurt Lucy like . . . like he hurt me," she said in a quiet voice.

Kelly studied Ellen for a moment as stray thoughts drifted through her mind. Another and another. Ellen's concern for Lucy. Not wanting her to be hurt. Hurt like Ellen. How had Derek hurt Ellen? By dumping her? That didn't make sense. Derek dumped every girl he slept with, according to Jennifer. No, it had to be something else, something more than getting dumped, something . . .

Suddenly, one thought crystallized before Kelly's eyes. That had to be it. Why hadn't Kelly seen it before? Ellen had become pregnant just like Lucy.

She leaned forward and touched Ellen's hand. "Ellen," she said softly, "were you pregnant with Derek's child? Is that why you're so concerned about Lucy?"

Ellen's head jerked up, and Kelly saw the truth shimmer in Ellen's eyes along with the pain. Ellen looked away and didn't answer, staring out into the nearly empty café. Kelly caught Burt's sympathetic glance as they sat and waited. Waited for Ellen to speak. Kelly could see the struggle inside reflected on Ellen's face.

"Yes, I was pregnant," she said at last. "Just like Lucy. Until Derek pushed me down the stairs. I lost the baby a few days later."

Kelly sat back in her chair, shocked by what she heard. "Ellen, I'm so sorry. That must have been awful."

Ellen nodded as she turned back to them.

"Can you tell me how it happened?" Burt asked in a low voice.

"I went over to Derek's ranch to tell him right after I got the news from the doctor. I was so excited, just like Lucy." Ellen's voice grew cold. "But Derek wasn't happy at all. He was furious. He didn't want a baby, and he didn't want me. Not anymore. He threw me out like a piece of trash. Pushed me out the front door. I pushed back, and he got really mad. That's when he pushed me down the porch steps. Then he threw some money on the ground and said he never wanted to see me again."

Kelly watched the emotions flash across Ellen's face as she stared at her hands. Kelly didn't have the right words, so she simply reached over and placed her hand over Ellen's and held it there. Ellen's mouth tightened, and her eyes started to glisten.

"That's why you've been taking such good care of Lucy, isn't it? You didn't want the same thing to happen to her, right?"

Ellen gave a little nod, but didn't say a word, simply wiped at her eyes.

"Is that why you called Derek?" Burt asked. "You called to warn him not to hurt Lucy?"

Ellen looked up, glancing from Burt to Kelly. "I didn't call Derek. What are you talking about?"

"The police have your message on Derek's phone. The message where you said he wouldn't 'get away with it this time,'" Burt explained. "You were warning him about Lucy, weren't you?"

"I told you, I didn't call Derek."

Kelly pulled her cell phone from her pocket and held it up. "I've saved your phone message from last night, Ellen. The police will be able to match the voices."

Ellen's face paled, and Kelly glimpsed fear dart through her eyes again. She sensed Ellen was on the edge, so she pushed and asked the question they'd come for.

"You went up to Derek's that night, didn't you? You followed Lucy in your car. Did you go there to protect her in case Derek got violent?"

Panic raced across Ellen's face for a moment, and then the anger returned, flaring. "I know what you're doing. You two are trying to pin Derek's murder on me, so that drunken slut, Diane, can get off. Well, it won't work. You have no proof I was there at Derek's. I left him a message, so what? You're crazy if you think I'm going to sit here and listen to this garbage." She grabbed for her briefcase, clearly planning to leave.

Burt reached over and placed his hand on Ellen's arm, gently holding her in place. "Ellen, your car was spotted parked at the bottom of Derek's driveway that night. A neighbor called in the license number because the car was blocking his driveway."

Once again, panic flashed across Ellen's face, but this time it stayed as all color drained away. She stared at Burt, then at Kelly, then she slumped in her chair.

"Why don't you tell us what happened that night? It'll be easier if you tell us first."

Ellen's lower lip trembled. "I . . . I didn't mean for it to happen. I just went up there to make sure Derek didn't try to hurt Lucy when she told him she was having a baby."

"Did you follow them to the barn?" Kelly asked.

"Yes, I slipped in the back and hid in one of the stalls. Derek started yelling at Lucy, and she was crying and . . . and it brought back all those old memories."

Kelly noticed a tear slide down Ellen's cheek. Release at last. "That must have been hard for you to listen to."

She nodded. "It was. Especially when he was shoving money at Lucy and yelling at her and pushing her out the door. I was about to come out of the stall when Lucy ran off to her car."

"What did you do then?" Burt prodded.

"I was going to confront him. Warn Derek that I wasn't going to let anything happen to Lucy. And he'd better stay away from her." Ellen stared off into the café again. "Then he took out his cell phone and called someone. Another girl, of course. And he starts sweet-talking her like he does at first. Lying to you, making promises, saying how much he loves you."

She paused. "Then he begged the girl to come up and spend the night with him. I couldn't believe it. I stood there and listened, and I . . . I couldn't believe it. He was doing the same thing all over again. Lying to some girl, sweet-talking her into his bed, just so he could walk all over her . . . the same old lies, over and over and over again. He'd never change. Never. I kept staring at him, listening to his lies, and . . . I don't know . . . I don't even remember coming out of the stall, but suddenly I was walking up behind him. I saw the shovel, and I grabbed it. All I could see was Derek, lying and lying and lying. . . ."

Ellen shook her head slowly. "I can't explain what happened next. I just wanted to hurt him, stop his lying, stop him . . . so I hit him. Hit him with the shovel. I only meant to hurt him, honest. I didn't mean to kill Derek, I swear. I only meant to hurt him. . . ."

Ellen's voice trailed off as she kept staring into the café. Burt reached over and touched her arm. "What happened when you saw Derek fall down?"

Ellen turned back to them with a sad gaze. "I woke up, I guess . . . I saw Derek lying on the barn floor, bleeding, and I panicked. I . . . I ran back down to my car and drove out of the canyon. I figured he'd come to, eventually. Believe me, I had no idea I'd killed him. Honest. And when I found out he'd died, well, that's when I really panicked."

Kelly watched Ellen Hunter and heard remorse creep into her voice as Burt asked her more questions. Clearly, Ellen had been obsessed with Derek Cooper. An obsession that swept away all reason and judgment. Obsession brought on, no doubt, by her heartbreak over losing her child. That pain must have spawned a rage that turned vengeful. How else to explain Ellen's behavior—stalking Derek, following and meeting his girlfriends, as she did with Lucy. Cultivating Lucy's friendship so she could keep track of Derek. All of it stoking a fire that was bound to blaze out of control as it did that night in Derek's barn. Obsession turned deadly.

Burt glanced across at Kelly. "Kelly, will you call Mimi and tell her I won't be coming over tonight, please?" Turning back to Ellen, Burt rose and held out his hand. "I'll go with you to the department, Ellen, and I'll stay with you while you give your statement, if you want me to."

Ellen stared up at Burt for several seconds, then nodded, before she gathered her things.

Twenty-one

"**Mimi,** this punch is delicious," Kelly said as she ladled more of the fruit juice mixture into her cup.

"Thank Connie. It's her recipe," Mimi said brightly, straightening the plates of holiday cookies, candies, and other tempting treats clustered on the library table.

"Did you spike the punch, Burt?" Kelly teased, watching Burt move a spinning wheel into an adjoining alcove. Lamb-spun family and friends were already drifting in for the afternoon party.

"Are you kidding? I don't want anything competing with my wassail," Burt said with a grin as he continued making space.

"Where is that wassail, anyway?" Jennifer asked as she pulled some chairs into the corner, away from the table. "You've been bragging about it all week, Burt."

"It's keeping warm at Pete's. I'll bring it over in a few minutes. I'm building suspense."

"I hope it's not too strong," Kelly said, gesturing toward the main yarn room where Lizzie and Hilda were chatting with Rosa and Connie. "Lizzie gets into enough trouble when she's sober. I don't want to think what would happen if she were tipsy."

"Don't worry about Lizzie," Mimi said with a laugh, carrying a plate filled with meringues. "Hilda will keep her in line."

Jennifer retrieved red and white wool from her bag and continued knitting what looked like another scarf. "I get the feeling that Hilda has spent her entire life keeping Lizzie in line."

Kelly snatched two tempting sweets and offered one to Jennifer before settling into a chair beside her friend. "These look like toffee bars," she said, sinking her teeth into the rich cookie. "Mmmm, yessss."

"I'll be five pounds heavier by the time this party's over, I know it." Jennifer gave a sardonic smile.

"You're not the only one, Jennifer. I've gained ten pounds this month already," Burt said with a laugh as he rearranged furniture. "By the way, Kelly, congratulations again. I know how much you wanted that ranch. Now you and Jayleen will be neighbors."

"Thanks, Burt," Kelly said as she nibbled another toffee bar, still surprised at her good fortune. Geri Norbert's beautiful canyon ranch would be hers at last. "I don't think it's settled in yet."

"She almost didn't believe me when I told her the buyer accepted her offer," Jennifer added.

"Burt, I hope I didn't wake you when I called last night,"

Kelly said sheepishly. "I knew it was late, but I couldn't stop myself. I called everybody."

Burt laughed. "Everyone likes to hear good news, Kelly. Believe me, you didn't bother any of us."

"Jayleen was pretty happy when I called. But she was even happier when I told her about Ellen Hunter's confession."

"I'll bet she was," Burt said as he moved more chairs away from the table.

"Diane said she nearly fainted with relief when Jayleen told her last night," Jennifer said as she worked the red and white yarns. Kelly spied a pretty cable design running down the length of the scarf.

"Have you seen Diane yet?"

Jennifer shook her head. "No, she's wiped out. She didn't even want to come to the party. Said she just wanted to sit by herself and watch snow falling on the mountains."

"Well, I can understand that," Kelly said, picturing the beautiful mountain views from Geri Norbert's canyon ranch. Soon to be *Kelly's* canyon ranch. The pride of possession warmed her inside.

"Looks like I came at the right time," Steve said as he walked into the room and scanned the library table, which was entirely covered by now with holiday sweets. He grinned and slipped off his winter jacket. "Wow, I see all my favorites here. We should cancel dinner plans, Kelly. I'll be stuffed."

"Better get a head start, because Marty will be coming later," Jennifer teased.

"Who invited him?" Steve asked, affecting a look of horror as he snagged a chocolate-layered brownie.

"Mimi did. So blame her," Kelly said with a grin.

"Well, I'd better get started, then, before old Marty shows up and wipes the table clean." He snatched a frosted cookie, a brownie, a toffee bar, and several other desserts, loading them onto his plate.

"Excuse me a minute, Jen," Kelly said as she rose. "Steve, if you can tear yourself away from the table for a second, I want to ask you something." Taking Steve's warning about Marty to heart, she snatched a brown sugar brownie and headed for the corner alcove, away from the crowded table.

"Where's that wassail Burt promised?" Steve asked, balancing desserts and punch as he smiled and greeted his way through the friendly group surrounding the table.

"I'm going to fetch it now," Burt announced, heading toward the café.

"Wow, have you tried this one?" Steve asked Kelly when he'd devoured the toffee bar.

"Those are deadly," Kelly said, leading Steve toward the doorway of the adjacent spinning alcove.

Steve closed his eyes, clearly savoring a lemony dessert. "What's up?" he asked, licking powdered sugar from his lips.

"I wanted to ask you something about the canyon property."

Steve grinned, his eyes twinkling. "You mean *your* canyon property?"

"Yeah, *my* canyon property." She returned his grin. "It's finally settled in that the place is going to be mine, so I figured I'd better start making some plans. And I've been thinking—"

"That's always dangerous."

"And I wanted your advice," Kelly continued, amused with the speed with which Steve had dispatched the desserts.

"Smart move," he managed after swallowing the last chocolate morsel and tossing the plate into the trash.

"Have you been taking lessons from Marty? Those desserts were gone in sixty seconds."

"Those were just the appetizers," he joked. "I dropped by the Old Town site, and forgot about lunch. Now I'm starving."

Kelly suddenly remembered Steve's new project, the one he'd dreamed of building in the turn-of-the-century section of Fort Connor's Old Town. She'd been so involved lately, she'd completely forgotten to ask him about it. "How's that going, anyway?" she asked. "Sorry, I've been so busy, I lost track of where you are in the process."

"That's okay, I figured you'd slow down to take a breath eventually," Steve said with a good-natured smile. "I'm actually drawing up plans now. Preliminary ones, of course. Just sketching out ideas and seeing what they look like on paper."

"It really helps being an architect, doesn't it?" Kelly said, allowing admiration to fill her voice. "You don't have to wait for someone to create your vision. You can do it yourself."

"Oh, yeah. I'm getting pretty excited, too. Lots of ideas are pouring out." They both stepped out of Connie and Rosa's way as they carried more dessert-filled plates to the table, eliciting oohs and aahs.

"We really do need to catch up over dinner, Steve," Kelly said, watching him eye the new culinary arrivals. "Providing you have any appetite left after the party."

He nodded toward the table. "Ready to go back for seconds?"

Kelly laughed. "Before you do, let me run a couple of things by you, okay? About the canyon ranch. I've been thinking that we'll probably have to tear down the house and the barns. They're both pretty dilapidated, and Curt doesn't think much can be salvaged. Neither does Jayleen."

"That means you'll be leaving the alpacas in Wyoming, then?"

"Until we can build a new barn. But I'd like you to come up to the ranch and help me decide where everything should be built. The house, the barn, the stables. I mean, the views are so gorgeous up there, I want to take advantage of it all. I want to be able to look out the windows and see the mountains."

Steve smiled into her eyes. "I'll be glad to, Kelly. I know what you mean about those views. Do you have any idea what style house you want? That makes a difference when you're trying to picture a setting."

"Well, that's the other thing I needed to ask you. I want you to help me design the house, Steve. I was hoping to take you up on that promise. I want you to build my house."

Steve's gaze deepened and Kelly felt the warmth. "You bet I'll build your house, Kelly," he said, taking her arms as he drew her closer. Then, he leaned over and placed his lips on hers.

Steve's kiss lingered, and Kelly felt its warmth all the way down to her toes this time. She placed her hand on his chest, feeling the cabled wool of his sweater beneath her fingertips.

"Merry Christmas," Steve murmured as their lips parted.

Oh, yes, indeed, Kelly thought as the warmth spread to her cheeks.

"Way to go, Steve!" Greg cried from across the table. "And they don't even have mistletoe."

"Would you be quiet!" Lisa scolded her boyfriend, jabbing him in the ribs at the same time. Greg simply cackled in reply and gobbled a brownie.

Kelly felt her cheeks flame now as she and Steve stepped away from each other. She glanced around at her friends' grinning faces. And who was that peeking around the corner of the yarn room and smiling devilishly at her? None other than Eugene Tolliver, Kelly's alpaca scarf tossed rakishly around his neck. Oh, brother, she'd be in for nonstop teasing now.

"We've gotta talk about your timing, Greg," Steve said as he returned to the table—and the desserts.

"Wassail, wassail, all over the town!" Burt's voice rang out as he marched to the table, glass punch bowl held high.

"Make room, make room," Connie said, directing the rearranging.

"Cups and napkins," Mimi announced, waving handfuls before she tucked them beside the punch bowl.

"Looks great, Burt," Kelly said, accepting the cup of spiced wine he offered her. Sniffing the heady aroma of cinnamon, cloves, allspice, and orange, she sipped and savored as she carefully made her way around the table to greet her friend from Denver. Eugene looked elegant but casual in his jacket and turtleneck sweater. "I'm so glad you could come, Eugene. Is Ronnie here?"

"Oh, yes, we've been here for nearly an hour. Mimi was kind enough to give Ronnie a private lesson and then let him loose. He's back there now, practicing with the spinning wheel. Mimi, brave soul that she is, told him to spin away."

"How did I miss seeing you?"

"Oh, I've been reveling in the yarns, that's why," Eugene said with a big smile. "Luxuriating would be more like it. I must say, Kelly, you did not exaggerate when you described this shop. The fibers here are, well, I cannot describe them all, they are so diverse. My head is spinning right now with ideas for some of our fiber artists at the studio."

Kelly grinned. "I told you this place was fabulous. Kimberly Gorman has come here several times. Bring some of your younger artists next time."

"I intend to." He stroked a fluffy yarn. "Kimberly told me she orders regularly. And I've heard from her that Sophia Emeraud, the designer, has placed an order for some yarns for her next collection. Now, that's exciting."

"Well, come in and enjoy yourself while Ronnie is spinning," Kelly said, beckoning Eugene toward the table. "Now that we've tempted you with yarns, we'll tempt you with desserts."

Eugene gave a nonchalant wave. "I don't want to intrude. This looks like a private party."

"Nonsense," Kelly said, taking Eugene by the arm. "It's for friends and family, and you're a friend. And here's someone you know."

"Hey, Eugene." Jennifer patted the chair beside her. "Keep me company and away from all that chocolate, why don't you? I'm gaining weight even as we speak."

"Jennifer, how delightful to see you again," Eugene said as he sat beside her. "Now you can introduce me to all your friends. I don't know a soul here except for you and Kelly and Mimi, whom I met an hour ago."

"Don't worry, Eugene." Jennifer patted him on the arm. "I'll fill you in on who's who. Believe me, Lambspun has a diverse group, and you can't tell the players without a program. Hopefully, that will keep me away from the toffee bars. And the lemon squares. And the chocolate everything."

"I'll do my best to distract you," Eugene said with a sly grin. "You can start by telling me who that handsome young man was, sharing a kiss with Kelly a moment ago. I sincerely hope he's the 'winner' you mentioned at lunch last fall."

"One and the same," Jennifer replied. "And you witnessed the first kiss that lasted more than ten nanoseconds. A truly historic event. I must congratulate Steve. He usually has to sneak up on Kelly. Kind of a kiss-and-run technique, I call it." Jennifer had returned to her knitting, adding red and white rows, the interesting cable design curving throughout the length of the scarf.

"Ignore her, Eugene. She exaggerates."

"Oh, really? Then why are you still blushing?" Jennifer teased with a wicked grin. "That must have been some kiss."

Kelly felt her cheeks regain their heat. "I'm going to get you a whole plate of chocolate," she threatened.

Eugene laughed softly, clearly enjoying the exchange. "Well, I'm glad I witnessed the escalation of the relationship. The young man is obviously captivated by you, Kelly. It radiates from him."

"Oh, please . . ." Kelly said, rolling her eyes. "I'm going to get chocolate for both of you so you'll stop teasing. I swear the only way to stop Jennifer is to feed her something sweet."

"See how cruel she is, Eugene," Jennifer said plaintively as her fingers deftly worked the rows. "She knows I've gained five pounds already."

"Serves you right for teasing."

Jennifer pointed across the room. "See those two elderly ladies? They're Lizzie and Hilda von Steuben. Spinster sisters and retired schoolteachers. And master knitters, of course."

"I'll be on my very best behavior, then," Eugene remarked, glancing their way. "The taller one looks like my high school geometry teacher." He gave a shiver. "She never did appreciate my sense of humor."

"Lizzie is the mischievous one, who has a curiosity that knows no limits, I've found. She insists on hearing all about my dating exploits."

Eugene stared at Jennifer in mock horror. "Are you sure that's wise, my dear? She has no heart problems, I trust."

"Don't worry. I edit my adventures."

"A wise decision," Eugene said. Glancing around the table, he gestured to Mimi. "Mimi is a charming person, truly. Very sweet and talented, too, from what I've seen. And her husband, Burt, appears to be a stalwart sort. There's a twinkle in his eye, I've noticed. I must try his wassail. I make a mean wassail myself, so I need to compare."

"Actually, Eugene, Mimi and Burt aren't married," Kelly said, grinning. "But you've got a good eye. They've started dating recently, so we've got our fingers crossed. They make a wonderful couple."

"Indeed, they do," Eugene concurred. "They already have that 'matched set' look that couples get when they belong together. Did they meet here at the yarn shop?"

Kelly nodded. "Burt's daughter sent him here to learn to knit after he had a heart attack following his wife's death. But Burt decided he'd take up spinning instead. He's a natural."

"So this shop has turned into a veritable love nest, hasn't it?" Eugene commented. "Burt and Mimi fell in love over the spinning wheel, and Kelly and her young man were kissing in the corner."

"Enough. I'm going to get that chocolate now," Kelly threatened the two of them. "You two deserve to gain weight."

"We'll sit here and gossip about you," Jennifer threatened.

"Oh, let's."

Deliberately ignoring the lighthearted banter behind her, Kelly proceeded to load two plates with a sample of every sweet dessert displayed. Carefully balancing it all, Kelly maneuvered around her friends, exchanging holiday greetings and accepting congratulations for gaining the canyon property at last.

"Here you go." Kelly presented the dessert-filled plates when she returned. "Now you can eat and gossip and get fat all at the same time."

"Kelly, you are truly evil," Jennifer said, eyeing the decadent sweets.

"I'll get some wassail . . ." Kelly stopped when she spied Curt Stackhouse approach the edge of the gathering. She raised her hand in greeting, beckoning him over.

"As I live and breathe, it's John Wayne," Eugene whispered to Kelly as he rose to greet Curt.

Kelly suppressed her laughter. "Curt, I'm so glad you could come and help us with all these desserts." She gestured to Eugene. "Curt, I'd like you to meet Eugene Tolliver. He owns a gallery in Denver and was really hospitable to Jennifer and me when we visited last fall."

"You mean when you went down there sniffing around for clues?" Curt said as he shook Eugene's hand. "Good to meet you, Eugene."

"My pleasure, Curt. So you're aware of Kelly's sleuthing activities?"

"Oh, yes, I'm glad you kept an eye on them while they were in Denver. Kelly throws a scare into us from time to time."

"Why does that not surprise me?"

Curt peered at Eugene for a second. "Kelly, Eugene's

scarf looks exactly like the one I saw you working on a couple of weeks ago."

"One and the same, Curt," Kelly replied, sneaking a bite of a toffee bar.

"Kelly was sweet enough to send me a gift for the holidays," Eugene said, holding up the gray and white alpaca wool. "It's lovely."

"Well, that's mighty nice of you, Kelly," Curt said. "Tell me, did you make a scarf for Steve, too? No offense to Eugene, here, but he works inside all day—"

"None taken," Eugene said with a sly smile.

"And Steve works outside all day. In the cold, I might add. Building houses, supervising all those workers—"

"Building houses, how noble."

"And I can't help but wonder why you didn't knit a scarf for poor, cold, hard-working Steve." Curt folded his arms across his chest and peered down at Kelly, eyebrow raised.

Eugene squared off with Kelly as well, arms crossed exactly like Curt's. "That's an excellent question. Why is that, Kelly? Poor, cold, hard-working Steve sounds like he could use a warm alpaca wool scarf."

Kelly knew where this conversation was going, and she already had her answer ready. "Rest assured, gentlemen, I wanted to knit a scarf for Steve, but they wouldn't let me."

"Did I hear my name in connection with a wool scarf?" Steve called from across the table where he was talking with Greg and Lisa.

"Yeah, you did," Curt announced, loud enough to stop all conversation around the table. "Eugene and I were wondering why Kelly didn't knit you a scarf for Christmas."

"Yeah, why is that, Kelly?" Greg chimed in. "I've got a scarf from Lisa."

"That's because you and I were already together," Lisa replied matter-of-factly, then sipped her wassail.

"Huh?" Greg stared at her.

"They wouldn't let me make a scarf for Steve," Kelly repeated.

"Who the Sam Hill are 'they'?"

Kelly counted on her fingers. "Lisa, Jennifer, Megan, Mimi, Connie, Rosa. Lizzie. Hilda. Everyone. They told me it would jinx the relationship if I knitted something for Steve. It's the knitting curse."

"*What?* That's the craziest damn thing I've ever heard." Curt screwed up his face.

"Hey, I'll take it as encouragement," Steve said with a wink, draining his cup.

"Strange as it may sound, Curtis, it is indeed true," Hilda intoned from the edge of the room, punch cup in hand. "Anecdotal evidence proves the knitting curse time and again."

"Oh, yes, yes," Lizzie jumped in breathlessly. "As soon as a young woman knits a personal item for her gentleman caller, then the gentleman ceases to call."

Curt stared at Hilda, then Lizzie and Kelly, then he rolled his eyes. "Women. I never will understand them."

"Amen to that," Jennifer pronounced from the corner.

"You need some wassail, Curt; don't worry about existential concerns," Greg joked. "Besides, I hear your nephew Marty is coming, so you'd better grab food while you can."

"Smart idea," Curt said as he surveyed the table. "That boy will wipe us out."

"Curt, could you bring us some wassail, please?" Kelly asked. "Eugene and Jennifer haven't had a drop and Marty could be here anytime." Curt nodded in reply, then headed for the punch bowl.

"Fascinating," Eugene remarked. "You weren't kidding when you said diversity, Jennifer. Incidentally, who is Marty?"

"A human vacuum cleaner when it comes to food," Jennifer replied. "We forgive him because he's the first guy who's ever been able to sneak past our friend Megan's terminal shyness."

"Surely shyness isn't terminal."

"I'll explain the details later." Jennifer sank her teeth into a lemon bar.

"Howdy, folks. Sorry I'm late. Had a ton of work up at the ranch," Jayleen announced as she strode into the room.

"Oh, my word, it's Annie Oakley," Eugene said, staring at Jayleen, who was clad in her usual Colorado casual—boots and blue jeans.

Kelly beckoned her over. "Hey, Jayleen, come and meet Eugene. He's visiting from Denver."

Jayleen strolled up and gave Eugene's hand a hearty shake. "If you're from Denver, then you must be Kelly's gallery friend. So you know she can't stop sniffing around for clues any more than a dog can stop chasing cats. It's part of her nature."

"Damn right," Curt said as he joined them, offering wassail cups to Jennifer and Eugene. "I've given up trying to steer Kelly away from sleuthing."

Eugene immediately offered his cup to Jayleen. "Please, I'll get some more."

Jayleen held up her hand and smiled. "No, thanks. Can't touch the stuff."

"Jayleen, have you ever heard about some cockeyed knitting curse?" Curt asked, sipping his wassail.

Jayleen looked up at Curt with a grin. "No, can't say that I have, Curt."

"Kelly's friends told her she shouldn't knit a scarf for Steve because it would curse their relationship, or some tomfool nonsense."

Jayleen hooted with laughter. "Curt, you know damn well men and women don't need knitting to curse their relationships. They manage to screw things up all by themselves. It's just their natures."

Curt snorted. "Now, that's the most sensible thing I've heard since I got here."

"Jayleen, come over here, I want to show you something," Mimi called from across the table.

"Excuse me, folks. Nice to meet you, Eugene," Jayleen said, backing away.

"You know, that wassail is mighty tasty," Curt said. "I think I'll grab some more. I heard that Megan and Marty are driving here as soon as they finish their tennis match. They're going for club champions, I think. My advice is to fill your plates while you can, folks." He gave them all a smile and headed for the table once again.

"Now, there's a matched set if ever I saw one," Eugene observed.

"You mean Curt and Jayleen?" Kelly said, surprised at his observation. She'd had that thought herself, once or twice. "Hmmmm, what do you think, Jen?"

Jennifer glanced toward the targets and nodded her head. "Yeah, I have to agree with Eugene. However, Curt would have a time trying to lasso that filly."

"Fascinating. Why is that?" Eugene asked.

Kelly spoke up. "Jayleen's had two bad marriages, plus she's a recovering alcoholic who's been sober ten years and is finally becoming successful in her alpaca business. I agree, Jen. Jayleen's gun shy."

"What about John Wayne?"

"Widower for six months now."

"Ahhhh, fascinating. I give him another six months before he starts practicing."

Kelly laughed. "Practicing what?"

"With the lasso," Eugene said. "Isn't that what cowboys do? Practice with cows, and . . . now who is this? I swear, this shop is a miniature Grand Central. People keep arriving."

"And they all have stories," Jennifer said.

Kelly zeroed in on the object of Eugene's attention and had to smile. There in the archway stood Megan and Marty, still wearing their tennis warm-ups and holding a silver trophy over their heads.

"I trust those are the tennis players you mentioned earlier," Eugene said.

Jennifer nodded. "Vacuum-cleaner Marty and our shy friend, Megan."

"Hmmmm, she doesn't look too shy now," Eugene observed.

Kelly watched the victorious twosome and noticed Megan joking with her friends and Marty, clearly enjoying herself. "That's because Marty showed up in Megan's blind spot. She never saw him coming. He sneaked up on her. And she forgot to be shy."

"Oh, I simply must come back," Eugene said, sinking into his chair. "This place is a veritable soap opera."

"Told you," Jennifer said, offering Eugene a brownie. "Chocolate?"

"Definitely," Eugene said, not taking his eyes from Megan and Marty.

*　　*　　*

"I say we build a snowman with Marty inside," Greg called over his shoulder as he bounded down the knitting shop front steps. "Payback for hiding that chocolate mint fudge."

"Hey, it was in plain sight," Marty said, holding Megan's arm as they negotiated the icy steps. "Everybody else was eating it, too."

"That fudge was lethal," Lisa said, catching up with Greg.

"Weapons grade," Steve added, zipping his jacket.

"Talk about death by chocolate," Jennifer said as she wrapped her scarf around her neck.

Kelly stepped outside the brightly lit shop into the cold December evening. "How're you doing, Megan?" she asked as she wrapped her colorful chunky wool scarf around her neck.

"Remind me not to have Burt's wassail again," Megan said. She snuggled into her fur collar.

Jennifer handed her a coffee cup. "Here, drink my coffee, Megan. Dilute Burt's brew."

"Hey, what do you say we go caroling?" Lisa suggested, pulling on her gloves. "How about that neighborhood down the street?"

Steve slid his arm around Kelly's waist. "Sounds like fun, but can any of us sing?"

Laughter bounced around the circle as the sounds of holiday merriment spilled from the shop. "Great idea," Marty said, zipping his ski jacket. "Maybe they'll be so pleased, they'll feed us."

"Don't tell me you're still hungry!" Kelly exclaimed.

"Dude, you ate a half pound of fudge."

"Marty plans to work his way through the entire neighborhood."

"Actually I was thinking about Megan," Marty said,

glancing her way. "She could use something to go with that coffee."

"I'm okay, really," Megan chirped. "Coffee's working. I'll be able to warble with the rest of you guys."

"We can take my car," Kelly offered, pointing across the driveway to her car parked in front of the cottage. "I can fit five inside."

"Okay, go fill up Kelly's car, then I'll take whoever's left," Greg offered.

"Marty, you and Megan and Jennifer come with Steve and me, why don't you?" Kelly said, beckoning her friends as she headed across the driveway. Digging in her purse for her car keys, Kelly walked around to the driver's side and then stopped.

Her car looked different somehow. What was it? Kelly stared for a second. It was lower. That couldn't be. It must be the nighttime playing tricks on her. And then Kelly saw the tires. All four tires were flat. The rims were touching the ground. No wonder her car looked lower.

"What the hell . . . ?" Kelly exclaimed, staring at the car.

"What's the matter?" Steve asked, coming up beside her.

"Look at that. Four flat tires! How can that be? Those tires are only six months old."

"Whoa, that's weird," Marty said. "You been doing any off-road driving?"

"That is strange," Steve said as he bent to look at the back left wheel, then walked around the car, examining the others.

Greg joined him. "Yeah, all four at once. That's not an accident, Kelly."

"Greg's right," Steve said. "I'm guessing someone slashed your tires. No way all four would go flat at the same time like that."

Kelly screwed up her face at the ugly suggestion. "You're kidding. Why would anyone do something like that? Especially now in the holidays." Her hand jerked out in exasperation.

"Vandals never need an excuse," Lisa said, shaking her head. "They were probably cutting across the golf course on the way to the shopping center and were looking for trouble."

"Listen, why don't we take my SUV," Greg suggested, pointing toward the café. "I'm parked right in front of Pete's. And we can all fit."

"Damn!" Kelly muttered, still staring at her vandalized vehicle. "That's so mean."

"Yeah, it is, Kelly," Jennifer said. "But Lisa's right. Some people don't need an excuse." Jennifer dug into her purse. "Here, have a piece of fudge. I was saving it for later. Now you can save me from myself."

"Whoa, I smell chocolate," Marty said as he and Megan followed Greg and Lisa.

Kelly kept staring at the car, refusing to be consoled.

"Hey, don't worry about it," Steve said, pulling her closer. "I'll come over tomorrow and we'll get them all fixed."

Kelly scowled at the hapless car for another moment before she allowed Steve to guide her toward Greg's SUV.

"We'd better start practicing," Jennifer said as she climbed into the middle seat with Kelly and Steve. "That subdivision is right down the road."

"Okay, how about 'Jingle Bells'?" Megan suggested as she climbed into the rear seat with Marty's assistance.

"Remember, we don't have to be good. Just loud," Marty added as he slammed the door.

"I can manage that," Steve said, slipping his arm around Kelly's shoulders. "How about you, Kelly?"

"I guess," she said with a dejected sigh.

"Here, Kelly, take the rest of the coffee." Megan offered the cup over the seat. "You need it more than I do."

Lisa started the holiday favorite, while Greg backed the oversized vehicle out of the driveway and into traffic.

Steve handed the cup to Kelly and snuggled closer. "Hey, coffee and carols. Can't do better than that, right?"

Kelly managed a small smile. The sound of her friends singing and Steve's warmth brought her back. She was surrounded by people she loved and cared about. She was surrounded by family. And she hadn't been this happy in years. There was no way Kelly would let some random act of vandalism ruin this happy holiday season.

"Oh, what fun it is to ride . . ." Kelly joined in the spirit of the moment, lifting her voice with the others, allowing the holiday merriment and off-key caroling to carry her along.

But in the pit of Kelly's stomach, there was a bad feeling that she just couldn't shake.

Cable Knit Scarf

LEVEL: Advanced beginner

SIZE: approximately 6" × 60"

MATERIALS: 275 yards of Aran-weight yarn (for example: Rowan Scottish tweed Aran); US size 10 needles; cable needle or DP (doublepoint) needle

GAUGE: 3–4 stitches per inch

SPECIAL STITCHES: "Cable 4"—slip the next two stitches to a cable needle or DP needle and hold in front; knit two stitches; knit two stitches from the cable or DP needle.

NOTE: The width of this scarf can be easily adjusted by increasing or decreasing the number of stitches within the [].

Cast on 28 stitches.

Rows 1–3: Knit.

Row 4: K3, P1, Cable 4, P1, [K10], P1, Cable 4, P1, K3.

Row 5: K4, P4, K1, [P10], K1, P4, K4.

Row 6: K3, P1, K4, P1, [K10], P1, K4, P1, K3.

Row 7: Repeat row 5.

Rows 4 through 7 establish the pattern. Repeat these four rows until scarf is the desired length.

Complete scarf with 3 rows of knitting.

Bind off purlwise.

(Pattern courtesy of Anita Meyer, LambShoppe Yarn & Coffee Bar, Denver, CO)

Maggie's Chocolate Mint Fudge

This recipe is an old favorite I remember from childhood. I've seen variations of it over the years in newsletters, magazines, cooking shows—everywhere there are chocolate lovers. My contribution has been to substitute peppermint extract for vanilla. Family and friends have loved it ever since. Enjoy!

1 medium-to-large jar of marshmallow creme
1 can evaporated milk
1 stick of butter (use regular salted butter—not *a butter substitute*)
3 cups granulated white sugar
1 teaspoon salt
2 12-ounce packages semisweet chocolate chips/morsels
1 tablespoon peppermint extract

A large thick-bottomed pot is recommended, to keep the fudge from burning.

Line two 8" × 8" pans with aluminum foil. Grease lightly with *butter* (not oil or margarine).

Place marshmallow creme in pot over medium heat, then stir in evaporated milk, stirring slowly. Cut stick of butter into eight pieces and drop into simmering mixture. Stir in salt. Adjust heat to medium-high and add sugar, one-half cup at a time, stirring well after each addition. Continue stirring as sugar mixture starts to bubble. Cook for *five minutes*, no more, STIRRING CONSTANTLY. I cannot emphasize this enough.

Remove from heat and immediately stir in the packages of semisweet chocolate chips/morsels, one package at a time, stirring vigorously. Add peppermint extract, stirring well until blended. Pour fudge into the two pans. Let cool on counter for several minutes, then place pans in fridge to set up and cool completely.

Makes two 8" × 8" pans of fudge.